PENNSYLVANIA AVENUE
A NOVEL

By J.A. Rich

To Pat + Michael

Thanks for the love
+ support

Enjoy

J.A. Rich

Acknowledgements

-For my wife, Essie
… without whom, this book would be just another daydream in my mind.
Love you, Hon.

-For my mother, Anita
...who taught me to read, encouraged me to write and inspired me to dream.

-Dedication

This, my first novel, is dedicated to my Aunts Ruth, Doris
& Shirley; who are the real-life <u>inspirations</u> for
Pennsylvania Avenue-A Novel.

BLACK MECCA

– "My momma sent me to the girl's finishing school on the Avenue. Class, real class. 'Taught me how to be a lady."

– "I used to run with one of the gangs down there. At night it got pretty rough, but in the daytime it was a different world."

– "I shined shoes down by the train station. Anybody who was anybody came through. One time non-other than Bill 'Bojangles' Robinson stopped for a shine. 'Tipped a whole dollar."

– "You should've seen it. Businesses, bars and movie houses; and colored folks, dressed to the nine. It was Baltimore's version of Harlem. Scratch that. Harlem was New York's version of Pennsylvania Avenue."

- Avenue residents

Prologue

'The Black Man's Paradise', 'Colored Heaven'. It was the commercial strip in west Baltimore called Pennsylvania Avenue; or what the residents affectionately referred to as 'The Ave.' The neighborhoods along that main strip, for over thirty years, had been a haven for blacks from all over the city and region. It was a place of safety, church, community and entertainment. One of the main colored neighborhoods in the city, to some it was 'Black Mecca'; to others it was Harlem in Baltimore. There were three and four storied row-house flats, most of which were converted storefronts; with gatherings of folks on the stoops, entering or exiting homes and businesses. Fancy signs, both neon and painted, hung above some businesses, adorned to attract consumers. The four lane street, two lanes for each direction, bounded by fifteen foot wide cement sidewalks, was always crowded with traffic; day and night. Doctors, lawyers, and teachers all lived, worked and played alongside sanitation workers, maids and shoe-shines. Hundreds of businesses sprouted up in the area; everything from bakeries to clothiers; from gas stations to barbershops. Anything and everything a neighborhood needed to sustain itself could be found along this main strip, and sometimes anything included 'alternate forms of happiness'.

Pennsylvania Avenue itself lived a double life; for with all its attributes, it had its vices and dangers. There were those who had a need to 'feel good', and they would pay good money to make it happen. Demand for the supply was strong, and vice versa. Entertainment was a large part of the lure of avenue nightlife, but vice and the men that made those vices possible had a greater lure. Gambling, prostitution, drugs and racketeering, were a reality of everyday life. It was symbiotic, pure and simple. Everything was mixed in; side by side, the wealthy and impoverished, the lazy and the motivated, the 'respectable' and 'not-so-respectable'. That was just the way it was. It was beautiful. It was Pennsylvania Avenue.

CHAPTER ONE

Baltimore, 1934

She adored her uncle. As long as she could remember, he was always there to look out for her and her mother. He was the closest thing to a father that she had ever known, and in her twelve years she had learned so much from him; life lessons that most times didn't seem to make sense to her. Nowadays, her uncle seemed to be more and more busy and came around less and less often, but he always made sure that she and her mom were alright.

It was a blustery and overcast fall early evening and she and her uncle were on an errand to the grocery store for suppertime ingredients. As they approached the block on which the grocer sat, they conversed about people, how those people acted and why they did the things they did; a subject on which she was becoming well versed, thanks to the many talks with her uncle. He always seemed to be 'coaching' her.

The grocery store was a typical storefront; an encased glass front separated by a walkway entrance. On one side lay fresh produce, boxed and canned goods. On the opposite side were nonperishable items such as silver & flatware and cleaning products. The sunset sky was fading from orange to black and a few people were milling about, on the sidewalk and in the store. In the middle of their conversation, the girl's uncle squeezed her hand, reflexively pulling her closer to him. Looking up at him,

9

she saw that he had seen something that made him hesitate. She followed his line of sight to a dark colored police squad car that sat just down the street on the intersecting corner. Beside that car stood a police officer that seemed to be a force of nature. He was white and wore his peaked cap pulled low, military style and though he was the only person of his type, no one in his immediate vicinity looked his way. The little girl knew only two things, this policeman was a bad man and that she didn't like him. Without hiding it, the policeman just stared at her uncle who had uncharacteristically begun to get nervous and jittery. The girl and her uncle entered the store. As she began to gather the ingredients and groceries for dinner, she saw her uncle signal the stock clerk over to him. From across the store she could see him reach in his blazer's inside pocket and quickly pass the stock clerk what appeared to be a revolver, which was immediately and discreetly taken to the back stocking area of the store. She seemed momentary shock at her uncle's possession of a firearm, but decided to ask about it later. She noticed her uncle's mood lift as he met her at the front counter with onions in his hand. Outside the store she saw the mean looking police officer casually pacing back and forth, occasionally glancing in through the glass door of the store. Then suddenly after a nod to someone he walked back in the direction of his squad car. The girl and her uncle quietly, to themselves, exhaled.

After paying for the groceries, they walked out the front entrance; bags in hand. Her uncle looked down the street, to the right of the store, to find the officer back in his vehicle on the corner, looking down into his lap as if reading a newspaper. Up the street, in the opposite direction they saw nothing out of the ordinary. But across the street in front of the hardware store, the girl noticed a woman dressed like one of those *nasty* women her mother told her to stay away from. She was trying to get her uncle's attention, signaling him to cross the street so they could speak. Her uncle hesitated, and then scanned the immediate surroundings.

He turned to his niece and said, "Listen, I need you to wait here. I'll be right back. Don't move."
He put his bag of groceries in her arms and then walked across the street to speak with the obviously familiar woman. The two spoke for just a moment before being interrupted by the cries of a boy of about thirteen or fourteen years old. The boy looked weak and lost as if wandering around in a fog.

He held on to passersby crying, "They shot him, they shot him."

It seemed that he suddenly recognized the girl's uncle because the boy ran directly to him.

Her uncle kneeled as the boy cried, "You gotta come! They shot him. They said he's dead!"

The girl saw her uncle's eyes widen from across the street. "Who's dead?!" her uncle asked the boy.

She saw the boy's mouth move but his voice was then drowned out by a passing car. Whose ever name the boy gave, put her uncle into a state of shock because he stood straight up, staring at the boy.

In a calm voice he told the boy, "Go home, now."

The little girl was very much afraid. Suddenly there was too much happening at once. Instinctively, she looked in the direction of the officer on the corner. He had just started his car and shifted his line of sight from the direction of her uncle to a shady character on the opposite corner. The officer then nodded to that character and pulled off, turning and driving south down the Avenue. She then watched the shady character tip his hat in the direction of her uncle who was on the same side of the street. She traced his line of sight to what looked like a kid. He was wearing an Elite Giants baseball cap and looked to be about fifteen years old. Her uncle was still distracted by what he had just heard from the crying boy. 'Not good' she thought. She started to panic. As the crying boy left for home, the girl could see the kid in the baseball cap walking towards her uncle with his right hand in his jacket pocket. The kid's pace quickened until he was about five feet away from his prey. He pulled a gun and aimed. For the girl, everything seemed to slow. The girl's uncle became suddenly aware. He had been in this situation before and his experience dictated his instincts and actions. He confidently turned sideways, making himself a smaller target and with a smirk reached to his shoulder holster for a weapon... that was no longer there.

At that very moment the man and his niece across the street made eye contact and shared the very same thought, "The gun... The gun, is in the store."
Blaamm!!!

The shot from the kid's gun knocked the girl's uncle back about eight feet on his back. Everything went silent. The girl was in shock; she couldn't move, she couldn't speak, she could barely breathe. Passersby ducked for cover behind whatever would offer them refuge. The kid in the baseball cap stood over the body of his victim, nervous but resolute. He offered a look down to the corner. The shady character, who was staring back, gave another nod then walked off. The kid shot his victim two more times in the chest.

Blaamm!! Blaamm!!

This snapped his niece, across the street, back into reality.

She dropped the bag of groceries and screamed, "NOOOOHHH!"

She had watched it all. The kid, not even noticing her, simply put the gun back in his jacket pocket, walked the way he came and vanished around the corner. The little girl hesitantly walked across the street afraid of what she would find when she got there. She could hear women screaming and people running but when she stood over her uncle, the same place his killer had stood only seconds before, she felt a calm fall over her. She didn't cry, she didn't faint, she just stared; with a single tear rolling down her cheek; processing the gravity of the moment.

"Cough." The body on the ground convulsed.

"He's still alive." someone said.

The girl, with a calm beyond her years, sat on the ground positioning her uncle's head in her lap. He bled from his mouth and struggled to talk. She managed a tearful smile trying her best to console him in the midst of his inevitable death. With her uncle's last muster of strength, he gently tapped his bloody finger to her temple as he lay bleeding in his niece's arms. In the dusk of the evening, his last, whimpering, dying word was...

Six months earlier

"So let me get this straight. We got thirty cartons coming in on the Sivas; Pier 2. In each carton there's ten boxes that contain 5 porcelain dolls; 'hollow porcelain dolls; that hold our '*surprise*'. The street value of each *surprise* is about five hundred. So by my calculations, that comes to...well, a lotta damn money; which can make us a lotta damn friends. The bosses get ten cartons each, off of which, *we* get a very small but hefty percentage; a finder's fee."

"Correct."

"Question."

"Shoot."

"My calculations, based on estimated profit as opposed to expenditures, minus mishaps and losses, tell me that shipment is for forty cartons instead of thirty."

A chuckle. "Damn girl, you are good. June said you would find it."

"Find what?"

"The discrepancy; the extra ten cartons."

"Well, why is it hidden?"

"It wasn't, from you. 'Just wanted to be certain before I brought you in. 'Keepin' this one close to the vest. My contact changed the figures at the last minute, something on their end. 'Time table moved up. That's why we had to drive down here on short notice. But your eye for detail is something else. That's why you're so important to the crew, among other things of course."

"Still, why the undercount?"

"You tell me."

"Hmm... hidden variables I know, but what?"

"Well you can say the extra ten cartons are for, let's say, expenses. Some people need to stay happy."

"But the greased palms, the police, and the uptown bosses are taken care of in the original numbers. Hmmm. So, I guess we can call it... an operator's fee. We kick upstairs to Goldie, again, and still end up with a nice chunk. And we don't have to worry about outside influences 'cause the Guineas and the Micks either hate us or scared to come uptown. But I heard that those Turks ain't so friendly with colored folk either; 'don't trust us. So how'd you finagle this meeting?"

"Well that's where the contact comes in. He's my go-between, my face."

A nod in acknowledgement.

A silence.

"Els."

"Yeah C."

"You got everything?"

"Yeah C."

"Just stay close. These things can derail real quick, so keep ya eyes and ears open, stay sharp and most importantly, back-me-up. Oh, and one more thing, no emotion. Got it?"

"Yeah. I got it." Sounding annoyed.

A sigh.

"You ready for this?"

Agitated, "Yeah!"

"This is the big one."

"I know."

"'The trucks behind us?"

"Yeah."

"OK, let's do this. We're here. I'm pullin' over."

A dusty gray 1931 Oldsmobile slowly came to a stop in front of an aged brick storefront. Elsie took a deep breath and opened the passenger side door clutching an old brown brief case. She wore a navy patterned knee length skirt with a matching blouse and jacket. It was early March and seasonably cool, and the wind that blew off the nearby water caused a chill in the air. Elsie was unfamiliar with this part of town and though she had known better, she could not help but to look around as if she were a tourist. 'Very dangerous in this neighborhood.' She quickly recovered and squinted at the store front sign sitting just above a weather faded green awning that read Kaufman's Wallpaper. It was like any of the numerous businesses that lined the western side of this busy street. The five-foot wide sidewalk pavement was so crowded with people that some resorted to walking along in the gutter for relief. There were residents and passersby of various descents, accents and dialects. A predominate colored neighborhood was just blocks to the south so it was not uncommon to see black faces peppered within the crowds. The sidewalk bustled and though dangerous at times, this area was one of the more commercially successful in the city; despite the great economic depression. The success was a direct result from its proximity to the docks and the rail-yard at nearby Camden Yards.

The gray Oldsmobile was followed there by an old furniture moving truck that had backed into the nearest available space across the wide street. The occupants just sat and waited patiently. The Oldsmobile's driver's side door opened. Out came the well-dressed leg of Clyde 'Pop' Hatch, a man in his early thirties. His black shoes tapped lightly on the cobblestone street as his six foot, medium-built frame exited the car. His suit indicated was frugality, while stating importance; not flashy, but enough to command the respect of those with whom he interacted.

The cobble stone street was a wide four laned thoroughfare, separated by two sets of street-car tracks for north and south bound trains in the median. On the other side of this street, across from the extended blocks of storefront commerce was one of its sources; the port. Elsie exited and walked around the car and joined Pop as they crossed the crowded street. Waiting for Pop, and leaning on the yellow and black safety rail of a buildings platform, was a young olive-skinned man who looked relieved at his arrival.

The man gave a quick handshake, and then said, "The boat just came in. Customs is...," with a smirk, "...'doin' their thing. We're good."

"Never doubted it for a second" replied Pop.

Elsie noted that the rapport between the two men was familiar but at that moment strictly business. The buildings that lined this side of the street were warehouses for the loading and receiving docks. The other side faced the port with piers that loaded and off-loaded goods and merchandise to be processed in a middle area by U.S. Customs agents.

"Nikos- Els, Els- Nikos." Pop uttered hurriedly.

"Hey hon', how you doin'?" said Nikos, as a matter of habit, half interested.

Elsie gave a cordial nod. Her training had told her that during business meetings she should hang back a few feet and only speak when absolutely necessary; and even then only with a consensual nod from Pop. Nikos was a man of medium height; bronzed skin and oily hair combed to the back. He was a young tough from the east side. Some called him Nikki the Spick because of his dark complexion and resemblance to Puerto Ricans. It was rumored that he was connected to the notorious criminal organization; the Greeks.

He took one long hail on his cigarette, flicked it and said, "Let's go."

His gray jacket and matching trousers waved in the breeze that came in off the harbor. The warehouse was dank and smelled of stale fish and bird droppings. The wooden floor creaked and had wide in-between spaces, broken up by various batches of offloaded goods and patches of sunlight. The three walked through the darkness of the warehouse toward the opposite pier side.

"You know the drill, P. Let me do the talkin'. These guys, they can be real touchy." Nikos said.

"Got it, but they *do* know who they makin' the deal with, right?" Clyde asked, affirming his position.

"Everything's been worked out already. All parties know. If this works out good, it could be the beginning of a beautiful business relationship." Nikki answered.

Clyde acknowledged with a quick nod. Just before exiting the warehouse on the port side, Clyde mentioned Nikki to 'hold up'.

Standing beside him, he mumbled, "Hey Nik, you know, I really appreciate you pulling these strings. Thanks."

Nikki answered, "What're you kiddin' me? We go way back, besides, after what you did for me, it's the least I can do."

Then suddenly spotting someone he said, "OK, there he is. It's Showtime".

As the three neared the loading dock, it seemed as if they were emerging from a different world. The air was a little cooler and slightly humid and smelled of salt-water and oil. The sounds of people, fog horns, ship bells and grinding tugboat engines were just barely drowned out by the squawking of hundreds of seagulls that fought for scraps in mid-flight and on the docks and roof tops of surrounding buildings. It was the Baltimore Harbor; the second busiest port on the east coast. Hundreds of ships visited this port every day, which spurred millions into the local and regional economies. The letter C shaped basin, called the inner harbor was surrounded on all three sides by warehouses, piers, and fish markets and was constantly crowded on land side with merchants and consumers, and on the sea side with skiffs, boats and ships of all sorts.

The ship docked on pier 2 was a large, gray merchant vessel. On the side read the M/T Sivas. Nikos gave a nod to a customs agent who was speaking with another man dressed in soiled traditional Middle Eastern garb whose name was Tariq. As the customs agent walked pass, Elsie thought, 'One of Nikki's inside guys. Good to know.' She breathed in the salt air, looking up at the filthy gray vessel. The Turkish flag's red field with white crescent moon and star billowed in the wind in contrast to the grayish overcast sky. Men onboard scattered about in preparation for the off- loading of the ship. A man who looked to be the captain walked down the M/T Sivas' gangplank followed by his apparent second in charge. Both seamen were unshaved and untidy with skin darkened by sunburn and dirt. They approached the awaiting party.

Nikos took the lead with Pop and Elsie a step behind, "Tariq, tell 'em I'm Nikos and this is their prospective business partner, Pop."

With an uncertain glare, Tariq gave a respectful bow then turned to the men and spoke in Turkish. He seemed to be introducing and reminding the captain of this unusual situation. The captain quickly examined Nikki, Pop and Elsie, with special curiosity to Elsie and then shrugged reluctant acceptance, responding back to Tariq in Turkish.

Tariq translated in a heavy Turkish accent, "He says he is Murat, the voice of the leader. He wishes to make this as quick and efficient as possible."

After more talking, Tariq translated, "He says that this is the shipment as agreed. And with, fifteen percent of the full load, plus an additional percentage added for every drop, we will settle at, let us say, 20,000 U.S. dollars?"

Murat gave his best poker face, as Tariq and Nikki gave a look to Pop, who then glanced at Elsie.

After a split second calculation, she nodded her head no, whispering to Pop, "17,000 with a five drop cap."

"17 with a five drop cap." Clyde confidently reiterated. "With a thirty percent gaining potential over your, 'other' option."

Tariq quickly translated and after a moment of counsel with his subordinate, Murat, somewhat impressed with this Moorish female's speed of calculation, reluctantly responded in Turkish.

Tariq, with a smile, then turned to the three saying, "It is agreed. Murat says his leader is grateful for finding an American associate to do business with, but remains cautious about certain, let's say 'specifics'. Such dealings are unorthodox, but if all goes well and without incident, he looks forward to a long lasting and prosperous relationship."

Handing over of the aged brown briefcase Elsie had and a round of farewell bows, the meeting was over. Murat turned and gave a hand signal to men on the ship's deck. The men immediately moved to offload merchandise. Upon seeing this, Elsie walked quickly through the shadowy warehouse to the loading dock and gave a nod to the driver of the parked delivery truck that had followed them there. Out of the back of the truck jumped two men dressed in caps and denim overalls who joined the driver and the passenger. Without acknowledgement, the men passed by Elsie, then Pop, Nikos and Tariq and began to transfer the M/T Sivas' off-loaded cartons onto the trucks.

'An instantaneous and fluid transaction,' Els thought. 'Solid.'

Tariq shook Nikos' hand, then gave a slight bow to Pop and Elsie. "Until the next time." he said in his thick middle eastern accent, and then walked down the short railed stairwell that connected the warehouse to the street and faded into the bustling mix of dock workers, sailors and residents. After Tariq's exit all vestiges of business and formality faded between Pop and Nikos.

"This is fuckin' great!" said Nikos. "'You know what this is gonna do for us? And you hon," turning to Elsie, "IpEroha!! How'd you add that up so quick? The brain on

21

this one, eh. This is it P. Now, we write our own ticket."
Elsie giggled at the relaxed change in the men.

With a huge grin Pop answered, "Yeah, things are
definitely looking up. And now the real work begins; but
the first thing I'm gonna do is take care of a few things,
sure up some loose ends."

"I hear that', I got some loose ends I need to tie up
myself." Nikki responded. "By the end of the week, I
should be done. Then it's rest and relaxation."

"Well if you really mean that, you might be
interested in some shindigery. Goldie's birthday! The 'get
together' next week. You should come by, meet him." Pop
suggested.

"You know what P? I think I will. Count me in. At
the Golden Touch?"

"You know it."

Nikos leaned over and gave Elsie a casual peck on
the cheek, "See you later, hon'. You too P."

The two men gave each other congratulatory
handshakes and hugs then Nikki walked down the
platform stoop and toward the street. With perfect timing,
Nikki was met in the middle of the street by a northbound
black '33 Buick. The car slowed down just enough for
him to jump in, then sped off. The men who hastily
worked to load the cartons onto the old moving trucks out
front were finished and pulling out of the loading dock.
Pop playfully offered Elsie his elbow. They strutted
across the cobble stone street. They got back in and
started the car, made a U turn and headed north-west
bound; destination Pennsylvania Avenue.

CHAPTER TWO

Uptown

Driving north and west from the port, piers and warehouses of the harbor, the two passed through the busy downtown business, legal and retail districts. The skyscrapers that lined the avenues gave way to marble and stone institutions of law and justice, and then to the large 'big box' department stores packed with shoppers milling about inside and out. Here, the faces were mostly white, but the further you drove from the city center, the more the crowds became gradually mixed, and then all black. Crossing the intersections of Franklin and Paca Streets, the unofficial northern and western boundary of downtown, one entered a cluster of neighborhoods, known to some as 'colored heaven' or 'the black man's paradise'. Its main artery was Pennsylvania Avenue; or what the residents affectionately referred to as 'The Ave.'

Turning onto Pennsylvania Ave. from Franklin St. and crossing Biddle Street, the dusty gray '31 Olds cruised for a block, and then came to a gradual stop at the next red light. The sky was still overcast, the sidewalks bustled with pedestrians and Pop and Elsie breathed a sigh of relief at their return to the neighborhood. Elsie casually starred out of the passenger side window. The Avenue looked normal enough, but she thought about all the issues behind the scenes. Violence was getting out of hand, lieutenants were getting caught in police stings, and even the Boss down 'The Bottom' was having legal issues.

He was usually known for running a tight ship, but now it was out of order, chaotic; something was definitely suspicious.

Elsie asked, "'You know if Sho is coming to Goldie's party next week?"

"Probably. If for no other reason, just to show respect." Pop answered. Then after a thought, "That's a random question. Where did *that* come from?"

Still staring out of her window, she answered with a sigh, "I don't know. Just driving through, made me think. It's getting wild down here. Sho need keep a tighter rein on his boys. I heard one of his lieutenants was found dead on the railroad tracks, and another one got pinched with a kilo of 'O' in his trunk; lookin' at some serious time."

"Law of the jungle. You can't get caught off guard in this business." Pop offered.

"Eh. Maybe you're right, but I think it's more than that. I smell a rat."

"Explain."

"Well you got all this chaos; men getting shot, bringing unwanted attention, scarin' people. Where's the leadership."

Giving the benefit of the doubt, Pop explained, "Well you know Sho is fighting 'nem cases hisself, trying to stay on the street. He's delegating. He probably can't see what's going on. He's lookin' at ten hisself."

"Yeah, and when he goes, and he *is* going, who'll be left standing? Bigg." Elsie stated.

"'Something to think about. He *is* ambitious, I'll give him that."

"Yeah, too ambitious. I don't know, he just rubs me the wrong ..."

24

"We're being followed." Pop interrupted, glimpsing at his side view.

"Mackey?", she asked.

"Think so."

"How long?"

"Not long."

"'The trucks?"

"They turned off to go to the spot already. Don't worry. He just wants me."

Two cars behind the Olds was a dark blue Baltimore City Police squad car. It had an ominous air about it, but it was nothing compared to the menace within. Sargent Sherman Mackey was a fifteen-year veteran of the force. Third generation Irish-American, he was the son of the famous Commander Erwin Mackey, who during the great fire of 1904 and the chaos and rioting which ensued, marshaled, deputized and led his men to restored calm and order in the streets of downtown Baltimore. It was said that this action alone salvaged what was left from the fires and allowed re-growth; in essence saving the future of the city. Commander Mackey was a hero, a legend. Sergeant Mackey was not. His father's heroism and years of service had obligated him to join the force but his commitment to law and order was iffy at best. Mackey had managed, through connections and favors, to get himself promoted up through the ranks. He became a relatively powerful man in the western district and though beneath his rank, he chose to personally patrol the district. He reveled his well-earned reputation as a hard ass, so when his siren blared, waving off the car in-between, and signaling the dusty gray Olds to pull over, the occupants, naturally, were a little apprehensive.

Pop watched Mackey approach from his side view mirror. He was a tall, imposing figure, uncharacteristically fit for a man his age. He wore the uniform of his rank, a navy blue city issued overcoat and trousers. His policemen's cap was pulled tight down on his head, military style. His eyes were in shadow. Standing in front of the driver's side window he tapped the glass three times with his nightstick. Pop, looking straight ahead, lifted his hand off of the stirring wheel and began to roll down the window. It was not wise to make quick movements in Mackey's presence for it could result in use of deadly force. Mackey bent down and looked in the window, first at Pop then to Elsie.

"License and registration."

"Sure. Is there a problem officer?"

Mackey shot Pop a look that could have frozen a flame.

"Maybe. But you speak when I say speak. Understand me, boy?"

Still looking straight, Pop calmly answered, "Yes." Pop handed his license and registration over to Mackey who carelessly glanced at it then threw it back into the car on his lap.

In a slow interrogative manner, and speaking as if he knew more than he had, Mackey asked, "Where you comin' from? Downtown?"

"Nope. East side."

"Kinda far from home for you, ain't it?"

"'Got a cousin, live offa Greenmount Avenue." Pop answered.

Moments passed in silence. Like a chess game each man studied the other, feeling the other out; silently, thinking, outthinking, waiting, sizing up. Elsie, nervously sitting still in the passenger's seat, didn't have to guess the reason for the high tension. This time she knew of the past these two shared. Mackey hated the old gangsters and their underlings. Due to the old back-room deals, kickbacks and payoffs, they all remained just beyond Mackey's reach. But in the wake of his promotion to Sargent, the previous Sargent being fired after having his relationship with a colored prostitute was conveniently exposed, his jurisdiction and power was growing.

In his strong east Baltimore accent Mackey leaned in close and said in a voice that was just above a whisper, "P's and Q's geechie. 'Cause when you go down, it's gonna be me that takes ya'."

His cold stare was maintained and only broken when he hocked and spit alongside the Olds.

"Carry on." he said with a nod standing straight from his hunched position. He walked to the rear of the Olds.

"And oh," taking his night stick and smashing the back driver's side break light, "your signal's out. Get it fixed."

With that, he walked back to his squad car, got in, and drove off. The few residents who bothered to stop slowly went back to their routine. The tension lifted slightly, but Pop sat behind the stirring wheel, hands still gripped; fuming. Though his eyes were staring straight, his mind was definitely elsewhere. After a few seconds, and a deep breath, he closed his eyes. Reopening them he restarted the car then pulled off, back into traffic.

After about two blocks of silence, Elsie, also staring straight broke it, asking, "What you gon' do?"

"What can I?" Pop answered, then after a thought, "As hated as he is, the heat from him vanishing, would be

27

bad for business." Then after another thought, "I guess we'll just have to *stay on our P's and Q's*." With that borrowed phrase, the tension broke even more, as they both chuckled. But neither was under any illusions about the seriousness of the Sargent's threat.

History

Up the Avenue they drove through moderate traffic. On the western side of the street were lined three-story row-house storefronts with residents and patrons going about their daily task. On the right sat the movie house and music venue The Royal Theater. With its black canopy and the white letters R-O-Y-A-L that centered and lined it, the theater for years had been an entertainment institution in Baltimore's colored community. It was flanked by various smaller movie houses and clubs, but none were as prestigious or famous. Colored performers from all over the country jumped at the chance to play the famous Royal Theater as it became the hub of Negro entertainment in the city.

The block on which the theaters sat, marked the northern boundary of the southern section of the avenue known as 'The Bottom'. Pennsylvania Avenue had been cut up into three sections, in accordance with the colored organized crime syndicate. This sectioning was the result of a compromise that arose from the 'Booze Wars' of the twenties. During the early years of prohibition, competition for the acquisition and sale of illegal alcohol was fierce. With twenty to thirty different outfits vying to be the suppliers, fighting became vicious and often times deadly. Some gangs were decimated while others consolidated to form larger gangs. Fear or racism kept the infighting homogeneous. The larger gangs became more organized and more influential. This resulted in four powerful organizations fighting it out on the streets. But with that fighting came fear from bystanders, loss of personnel, negative attention from the press, and heat from the authorities; all of which was deemed bad for business. Something had to be done.

It was said that Thomas 'Goldie' Richardson, a charismatic leader of one of the larger outfits, called for a 'sit down' to work out an arrangement. The leaders of the other three organizations agreed, and all met at a neutral place. There, they worked out a plan that would be amicable and lucrative for all parties. Pennsylvania Avenue would be broken in to the three sections according to specialized earning potential and each leader would be designated 'boss' of a section according to his area of expertise.

Because of the concentration of entertainment establishments along the southern section of the Avenue, Sho, an eastern shore native, assumed control of it and all things that went along with it, including and especially narcotics. Because of its geographical position, this section was known as 'the bottom', though by comparison it was by far the ritziest. Shiny cars lined the street. By day, the famous could be seen walking in and out of theaters and jazz clubs, by night the neon signs and flashing lights there were rivaled only by those in New York's Time Square. With his dark suits and derby complementing his rotund frame, Sho, short for 'Showtime' gained influence from the politicians and judges he rubbed shoulders with at his establishments. He loved the lime light and fancied himself, a celebrity of sorts, and either owned or got a piece of every hot spot, and narcotics deal on his part of the strip. Show business was truly Sho's business.

Just north of 'The Bottom' was the section of the strip that was referred to as 'The Shop'. 'The Shop' was the main shopping district of the Avenue, so known for its concentration of clothiers, food markets, and other retail stores. Arabbers with horse-carts full of fruits, vegetables and meats, crowded the already packed sidewalks and all were made to pay tribute for protection. By day, it was by far the busiest part of the avenue, but by night, the shopping didn't change, just what was being bought and sold. After the sun went down and the shops closed for the night, out came the ladies. Prostitution was the cash cow in this section and gangster Cleveland Black was the man to control it. Named for the President at the time of his birth, Grover Cleveland Hayden, was a pimp and easily the most violent of the Avenue bosses.

In contention with Cleveland Black was east-side native and former heist man, Wilbur 'Foxx' Long. Foxx was a thief, and a very good one. He had gotten his start as one of the main 'fences' on the Ave. Both men felt deserving of the territory. Both were stubborn and proud, both were powerful, and both had notorious tempers. Delicate skill and diplomacy were needed. The heated and volatile competition for 'The Shop' was settled by Goldie, who suggested that Foxx's background in larceny and roots on the east side made him the perfect choice to head the newly established organization in the colored neighborhood near the East Baltimore Rail Yards. The tons of materials and goods, including booze, which came through those yards monthly, closed the deal for Foxx.

'Up Top' was the mostly residential section of the Avenue. It was concentrated with specialty shops, and the professional offices of accountants, doctors and lawyers, but like any other neighborhood, it felt the pain of the depression on everyday life. Any chance to ease that pain was seized, and to some, that chance was in the form of 'playing the numbers'. 'Playing the numbers' or 'policy' involved gambling a small investment for a big payoff. Placing a penny bet, at five hundred to one odds could net fifty bucks; a gold mine. Running numbers and gambling were the big money makers here and every policy house, every card game, dice game, even pitching pennies, all paid tribute to Goldie. Tribute was the street tax that the under world paid for 'protection' from thieves and those who sought to take their ill-gotten earnings. For most, it was just the cost of doing business. All in all, business on the Avenue was mutually beneficial. Bosses were free to deal with whomever and earn however they felt as long as it did not infringe on the other's earnings and businesses. And so was the peace and prosperity during prohibition, through the roaring twenties, and up to the present day.

Trench

The taps of freshly shined shoes echoed in the marbled hallway of the Slatemore Hotel. The wearer's, husky build walked so quickly, that the passing scenery became a blur. He wore a dark green trench coat and his quick stride indicated that he was a man on urgent business. It was a Sunday morning so there was little to no foot traffic on the street nor within the hotel. Though smaller in comparison to the downtown varieties, it was in the style of early Victorian with sculptures, polished

31

wood, carpet and rich print draperies. It sat on the corner of Pennsylvania Avenue and North Pearl Street, just on the edge of downtown and catered to the colored elite. The few hotel staff on duty barely noticed or acknowledged the man. The last 'sitting room' off the grand hallway was converted into an upscale barber exclusively for the hotel's upscale patrons. Upon entering the shop, the man in the trench saw two stone faced gentlemen sitting in the waiting area conspicuously reading newspapers. They both rested their papers on their laps and watched the trenched man while the barber caked shaving cream on the face of a customer in his barber's chair. The barber's had all the trappings of an average shop including chairs, hair and shaving products plus the trademark barber's pole. The barber went about preparing his tools without even once glancing up. The man in the green trench was impressed. He waited silently and patiently a few feet away from the occupied barber's chair. After a moment, the customer in the chair, obviously someone of influence, with lower face still covered with cream, spoke.

"You Green?"

The man nodded yes. "With three E's."

And then after a quick glance at his trench, the customer said, "Kind-a obvious, no?"

Greene hunched, "Eh, Whatchugon'do?"

Laying his head back to continue his shave, the customer said, "On the chair, between the bookends." Greene looked opposite the customer to the where the stone-faced gentlemen were sitting. Between them, in the empty chair was a folded newspaper, thicker than it should've been. He walked over and reached for it only to have one of the men sitting, block his hand.

Keeping his patience, he heard the customer, from behind and still in the lying position say, "I want this clean, not a trace. Use a safe house first so it don't get loud, then after a few days, do what you want with her. Understand?"

"Understood." the man answered.

The bookend moved his hand. Greene picked up the bulging newspaper and slid it into the side pocket of his green trench. He then nodded, turned and walked out of the barber shop, through the hotel lobby and out onto the street.

CHAPTER THREE

The Git-Together

It was about a quarter after ten pm and the cool, misty spring night closely resembled a scene from a Sherlock Holmes novel. One block in any direction was shrouded in fog, and the condensation that collected on the street and on vehicles gave a false indication of rain. The streets were comparably empty save a few night workers and street people. This was close to 'the top' of the Ave. and a few residents walked quickly to their destinations as two lone men in overcoats stood at the intersection of Pennsylvania Ave. and Baker Street. They looked to be hired goon security on watch as there was no other apparent purpose to loiter, aside from a casual peep toward the storefront, two businesses up from the corner. Mostly converted row houses, most properties along the block had glass fronts and fancy floor tiles that invited people in. The store front, two businesses up from the corner had two opposing platforms separated by a short marble path that advertised male manikins sporting the latest style in men's fashion. The manikins stared from behind thick rounded glass and the faint sounds of jazz could be heard, muffled behind the wooden framed, thick glass door. Light spilled from the seams of the door shade along with the sounds of people making merry. One of the security goons glanced back with envy, and then resumed his watch.

Those muffled sounds of celebration were momentary surpassed by the tire thuds and low hum of the '31 Oldsmobile. The Olds' slowly came to a stop on that corner and the goons immediately sided the driver and passenger side doors to assist the riders. It was Pop and Elsie. Doors were open, greetings given and assistance for the lady was gladly accepted. Pop, who had cleaned up nicely with a brown pin striped suit, dark shoes, a beige button up and tie with fedora, stepped out. Elsie, his escort, was stunning with a light beige form fitting textured dress that fell just below the knee, a matching jacket with loose puffy shoulder sleeves, and a frilly shear shawl that traipsed across the front. A small matching bonnet style hat with brown ribbon, tilted to the side and a brownish grey mink fur wrapped around her shoulders completed the ensemble. Pop rushed around to the curb side and offered her his elbow.

"Y'all lookin' mighty fine tonight," said one of the goons, closing the car door, "y'all have a good time."

With a look of acknowledgement Pop responded, "Thanks, soldier. In 'bout another hour I'll get somebody to cover y'all shift for a while, so y'all can get something to eat."

"Much obliged." the other goon responded, giving the same respect that a servant would give his boss.

As they approached the muffled sound got louder until they both stood in front of the entrance. It was like a 'Jack in the Box' of light and music at the end of the 'pop goes the weasel' song. Pop and Elsie were actually nervous from excitement. They had been to the little clothing store many times on many occasions, but this time seemed different... special, as they stared up at the store. The sign above the door read 'Golden Touch Clothier'.

It was Goldie's place and this was Goldie's night. When the door opened, everything amplified; sight, sound and smell. As Pop and Elsie entered they were instantly enveloped and welcomed into the room. A clothier by day, furniture had been moved around, manikins removed and clothed tables set out. The only thing that remained was the custom made brass cash register that set on a glass counter to the left of the front door, which fit in quite well with party decorations. Small square tables were arranged checkerboard style with a walkway up the middle. And the rectangular shape of the widened row house storefront gave the room from the inside, the look of a small hall. The lights dimly lit the inside of the smoke filled room and the crowd consisted of some important men of Colored society, including organized crime figures, business owners, professionals and politicians.

A man, close to the dance floor, waved the two over. Pop knew the man, saw the wave, and acknowledged it. Elsie acted as if she didn't see it at all.

"There's a table, I'm going to sit down." she whispered from the side of her mouth.

"The hell you are. You gon' suffer through this with me", Pop answered in a similar fashion; locking his arm with hers, pulling her closer.

Reluctantly, and with clasped arms, he put on a good face and dragged Els in that direction. He hated the politics of 'business', but loved the man calling on him.

"You owe me Pop", Els whispered angrily.

The man waving the two over was a very important man in Goldie's organization. Unlike Pop and the others, he did not have a crew of associates that worked under him. He seemed to serve as the on-site representative of the organization and workers mostly reported to him. He was amongst the senior of the lieutenants and the widely considered 'third in line' to be 'Boss Up Top'. People called him 'Street' because from the time he first hung in the street; he never liked to go home, always fearing that he would miss some action or the next big score. As he grew in wealth and power he maintained his presence on the streets though he owned one of nicer homes in Sugar Hill, the adjacent ritzier neighborhood. His loyalty and his knack for having his fingers on the pulse of streets endeared him to Goldie; personally and strategically. He had earned his place in upper management, but didn't like the stress or restraint of high leadership. Elsie thought to herself, 'He seems to be a man on the brink of retirement.'

As Pop approached, Street gave a gregarious laugh, hugged him from the side and introduced him as if he were a proud uncle. The people to which he was being introduced seemed intrigued and impress. There was the city councilman from ward 17, his wife and two union delegates enjoying martinis.

"Meet the future of 'Golden Touch Clothiers'", Street said with knowing smile, "a friend of mine, Mr. Hatch". Pop gave a modest nod, then introduced Elsie who was nudged back into reality.

Playing back Street's last statement in his mind, 'Future', Pop thought to himself, 'Now that sounds good, but it ain't happening no time soon.'

37

He thought this in spite of the increased responsibilities and tutelage he had been receiving from the top three. As Street bragged over him, Pop scanned the room. Since the conversation had little to do with him answering technical questions, he allowed himself to devote only half of his attention. The other half observed. He saw the six piece band pumping out jazz to a few couples on the dance floor while others enjoyed from their tables. He saw a few of his 'colleagues' within the outfit. They good-naturedly regarded Pop as 'Goldie's golden boy' and genuinely liked and respected him. From another glance across the room, he saw the boss from 'The Shop', Cleveland Black, with his second in charge and some lady friends. Across from them was Foxx, the east side boss, who sat at one of the larger tables, accompanied by all ladies; one of which gave and received whispered messages in his ear.

'She must be the rumored second in charge; Interesting.' Pop thought. He was nudged back by Elsie, who smoothly answered a casual question directed at him from the councilman's wife.

"No, it's strictly a business relationship, though the way I take care of him, you can hardly tell the difference." she said jokingly.

Laughs went around the table.

Street concluded, "I'm gonna let you kids go, but I want you to relax and enjoy yourself tonight, 'cause tomorrow, we got work to do."

Clyde and Elsie graciously bowed and left the table. The two walked away, smirking as if narrowly escaping an ordeal. A waiter showed them to their table near the wall.

As they sat, they gave their drink orders. Finally getting relative peace and quiet, Elsie sat exhaling. The band had just finished an up-tempo number and were winding down for their break. They were accompanied by a female vocalist, for a mellow version of *Honeysuckle Rose*, Elsie's favorite.

In a low tone, she sang along.

"Say, I have no use for other sweets of any kind, since the day you came around.

But from the start I instantly made up my mind, no sweeter taste can be found."

To her surprise, she heard Pop chime right in, with the following lyric, imitating Satchmo,

"You' so sweet. Can't be beat.

Nothing sweeter ever stood on feet. Yeeaahhh."

To Els, everything faded. There was no longer music, no chattering people, no restaurant; just those eyes and that voice. Eyes and a voice that she had seen and heard countless times. But not like this.

'Whoa.' She thought, snapping back into reality. 'What am I thinking? He don't see me like that, and I shouldn't see him like that either. Bad for business. Old schoolgirl feelings. Gotta push 'em back. Way too much ambiance here. Still, not a bad dream.'

They both laughed that intense moment off. After another moment Pop said, "Els, can I ask you a question?, off the record."

"Shoot." she answered mockingly.

"About what you said over there to the councilman's wife. I was half out of it, so..."

Just then, Elsie's eyes shifted to a figure just across the room. This figure waved to her and signaled for Clyde. It was June. June had been at the celebration by

39

then for about an hour, but was preoccupied with last minute details of a potential business venture. He was tall and medium built, sporting a navy pinstriped suit and white shirt which heightened his dark complexion. He had piercing dark eyes and spoke in a baritone voice; and he was Pop's right hand. Over the years, he had earned his reputation as a street tuff and had become a brilliant gang warfare tactician; working sometimes directly with Goldie's second in command. He had the respect of the streets; friend and foe alike, and had made his bones hustling along the Gay Street commercial district on the east-side. Legend has it that the two met as teenagers when Pop negotiated for the life of June's kidnapped sister and her son. Once they were safe, Pop helped June personally executed the assailants and their associates. Feeling personally indebted to Pop, June stood by his side during his rise, solidifying their bond.

CHAPTER FOUR

Upped

Upon making eye contact with June, Pop stood up from the table, looked down at Elsie and said, "We can finish this later. 'Gotta meet with Goldie. Be back in a few."

He left the table traversing his way through the crowd toward June who stood waiting on the left side of the room at the foot of a steep narrow exposed stairwell.

"That thing, down in Pig Town is good. Everybody's on board. We're in." June said in a low voice as Pop approached.

"Solid." he answered.

June let him pass and then followed up the stairwell. At the top of the stairs, on the balcony-like level, Goldie, with a cigar clinched grin, greeted Pop with open arms.

"Come here you." The two embraced and grinned.

"Happy Birthday, Gold. Many more."

"Thanks kid. Let's hope so." Goldie answered. There was a sitting area wide enough for only a walkway and three exquisitely made tables that lined the width of the store and overlooked the celebration below. The lighting was comparatively dull, but encased table candles gave an intimate glow, which meant one thing; business. The two followed Goldie back to the last table. Goldie sat in the chair with its back against the far wall.

"Sit down." he said in a commanding yet fatherly way.

Pop took a seat opposite Goldie. Giggy, Goldie's number two or second in command, sat between them at the table's twelve o'clock. June was mentioned to a chair at the table directly behind and to left of Pop. The chair had been turned to face the meeting, but was noticeably apart from Goldie's table; a subtle reminder of June's rank in the hierarchy. Duly noted, accepted and respected by June. The dimly lit area provided a semi private setting to do business. And with the hovering smoke and low set lights one could barely see through the smoky veil that seemed to separate the levels. The two old men seemed to be more grim than usual. Not from words or mannerisms, but more from the lack thereof. Pop had dealt with Goldie, through Giggy mostly, so the two were well acquainted and had a good business relationship, but in recent months Goldie had been communicating directly with Pop; their relationship becoming more 'business/personal'. He had wondered if this had caused a rift between the old men or even worst, an issue between him and Giggy. That was a situation he wanted no parts of, yet he still wondered. He hadn't heard any rumblings of friction and Goldie's conversations were strictly confidential, so 'maybe this paranoia was just a conjuring of the mind', Pop thought.

"What you guys drinkin'? Hey hon', get 'em a couple of shots of whiskey." Goldie said to the assigned waitress. As she hurried off to get their drinks, they began small talk. The acoustics were such that there was no need to over talk the music from below. The amphitheater like surroundings pushed the band's music outward and not upward.

Goldie relit his half smoked, soggy mouth-ended cigar, and then spoke.

"Congrats on that thing downtown. That's a big take for a kid your age."

"And a big connect", Gig added, "How'd the hell you pull it off?".

"Old favors, Old friends. One of which you'll be meeting real soon. It all kinda fell in my lap.", Pop answered modestly.

"Things don't just fall in laps kid. In this business you make things happen, and that takes smarts. You got smarts, kid." Gig retorted.

"I gotta agree. We've been building this business for almost twenty years and I gotta say, you been pretty consistent with your end." said Goldie.

"Thank you, sir." Pop was instantly relieved. He wasn't here to settle any beef. The old guys seem to be praising him.

"You respect the chain, you listen, you think and you earn. Very important if you wanna survive in this line of work."

Pop nodded more thanks. He was careful not to be too thankful or say too much as not to sound disingenuous. 'Just take your praise like a good soldier' he thought once again to himself.

"It looks like you surrounded yourself with a good crew. Remember," Goldie leaned in. The music seemed to fade to mute as the moment was so intense. He seemed to be lecturing from an earlier conversation. "there's always opportunity for disloyalty, reasons for betrayal. From within,... from without. But when you can see it coming, find ways to avoid it, to navigate around it, to make it work in your favor, that's when you can truly be successful."

Goldie sat back in reflection, as the mood lifted; more in a conversation with himself.

"And when you get to a certain point, it seems like only then, do you truly realize what success means."
He glanced over at Giggy who knowingly nodded back. Pop's face betrayed a look of confusion as he traded a quick over-the-shoulder glimpse with June, who was equally baffled. These old guys were two of the sharpest men in the underworld, yet they were hot and cold. One minute praising him, the next, what almost seemed like a warning. 'What were these old geezers up to?' the younger men thought.

"All due respect, sir. I don't understand." Pop said.

"I'm coming to that son." Goldie over-talked . "But let me ask you something. Off the top of ya head, about how much do you think I'm worth?"

Pop, confused once again looked at June, then back, thought a moment then said, "I don't know, 'bout a million."

"Whew! That's a big number." Goldie answered, suggesting that he was of more modest means, then said, "Try four mil."

Pop's and June's jaws dropped. Goldie gave them a second to recover then said. "And you know what?, I wanna enjoy it." He thought for a moment, reflecting; thinking of the right thing to say then coming out, bluntly, "I'm sick Clyde." Pop, stunned, took in the moment. He noted the use of his given name. He looked down silently, and then back at Goldie.

"'You mean sick as in dying?" Pop asked.

Goldie shrugged, "Well more old than sick, but still not a good mix. I guess it's just the complications of stress and being old. 'Happens to us all."

"Maybe you should take a little time off." Pop suggested, concerned.

Goldie replied, "Well that's the second part of what I wanted to discuss. I am taking time off. A lotta time. I'm leaving; the game, the neighborhood, the city. 'Doctor says I need plenty of rest and relaxation. Besides, I'm getting too old for this. The hustle..." he sighed. "The hustle. It's a young man's game. I figured I'd go to California; live on a farm. No more cold. No more snow. Besides, I got the money to do it, why not?" Goldie turned to Giggy asking, "That's what we work so hard for, right?"

Pop, in mild disbelief, responded, "Whoa. You mean you ready to walk away from all the power, all the money?"

Goldie gave a knowing reflective chuckle. "A wise man once told me, no matter how much you have, you can't take any of it with you."

After another moment, Clyde and June, coming to a realization, moved their glances from Goldie to Giggy.

Knowing what the two were thinking, Giggy chuckled. "Obvious guess, but wrong. I'm leaving too. 'Goin to Arizona. Getting into the landscaping business in some small town called Phoenix. 'Weather's great."

Goldie, darting a solemn look of approval through his latest puff of cigar smoke, said, with much insight, "I think I'm leaving the business in capable hands." He continued tapping his finger on the table, "Good strategist, a strong leader, solid crew, and you done a pretty good job of that without getting too cute or over stepping." Goldie seemed to be wrestling with something. An anxiety; to pass a burden, or leave. He leaned forward once again resolutely addressing both young men. "I'm leaving. Out the game; retiring. And dat's dat" he said brushing his hands together in two strokes.

Then reading Pop's deciphering face, he answered, "Where *you* come in? You're the new me. You're the one. The boss." Pop's poker face was impassive but his lost for words gave his feelings away.

Giggy queried, "Kid, you didn't see this coming? We gotta work on that."

Pop answered, "I assumed chain of command; next in line. You, Street, one of the other captains."

Giggy answered back, "Your crew exhibits the model for business success in this game. Huh, one day you might even find a way to go legal." Pop's silence made Giggy chuckle, "Christ, kid. What the hell you think we been grooming you for the last few years." Then with finality in his voice and raised eyebrows, he pointed, saying. "You're it."

Pop sat back in his chair glancing back at June. His body language suggested overwhelming, acceptance, and then resolve.

Goldie, a good reader of situations and people continued, "Me and Gig'll be leaving in two weeks, me to California, him", nodding to Giggy, "him to Arizona. So as not stir up any unnecessary vacuum issues, word will be sent out to those that need to know; when they need to know. Other than that, you keep doing what you're doing and you'll be fine. Remember, you gotta stay at least three moves ahead of everybody else; Very important."

"What about Street?" Pop asked, adding things up in his mind. Goldie answered, "Street is gon' stick around for a little while longer. Tie up some loose ends, help with the transition; advise you and June where you need it. Then he's gonna retire down South Carolina; on a farm of all places. I guess city life has finally caught up to him, too. 'Got it all set up down there with family and what not. I guess when he's ready, he'll go. Shouldn't be too long though. But he is 'at your service'."
They all had a snicker.

Giggy added, "You know he's crazy about you. 'Tries to take credit for your fortune. A father's pride." Pop smiled as he gave his thanks and gratitude for the stripes and the extra tutelage from Street. Then he thought as he looked down on the dance floor and tables, 'So this was about them leaving and grooming me to move up to run the outfit. More responsibility, more money, more respect. 'Yes' he thought. But then it hit him. Goldie had said, 'I'm leaving'. Giggy had said, 'I'm moving', and Street was leaving too. These men, who had given him his start, who had been his father figures, his mentors and more importantly his friends, were all leaving. His selfish outlook on the future was replaced by a sadness that was evident on his now not-so-convincing poker face. Giggy and Goldie took notice.

The meeting was officially over. What needed to be said was said as the men all stood, shook hands and raised glasses in a toast. It was then, that they noticed some of the people below heads turn toward the front door. Through the veil of smoke they could see on the party goers' faces, looks of curiosity as three white men walked in, had their coats taken and were being shown to a table.

47

For a moment Pop hoped that they weren't the cops here to ruin the night, but upon a closer examination, he saw that it was Nikos.

Pop turned to Goldie and acknowledged, "That's my face downtown. I want him to meet you. You mind if..?"

Goldie gave a shrug, "Sure."

Pop gave a nod to June, who immediately got up, walked down the stairwell, intercepted Nikos and his party and redirected them back up to the balcony level. At the top of the stairs Pop again scanned the room as he awaited Nikos. Off in the distance, in the far front corner of the room a face caught his attention. A face with a gaze. A gaze that seemed to be studying him with eyes that sat in shadow between a dark gray derby and a lit smoking cigarette. Pop knew almost instantly who it was; Big Shot, heading his own table. Puzzled, Pop thought to himself, 'Was he just staring at me?'

"P! How ya doin?" Nikos interrupted with a sincere hand shake.

"Good. Good Nik. Glad you could make it." Pop answered, refocusing his attention.

"This is a friend of mine Adrian, and my cousin, Dom." Nikos said introducing his associates.

"Welcome gentlemen. As the saying goes 'Any friend of Nikki's....'"

With that Pop made eye contact with the matre'd, gave a head gesture, while pointing at the two.

"Take care of these two; their money's no good here." then to Niko's companions, "Fellas, let me borrow him for a minute."

As the men were escorted by June to the table where Els sat, Nikos followed Pop up the remainder of the stairs and over to Goldie's table.

"Goldie, Gig, allow me to introduce a friend of mine, Nikos, from the Town."

Nikki extended his hand. "It's an honor." Goldie and Giggy remained seated but was genuinely pleased at the respect shown.

"And we hear nothing but good things about you." Goldie responded as they exchanged shakes. "Pop, get 'em a drink."

Pop poured four shots of whiskey. The four lifted glasses in a toast.

"To a long, prosperous relationship." Toasted Goldie, "And since I have one more pressing matter of business before enjoying my own birthday gathering, I will see *you* to the business of enjoying yourselves. Gentlemen." And with that and a gesture, Pop and Nikos rejoined the celebration below.

Trouble

At the table shared by both their parties, there was merriment and talk of earlier successes. But Pop's mind seemed to be yet again, elsewhere. June recognized Pop's tense preoccupation. In the middle of a group conversation, Pop took off, walking toward Big Shot's table. June excused them both, then quickly caught up. An up-tempo jazz tune was being played as Pop traversed the tables. He thought to himself, 'I hope this is not the night I go to jail.' June followed closely behind until they both stood at the foot of Big Shot's table.

After a brief sizing up, Pop spoke with a nod. "Thanks for coming through. Goldie appreciates."

Taking a hail from his cigarette, Big Shot responded. "I *AIMs*, to please. But more importantly, congrats."

"Congrats? On what?"

"On the stripes. You got upped, right? You *is* the heir apparent." Big Shot said mockingly? "It's a time to celebrate. I'd've sent a bottle over if you niggas didn't already own the joint."

Pop thought in a flash, 'How'd the hell he know? A spy. A snitch. Naw. Probably just a clever guess. Even though, this guy might be a little too smart for his own good. Gotta watch him. Gotta be careful.'

After a quick pokerfaced glance to June, Pop answered with a shrug. "I appreciate your confidence in me, Biggs, but your congratulations are totally unnecessary. Business is still business. No changes; not yet."

Eyes still locked and with a grin Biggs said, "Ok, whatever. That being said, if you could run tell your boss, Sho sends his best. He's sorry he couldn't make it. With the trial coming and all, 'wouldn't look good if he were seen here with such, unsavory characters." Big Shot snorted, nudging his associate.

"Yourself included. But I guess you won't have that problem soon." Pop quickly shot back, as he thought, 'Run tell', 'unsavory'. 'The balls on this guy. I should... naw, wait. This is Goldie's night, mine too. Can't let nobody ruin it. Just relax, placate, deal with it later.'

June, equally offended but less restrained, wolfed in his baritone voice, "Nigga, do I need to remind you where you are? Watch ya mouth, and show some respect!"

Pop gave June a glance of 'de-escalation' then politely interjected, "I will, 'relay', the message. I'm sure he'll appreciate your coming and representing *the bottom'*. Gentlemen."
With that, nods were exchanged and Pop and June turned and left the table.

Walking away, in a low tone to Pop, June mumbled, "You know we gon' have to deal with that soon. Real soon."

Pop responded gravely, "I know."

Back at their table, listening to the band play, the party sat in relative quiet for a moment. Nikos broke the silence.

Taking a puff on his cigar, he exhale then said to Pop, as if finishing a conversation, "I don't like his face. P, I don't wanna get into your business or nothing but, be careful with him. I've been watching him from here and I don't like his face."

"Eh. 'He's just a little ambitious. Ambition ain't never hurt nobody."

"Yeah, tell that to Masseria."

"Duly noted."

"Other things." Nikos said, changing his demeanor. "We made a nice piece of change downtown. How ya celebrating?"

"Thinking 'bout opening a barber shop, maybe a drug store." Pop answered. "Clean the money up. Then I got some properties out in the county. Make sure my sis is good."

"Look at you; always thinking." Nikos chuckled. "Me. I'm putting some back into the family restaurants. I got this meeting in a couple of weeks with some Micks down by the water. Should get me closer to what I need, to do what I want. But we'll see. What about you hon'?" Nikos asked Els.

"Still working on it." She answered, nursing her drink.

One of Nikki's associates nudged him and whispered something in his ear. Nikki agreed to what was said then stood up signaling the coat & hat check girl.

"Hey P, I gotta go. I got that thing. Thanks for having us."

"Thanks for coming." Pop responded. "Talk to you soon."

The two crews shook hands and nods goodbye around the table. June saw them out as Elsie sat at the table staring smilingly at Pop. After a moment he noticed.

Rolling his eyes back, he said, "What?"

"Don't play with me." Elsie answered staring in his face, smiling.

"What?"

"Don't play."

"Here we go."

"Look tough guy, don't think I ain't notice. You went up to that meeting one way, and you came down another."

"I don't know what you're talking about, Els. Everything's good."

"I bet it is." Then a moment more, "You're really not gonna say nothing."

"Say what? What am I supposed to say?" replied Pop with an agitated, weak attempted pokerface.

"That you got upped."

Then after studying Pop's face and realizing she was right, she excitedly whispered, "You got upped!"

Pop's eyes popped, non-verbally hushing her.

Elsie quickly regained her composure, "I'm sorry. I'm sorry. I'm just happy for you. For the crew." She brimmed with giddiness. "What are the terms?"

Like a man of control and confidence, Pop grabbed her hand. "Don't worry about the terms. Don't worry about agreements. Don't worry about business. Just know that we have arrived. We got a lot of hard work ahead of us, but tonight, we relax. Tonight, We have a good time. Tonight, we celebrate."

And with that, at Goldie's birthday celebration, Clyde, Elsie, & June partied the night away.

CHAPTER FIVE

Officer and the Tough Guy

Officer Wright quietly pulled his squad car into the alley and shut off the engine. He and his partner, Officer Bennett, exited the car and walked up to the back door of a flat in Sandtown; one of the neighborhoods off the Avenue. It was close to dusk and as his partner looked out, Wright, gun drawn, listened through a decrepit back door. He could hear voices coming from inside, most likely from one of the adjacent rooms. He signaled Bennett to follow him as he opened the door and silently entered. They moved quickly as not too draw attention to their white faces; faces that obviously stood out in this colored neighborhood. They secured the back room kitchen, then quickly moved down the middle hallway. Voices and movement could be heard coming from the middle room. From the hallway they sounded like they were gambling. The peeling wallpaper and broken scattered ceiling plaster that covered the floor gave the indication of an abandoned house.

'Good, no civilians', Wright thought.
The officers stood on either side of the closed-door waiting to rush in, when the door opened and a man walked out.

Officer Bennett pressed his service revolver's muzzle against the man's neck, whispering "Don't move."

The man's hands went up as Wright bent the corner into the room, shouting "Freeze!"

Immediately all hands flew up in the air. The room was in the same condition as the rest of the house, dilapidated. Securing two other prisoners, Wright approach the last man, who stood red handed, dice in one hand, money in the other. Upon closer inspection and to Wright's surprise, that last 'man' looked to be a boy of about 15. And even stranger, the boy seemed to be in charge.

"Is there a problem officer?" The boy said with an arrogant smirk.

Wright stood face to face, meeting the boy's gaze. "'Little young to be in the company of degenerates, don't you think?"

The boy answered wryly, "Degenerates? You talking about them, or me?"

Analyzing the boy's answer, after a moment, Wright asked, "What's your name?"

"Melvin. And I don't appreciate it when...." Melvin's sentence was stopped short when he was forced down on his knees and handcuffed alongside his gambling partners.

"No monologue-ing kid. This ain't the funnies". After a studied glance around the broken-down room, Wright asked, "You got something you wanna tell me, or in the very least show me?"

Melvin stared quietly at the wall in front of him; his arrogance had been halted before it could get started. Officer Wright scanned the room once again. This time his eye caught a slight bulge in the wallpaper, on the opposite wall, by an old radiator. A quick glance back to Melvin told him what he wanted to know, because the kid, facing the wall, shot look over his shoulder, then quickly back. Wright walked to the opposing wall where a radiator sat. He felt along the wall near the floor where the wallpaper budged. Where the paper seam met the floor borders he pulled the loose unglued flap up. It gave little resistance and revealed a fist-sized hole in the wall.

He looked back at Melvin, "You sure you got nothing to say?"
Wright saw the once arrogant gambler revert back to a frightened teen looking like he had something to say.

"Too late, kid." he said as his hand felt around inside the wall's hole.
When he brought his hand out, he had in it two small waxed paper packages containing a powdery substance. He opened them and immediately recognized what it was; heroine.

"That yours?" asked Officer Bennett.

"Nope." answered Melvin. "Must be plaster from the wall."

"How's about I plaster your face all over this floor?"

"No need, partner." Wright happily interrupted, calming the situation. "We got this little fella right where we want 'em."

"'Lotta good it's gonna do. Bennett said. "He'll probably end up in his second home, 'juvie'. Then what we got?"

Wright turned to Bennett then whispered, "I've been on this one for a while. I'm thinking he can lead us to one of the big fish, this kid."

"Come on, you and you." Bennett ordered Melvin and one of the other two men. "Let's take a ride. You two, beat it."

The remaining two men walked nervously out the room, down the hall, and out the front door of the house as the officers escorted their captives to their squad car. Once the captives were secured in the back seat, the car crept though the alley, turned onto the main street, then headed to the Western Precinct headquarters. As he sat quietly in the back seat of the squad car watching the marble-stepped row houses fly by, Melvin thought to himself that this was the longest ride of his life. He had done a lot of things but this was the first time he had ever gotten arrested for any of it; and his first pinch was this? His boss would not be happy. He was still young but had quickly worked his way up from an unknown and had gotten noticed because of his 'ambition'. His boss had promised him a big job if he could consistently show his worth, but now he sat in the back of a squad car on his way to jail.

'Damn!' he thought.

The squad car pulled into the back parking lot of the precinct headquarters near the prisoner intake door.

"I believe this is your stop, gentlemen." Bennett said with a chuckle.

The police headquarters was the conventional brick and mortar two-level building with parking lot and prisoner entrance in the back. Melvin and his partner were escorted in, processed and sent to a holding pen. While in the pen, Melvin looked through the bars, noticing the guard on duty. As if remembering some sort of protocol, he mentioned the guard over to him. The men in the cell with him thought he was insane as they saw him whisper something in the guard's ear. Whatever was whispered immediately inspired a sense of urgency in the guard as he with some reluctance, walked off quickly. Even more amazing to his fellow prisoners was that fifteen minutes later, the guard returned to the pen.

"You," the guard said, pointing to Melvin, "follow me." Melvin stood arrogantly and strutted toward the opened bars, not even looking back.

"What about me?" asked Melvin's coconspirator, as he rushed toward the gate.

"Not you scumbag, just him. Now sit down." barked the guard as he cuffed Melvin, secured the gate and the two vanished down the hall and into the receiving area. In the front lobby, a few officers talked and joked to pass the time until their shifts ended or until they received their next assignments. Among them were Officers Wright and Bennett.

In the middle of a story that one of the other officers was telling, someone yelled, "Ten hupp!"
All the officers stood at attention and saluted as Sargant Mackey passed by.

"As you were, men." Mackey said.
Everyone stood at ease. They all knew him as a no-nonsense commander, to be respected and feared. Mackey seemed rushed as he whisked by. Out the corner of his eye, Wright saw Mackey being intercepted by one of the detention guards and what looked like that 'kid' he'd just brought in for booking.

'What the hell?' he thought, as he saw the guard nod toward the boy, then whisper something to Mackey.

"That's my collar." he said to him self.
In disbelief he saw Mackey personally uncuff the kid and give him the thumbed hand gesture for 'beat it'. It was like slow motion as Wright watched the kid walk right by,

recognize him from earlier and quickly eye the ground as he exited. It was all Officer Wright could do to stop from grabbing the kid by the neck and slamming his face into the nearest wall. With a mixture of disbelief and rage, he regained his composure, took a breath and made a focused stride toward the Sargent.

The Sargent stood speaking with one of the lieutenants when Wright interrupted, "Sir. A moment of your time, sir?"

Before Mackey could respond, Wright spoke, smoldering, "Sir, that boy fit the description of a perp I arrested and brought here to be booked."

"What boy, Officer..." Mackey paused to look down at Wright's badge, "...Wright, Is it?"

"The one that just walked out, right pass a lobby full of policemen including his arresting officer." Wright restrained his voice, despite the confusion and anger that boiled up inside him. Mackey, taken aback for a second, glanced around to see who was looking. Naturally anyone who *was* staring, wasn't anymore.

He gathered himself, cleared his throat and answered, "Oh him, ah, he was a special case that was brought to my attention. Don't worry about it; It's been taken care of." Mackey grumbled, trying to sound official and passively dismissive.

"I haven't even put the paperwork in yet." Wright complained. "How can it be taken care of?"
With that, Mackey shot him a look full of daggers and menacingly turned to face him. Sensing he'd overstepped, Wright took a more passive tone.

"Sir. Not to interfere, but that kid was a big part of my investigation. I have evidence that could tie him to a lieutenant in the ..."

"Officer?" Mackey interrupted in a sharp steely tone. "How long 'you been in uniform?"

Wright stiffened up, "In my third year, sir."

"What's your rank?"

"Officer, Sir!"

Tapping the wings on his shoulders, Mackey asked, "And what are these?"

"Sargent's wings, sir."

"You know what that means, Officer?"
Wright stood quietly; intimidated to silence.

"It means, I am not in the practice of explaining myself to subordinates." Mackey then moved so close, they breathed the same air. "It happens again, and it gets bad for you. Understood?"

"Understood Sir." Wright chanted with eyes straight ahead, stiffened back and a saluted hand to brow.

Mackey utter three words that made Wright's blood run cold. "Consider yourself, 'noticed'."
He stepped back, glancing at the officer with whom he had the earlier conversation. Wright, all anger replaced by fear, remained paralyzed until Mackey, after a moment said one more word, "Out!" Wright could not get out of the Sargent's presence quickly enough. He walked out the door of the western precinct district headquarters into the visitors parking lot followed by his partner Bennett.

"Shit man, what was that?" Bennett asked looking around.

"I don't know. It started one way, ended another." Wright answered, gathering himself.

"You must've really ticked him off. I saw you going over there, I even heard you. No one questions him. No one even approaches him, what the hell were you thinking?" Bennett asked.

"I didn't know."

"Whatdaya mean ya didn't know? You kidding me?"

"I've only been transferred here for three months." Wright offered.

Bennett shook his head. "Well, now you do. You might wanna stay outta his way."

By then, dusk was night and the two officers' shifts were over.

After a moment Bennett asked. "You wanna get something to eat?"

Wright simply answered, "I'm usually dry, but if it's all the same to you. I'd rather have a drink."

"First two rounds on me." Bennett said as the two walked toward his car, got in, then pulled from the precinct parking lot; headed for 'happiness in a bottle'.

CHAPTER SIX

House on the Hill

Tap tap tap, tap tap tap tap.

"Sis!" No answer.

Tap tap tap tap.

"Sis!" Still no answer.

Pop tapped on the wood framed glass door of a row house in the Winchester neighborhood adjacent to the Avenue. Like the buildings on the avenue, these row homes were separated from the street by a wide cement pavement. Unlike the commercial district, these houses were identical brick front, three storied flats with marble steps and rails. Pop's '31 Oldsmobile was one of the many nice cars that lined the street, on one of the more 'well to do' blocks of the community. There was hardly any trash, save that which was carried by the wind, and small children and the elderly could be seen playing and talking quietly on the stoops where they lived. It was a relatively quiet block, a few streets off of the Avenue.

About four months had passed since Pop's boss Goldie, along with his underboss Giggy had left town. They had totally broken off contact, leaving it all behind and evidently enjoying their new lives. Street, who had remained behind, advising, sitting in on meetings and ensuring the changing of the guard, had left just a month before, and was by now, settling in on his new farm home in South Carolina. Middle management and street soldiers had fallen in line, and Pop's position atop the organization was secure. The transition and other matters had kept him, June and Elsie very busy on functional and operational levels, but business had eased enough to allow Pop to make a social call or two.

As he stood on the steps of his sister's house on North Stricker Street, he wondered why no one was answering the door. In between knocks, he looked up at the second and third floor windows, both of which were open and letting the breeze in. He knocked again, for the last time, he thought.

"Sis!" he hollered, this time up to the windows. A head poked out of the third floor window. Looking down at him, the face changed from a look of irritation to one of delighted relief. It was Pop's older sister Lillian.

"Oh, it's only you. Don't you have a key?" she questioned jokingly.

"I must've left it at my apartment. Gimme a break." Pop answered.

"Alright hold on, I'll be right down."

"Don't sound so happy to see your baby brother." Pop replied sarcastically.

As he waited, he observed the block on which his sister lived. He had bought the house for the three of them years ago when Lillian's husband, Israel Tucker, a railroad laborer, died from a stroke on the job. She had his small pension, but had a baby girl to care for, and Pop, who was just starting to make some real money, purchased the home outright. He would make sure his family was safe and secure; it was the least he could do. Growing up, it was Lillian who had raised younger brother Pop, when their parents died in the influenza epidemic of 1918. It seemed someone was always dying and leaving a burden to someone else. Early on, Lillian had tried to shield her brother from the streets, but she soon realized that not only had she failed, but he had proved to be a well adept street person. Though constantly afraid for her brother's safety, she dealt with his reality, and secretly dreamed of the day when they could leave it all behind.

The door unlocked from the inside, then opened.

In a flower print housedress, Lillian gestured with her hand, "Well, little brother, come on in."

Pop followed. She was just a few years older than him, barely forty, but she had the look of a woman ten years younger. The vestibule and hallway were neatly draped in wallpaper of silver spearheads on a field of navy. Baseboards and trims were a neat eggshell white and the hardwood floors were kept immaculately polished. The living room was furnished with a simple three piece beige, Victorian print set and coffee table, while the dining room had a full oak table and matching chairs. Both rooms looked like they were barely used.

"'Like what you've done with the place. My poor niece, growing up in a museum." Pop said walking through.

"Ha, ha, ha. Very funny, smart ass." Lillian shot back.

"Where is my baby niece, anyway?"

"Your '*baby*', is around the playground with her friends." she replied. "She should be back soon."
She lead led him to the kitchen. The wide rectangular shape of the row houses' floor dimensions, allotted the living space of the living room, dining room and kitchen on the right side facing the back, with the hallway going

64

the length of the left side of the house. They sat at a small square table in the kitchen.

"Coffee?" she offered.

"Naw. 'Got any iced tea?"

"Yup. Got some cake too. Coming right up."

As Lillian gathered food and drink, she light heartedly asked, "So, to what do I owe this visit from my successful brother?"

"I gotta want something?" Pop asked defensively. "I can't just stop by to see my darling older sis."

"Watch it, with the *old*" she said "I look younger than you."

"What ever you gotta tell yourself to sleep at night." They laughed.

"I do wanna talk, though." Pop said with a more serious tone.

Lillian turned around with a glass of iced tea in one hand and two small plates of cake in the other. "So talk." She sat down placing the tea and one plate in front of Pop and the other in front of herself.

He started, "Well, as you would guess, my new position has put me at a higher level of finance. That level opened a lot of doors for me. 'Made me a lot of friends, but at the same time, it's made a lot of enemies too. 'Upside to that is, people trying to get in my good graces, going out their way to try to *help* you or *please* you, since they know who you are to me. That could get real annoying, real quick. 'Downside is somebody who's trying to hurt me. They probably won't be able to get to me, so who's the next best thing, you."

Lillian shifted in her chair. "Enough with the preamble," she said impatiently, "Get to it."

65

"I am. I am." Pop agreed. Then after a moment, he restarted, "Bottom line, I get real busy and I can't come around as much to keep an eye. I worry. I've been making arrangements, for the family; for the future."

He thought for a second, and then instead of further explanation, he reached in the inner side-pocket of his blazer. From it, he pulled a round folded manila envelope with documents inside. He placed it on the table in front of Lillian. With a touch of apprehension mixed with curiosity, she grabbed the envelope, opened it and skimmed the first two documents. Confusion, then realization came over her face.

"Is this what I think it is?" she asked. Pop responded with a nod. "This is... great. I think."
He had given Lillian the Deed and Title to a new home that sat on a patch of land.

"It's all yours. All paid for. Just sign it into your name."

Instead of an elated response that Pop had expected, he was baffled to see his sister starting to worry.

"I don't understand. This is so out of the blue. Is there a reason we have to leave? Are we in danger?" she asked nervously.

He cut her off, "Sis. Relax." Then he grabbed her hand and with a calming voice, said "Nothing's wrong. In fact everything is copasetic. I would just feel better if y'all was set, just in *case* anything bad happened; which it won't." he added reassuringly.

Lillian said holding the forms up, "This is a big step, a big move. Can we afford to do this now? You're always so busy."

"Its not for me, its for y'all. Look, you still got Israel's pension, and we got a lot of money here in the safe, but I put a lot more of it away at the new house. It'll be fine. Besides, that's why we do it, right? A wise man once said, 'Why work so hard for if we can't look out for our families'?"

Lillian reluctantly agreed, "I suppose so." A look of calm and understanding came across her face. She looked down inspecting the paper work once again. As she skimmed, an eyebrow went up.

"Interesting." she said under her breath. "You got some land up on 'The Hill'." Then looking up she asked, "Is it close to the family plot?"

"Right beside it." Pop answered.

Lil's eyes welled.

'The Hill' was a colored community in the town of Cockeysville, Maryland, just north of the city. Pop's and Lillian's grandparents had owned a small home off of one of the winding roads, and though their mother moved to the city when she was married, they visited 'The Hill' every summer. The old house, to them, was home.

"Back to 'The Hill'." she said almost to herself. "The more I think about it, the more I can't wait."

"Good," Pop answered. "'Cause I've already made the arrangements. The ball is already rolling."

He sifted through the documents, folding the ends of signature pages. He placed the pages on the table in front of Lillian.

"We got business first." Pointing at the lined spaces, "Sign here, here, here and here." As Lil signed, Pop continued, "Tomorrow morning, I'll take it to my lawyer.

We can trust him. He'll process it. In three days I got the movers coming by."

When she finished, Lillian's, eyes welling up, pushed her chair back, walked around the table to where Pop sat, kissed him gently on his forehead and simply said, "Thank you."

Ruthie was very fond of her Uncle Poppy. He had always spent time with her and had taught her lots of things. Though she was only twelve, Ruthie seemed to be more mature, more aware, more calculating. Apart from those qualities, she was like any other neighborhood girl. She had pretty brown skin with almond shaped eyes and her hair was pulled up into three thick plats, one of which fell on her forehead. Her mother Lillian told her that her Uncle had visited the day before and would be returning the next day; today. She sat at the neighborhood playground, playing jacks with her best friend Doris. It was getting late and she decided that it was time to be getting home; besides, she didn't want to miss her uncle's visit.

"Ru Ru, when are you gonna ask your uncle to drive us around in his big car?" Doris asked as the two made their way from the playground.

"I tried. He don't come around as much, probably because of his new job."

"New job? I thought you was his favorite niece?

I'm his *only* niece, and I'm working on it. He keeps saying he too busy to drive two little girls around."

Doris thought, then offered, "What if I brought my little cousin? Then it would be more of us."

"Jacks?" Ruthie sneered. "I don't know. She's too little and too sassy. She'll get us in trouble, again."

"Well, we gotta do something. I'm getting tired of walking everywhere."

"He ain't your personal driver." Ruthie laughed.

As they walked onto their block, Ruthie noticed the '31 Oldsmobile parked in front of her house. Her pace quickened to a skip, almost leaving Doris behind. As she neared her house, the front door opened. Out came her Uncle Poppy followed by her mother. Ruthie was elated. When he turned to see her, his smile grew.

"Hey, baby niece!" he shouted as he walked down the house's marble steps, arms wide. "Gimme my sugar."

Ruthie ran and jumped into her uncle's waiting arms. "Uncle Poppy!" She was the only one who called him Pop*py*.

"Thought I wasn't coming, didn't you?" he asked.

"Nope. Mommy said you'd be back today, I just didn't know when." she answered.

They hugged then he put her down. He noticed his niece's friend standing just behind her.

"And how 'you doing? little person."

"Fine." Doris bashfully answered.

Ruthie cut in, "Oh, you remember my best friend Dorie, from down the street."

"Hi Mister Uncle Poppy. You got a funny name." Dorie said.

"Well we all can't have a pretty name like Dorie, can we?"

Doris blushed. "Thank you." She turned to Ruthie. "I gotta go, I'll see you tomorrow. Bye Mister Uncle Poppy. Bye Miss Lil."

Doris went home; Ruthie sat on the stoop and the adults talked. Her mind drifted as she thought of school and her uncle's nice car; and that lady she would see him driving around with sometimes.

'Was that his girlfriend or something,' she thought, 'yuck!'

Then she thought about all the nice stuff he had and how everybody liked him. She was snapped back into their conversation, seeing a big envelope and hearing them talk about a house on some 'hill'.

'What's the Hill?' she thought.

Lillian, stuffing the weird envelope in her apron said to Pop, "This is definitely a day for celebrating. You know what?, me and Ruthie are gonna take you out to dinner. Our treat."

Pop reluctantly, suggested, "Maybe being out with me, in public, ain't the best idea right now." He saw Lillian frown, and then added, "But I could use a good home cooked meal."

Lillian's frown reversed into a gentle smile.

She quickly conceded, "OK. A homestyle dinner; here, tonight. It's the least I can do. 'Cause God knows that little skinny heifer you hang around with can't cook." They laughed.

Pop asked. "What's on the menu?"

"I'll make your favorite. Pork chops, mashed potatoes and kale, smothered in gravy."

"Man. You sure know how to close the deal, sis."

She agreed, and then with a quick thought she said, almost to herself, "Damn, I gotta go on the avenue to pick up a few things. Could you wait here with Ruthie? I'll be right back."

Pop put a hand up in protest. "Naw, don't worry about it. You stay here, *I'll* go around. Just tell me what you need."

Lillian quickly jotted ingredients down on a brown piece of wrinkled paper and handed it to her brother. As he pocketed it, Lil gave him a sincere look.

She said mockingly, "You're the greatest little brother of all time."

"And don't you forget it." Pop replied, then turned to his niece, and jokingly said, "You. You're coming with me. Your mother is putting me to work, but I won't slave alone. Come on."

"Ok," Ruthie said offering her hand.

"We're walking." he said throwing his keys back to Lil, as the two walked pass his car. "Be back in a few." Lillian stood in the doorway watching her daughter and brother cross the street, and walk around the corner; adoring their loving relationship. She smiled and went inside.

The weather had suddenly become a bit blustery as Ruthie buttoned the sweater her mother had made her wear earlier. As the two walked to the grocers, she observed the warmth with which the older folks from the neighborhood treated him. It seemed, the closer they got to the Avenue, the more he was treated like a celebrity. She grabbed her uncle Poppy's hand with pride.

Looking up at him she asked, "Do you know all these people?"

"Well, kinda. We're all from the neighborhood. I've known some of them since I was a kid."

"They all act like they like you, or scared of you, or something. I can't tell which one." Ruthie thought for a second. "Is that because of your new job?"
With one brow raised, her uncle turned to her. He wasn't quite sure if she knew what he did, but he suspected.

"Full of questions you know all the answers to, huh?"

"No. Just curious." she answered nonchalantly.

As they crossed the intersection of a side street, she asked "Unc', do you like when everybody knows who you are?"

He thought reflectively, then answered, "Baby girl, sometimes I think it would've been better if nobody knew who I was. It can slow you down when everybody knows about you." Then, staring off, almost talking to himself he said, "Goldie always said, great things...are better done... in secrecy."
He sighed. They could now clearly hear the sounds of music, people and traffic on the Avenue. Reflecting and talking as if reprimanding himself, he lectured, "You gotta be focused Ruthie. You gotta stay sharp. Think things through." Then looking off into the distance, he chuckle to himself, "Hmm, I'm one to talk. I've been so focused on making sure y'all alright, *I* lost focus; lost focus out here on the streets."
He looked down to notice Ruthie's confused frown.

With his free hand he playfully rubbed her hair, "Don't worry about, squirt. Someday you'll understand."

She gave a reassuring smiled as they walked onto the busy thoroughfare that was Pennsylvania Avenue.

Once Again

As they approached the block on which the grocer sat, Ruthie and her Uncle Poppy conversed about people, how they acted and why they did the things they did; a subject on which she was becoming very well versed, thanks to her many talks with him. He always seemed to be 'coaching' her. The grocers had the look of an average storefront; an encased glass front separated by a walkway entrance. On one side lay fresh produce and canned goods, on the opposite side were nonperishable items such as silver and flatware and cleaning products. It seemed to be an ordinary mid-evening with a few people on the street and in the store.

Their talk had become less serious, more about school and the movies, when in the middle of their conversation, Pop squeezed Ruthie's hand, pulling her closer to him. Looking up at him she saw that he had seen something that made him hesitate. She followed his line of sight to a dark colored police squad car that sat just down the street on the intersecting corner. Beside that car stood a police officer that seemed to be a force of nature. He stood tall and trim with a with his peaked cap pulled low, military style and though he was the only one of his type, no one in his immediate vicinity looked his way. The little girl knew only two things, this policeman was a bad man and that she didn't like him. Without hiding it, the policeman just stared at her uncle who had uncharacteristically begun to get nervous and jittery.

As they turned into the grocer, Pop held the door open for her, trying to fake normalcy, "You first." They entered the store. As Ruthie began to gather the ingredients and groceries for dinner, Pop signaled the stock clerk over to him. From across the store Ruthie could see him reach in his blazer's inside pocket and quickly pass the stock clerk what appeared to be a handgun, which in turn, was immediately and discreetly taken to the back stocking area of the store. Ruthie was frightened to know that her uncle carried a gun, but quickly reasoned that it was probably just part of his 'business'.

Pop's mood lifted as he grabbed some onions and met her at the front counter. Outside the store Ruthie saw the mean looking police officer casually pacing back and forth, occasionally glancing in. She watched intently as suddenly the officer seemed to nod to someone out of view, and then walked back in the direction of his squad car. Ruthie and Pop quietly exhaled. After paying for the groceries, they walked out the front entrance. A cursory glance revealed the officer now, to the right of the store, in his vehicle looking down in his lap, as if reading a newspaper. Another glance in the opposite direction showed nothing out of the ordinary. But across the street in front of the hardware store, Ruthie noticed a lady dressed like one of those nasty women her mother told her to stay away from. The woman was trying to get her uncle's attention, signaling him to cross the street so they could speak.

Pop turned to Ruthie, "Listen, wait here. I'll be right back. Don't move."

He put the bag he was carrying in Ruthie's arms and walked across the street to speak with the obviously familiar woman. Pop and the woman talked for a few seconds when they were interrupted by the cries of a boy of about thirteen or fourteen years old. He looked weak and lost as if wandering around in a fog.

He held on to passersby crying, "They shot him, they shot him." It seemed that he had suddenly recognized Pop because the boy ran directly to him.

Pop kneeled as the boy cried, "You gotta come; you gotta! They shot him. They said he's dead!"
Ruthie saw her uncle's eyes widen from across the street.

"Who's dead?!" Pop reluctantly asked the boy. Ruthie saw the boy's mouth move but his voice was drowned out by a passing automobile. Whatever name the boy gave put Pop in a state of shock because he stood straight up, staring at the boy.

In a calm voice he told the boy, "Go home, now." Ruthie was very much afraid now. There was too much happening at once. Instinctively, she looked in the direction of the policeman on the corner. The officer had just started his car and shifted his line of sight from the direction of her Uncle Poppy to a shady character on the opposite corner. The officer nodded to the character and pulled off, turned left and drove in the opposite direction down Pennsylvania Avenue. Ruthie then watched the shady character tip his hat in the direction of her Uncle Poppy who was on the same side of the street. She traced the character's line of sight to some kid wearing an Elite Giants baseball cap. The kid looked like he was in his mid-teens. Her Uncle Poppy was still distracted by what he had just heard from the crying boy.

'Not good' she thought.

She started to panic. As the crying boy left for home, Ruthie could see the kid in the baseball cap walking towards her uncle with his right hand in his jacket pocket. The kid's pace quickened until he was about five feet away. He pulled a gun and aimed at her Uncle Poppy's chest. Everything for Ruthie seemed to slow. Pop became suddenly aware. He had been in this situation before and his experience dictated his instincts and actions. He confidently turned sideways, making himself a smaller target and with a smirk reached in his shoulder holster for a weapon... that was no longer there.

At that very same moment Pop and Ruthie shared the very same thought, "The gun... The gun is in the store." Blaamm!!!

The shot from the kid's gun knocked Pop about eight feet onto his back. Everything went silent. Ruthie was in shock; she couldn't move, she couldn't speak, she could barely breathe. Passersby ducked for cover behind whatever would offer them refuge. The kid in the baseball cap stood over the body of his victim, nervous but resolute. He offered a look down to the corner. The shady character, who was staring back gave another nod then walked off. The kid shot Pop two more times in the chest. "Blaamm, Blaamm!!!"

This snapped Ruthie, who stood across the street, back into reality. She dropped her groceries.

"NOOOO!"

She had watched it all. The kid, not even noticing her, simply put the gun back in his pocket, walked the way he came and vanished around the corner. Ruthie crept across the street afraid of what she would find when she got there. She could hear women screaming and people running but when she stood over her uncle, where his killer had stood only a minute before, she felt a calm fall over her. She didn't cry, she didn't faint, she just stared; with a single tear rolling down her cheek; processing the gravity of the moment.

"Cough!" On the ground, Pop's body convulsed.

"He's still alive." someone said.

With a calm beyond her years, Ruthie sat on the ground positioning her uncle's head in her lap. Pop bled from the mouth and struggled to talk. She managed a tearful smile trying her best to console him from his inevitable death. With her Uncle Poppy's last muster of strength, he gently tapped his bloody finger to her temple. And as he lay bleeding in his niece's arms, his last, whimpering, dying word was... "Ruthie".

CHAPTER SEVEN

1942

From a Pennsylvania Railroad steam-liner's passenger car, reserved for colored patrons, a young lady sitting in a window seat stared though the thick glass. As the train pulled into the upcoming station, she saw that the platform was full of people waiting to board the 529 local to Washington DC; the train on which she rode. It seemed an equal amount of people prepared to exit the train as were waiting to board it. The young lady was amongst the exiting crowd. Standing, she gathered her belongings; two medium sized suitcases and an old circular hatbox, then moved toward the doors.

"Now entering, Penn Line's Wilson Street Station. Please watch your step." the conductor's voice announced over the intercom.

Train porters, neatly dressed in dark brown uniforms, assisted passengers on and off the trains.

"Take your bags, ma'am?" one asked the young lady as she disembarked.

"No. I got it." she answered.

With a suitcase in each hand and her hatbox under her left arm, she walked onto the platform, excusing her way through the thick crowd. She noticed that most of the people entering, leaving and working in this particular station were colored, but she didn't wonder why. She already knew. This was the train station that served one of the colored sections of the city; the neighborhood of

Upton. The station's underground tunnel intersected the neighborhoods busiest street, Pennsylvania Avenue. Its boarding platforms were near the main commercial district and set below street level, bookended by double tracked tunnel openings. The easternmost opening sat below the station building's entrance that faced the avenue. The surrounding buildings gave the submerged platform a gorged look, as above and beyond the station walls, it was opened to the sky and the elements. Fortunately, this was a sunny, warm late morning.

Patrons had to ascend from the platform by steps, which opened into the building's ticketing and waiting area. The young lady trudged on while people pushed by and bumped her. She felt like a snail in a horse race, but took no offense to everyone else's haste. She was just taking it all in. She had just made the short trip from the country, where she lived in a farmhouse with her mother. For one reason or another she had decided that she needed a change of scenery. Once in the big city, she was so obviously out of place, from her clothes, a simple light brown flower print dress, to her demeanor. She looked like a bumpkin and eventually made her way through the waiting area to the street. People buzzed about, going in and out of the train station's front doors.

"Can I get you a taxi, Miss?" a bellhop asked.

"No. I'm OK." she answered.

"Well you have a good day just the same miss."
He tipped his cap, and then went off to help someone else. The young lady found a place outside and up the street and just beyond a cab stand; waiting for someone who had not yet shown up. She reached in her jacket pocket and pulled out a piece of paper with an address on it. She

looked at it sighing, and just as she made a decision to walk and find that address, her path was suddenly blocked.

"Well, well, well. You was about to leave. You ain't think I was gonna be on time, did you?" There, stood a solidly built young woman with a light brown skin, a thick nose and a smirk.

It took less than a second for the young lady to recognize her.

"Well, technically, you are, by about two minutes." she said with a wry smile.

"Ruthie!"

"Dorie!"

The two squealed and hugged each other excitedly.

Doris stood back and looked her friend up and down, "Girl, it's good to see you. Look at you; all grown-womanish."

Ruthie struck a playful pose, like a pin-up girl.

Doris smirked, "Don't get carried away. I said *looked*. Twenty don't make you grown."

"Well you think you' grown, and we the same age, so..."

"Ooh, you done' got sassy out there in the sticks. Girl, how was that train ride in?"

"Crowded, but at least it was short. I'm just glad to be here. That farm was driving me crazy. I needed this change. Thank you so much for puttin' me up."

"Please, you're like my sister. My long lost sister, but my sister, none-the-less."

"Thanks again girl, and look at you." Ruthie said observing Doris' outfit. "Lena Horne ain't got nothin' on you."

"Dorthy Dandridge either, and don't you forget it."
They chuckle.

Doris continued, "We gon' have so much fun. It'll be like old times. We got a lot of catching up to do."

"Well if you don't mind," Ruthie said, collecting her luggage. "Let's do some of that catching up, and walking at the same time."

Doris grabbed one of Ruthie's suitcases and the two walked one block up the moderately busy Avenue, turned right at Laurens Street then walked and talked all the way to Doris' apartment.

As they walked and reminisced, Ruthie felt like she was in a time capsule; all the good times began to come back to her. She was like a tourist visiting home. They ended up in front of a wide, three storied, Victorian styled corner house. It had been converted into apartments and Doris' was on the second floor back. They walked up the front marble stoop, through the vestibule doors and straight up a hallway stairwell. On the second floor Doris unlocked and opened the door to a very neat and clean living space, which included a couch, a chair, a small magazine table and a radio. A kitchen area was to the right of the entrance, across from a very small bathroom, with her small bedroom to the back.

Doris presented the couch. "You're suite, M' lady." she said in an English accent, with a mocking grin. Ruthie dropped her luggage and flopped down on the couch.

"Thank you, fair wench." she responded jokingly. Doris stared at Ruthie. It was the first time she had really seen and looked at her friend in years. Ruthie's simple flower print dress was a direct indication that she was indeed a country girl. Though she was from the neighborhood, Doris figured that since she was gone for so long and since she spent most of her formative years on a farm, the Avenue was probably a different world to her.

The two rested for a moment then Doris got up to turn on the radio. There were some commercials for the new cartoon movie, Bambi, a few automobiles ads, some local news and the inevitable news from the war. The announcer spoke of yet another naval defeat by the Empire of Japan on some far off pacific island. It had been about four months since the Second World War had started, but it seemed that the news was always getting worse. Japan was winning battles and the U.S. hardly seemed prepared. People were scared. Some in California feared bombing or worse, invasion. And because of this city's port and armaments facilities, Baltimore was thought to be a main target, but not for Japan, but for Nazi Germany. The Port of Baltimore had been refitted and retooled for the war industry; from war ships to terrain vehicles to bombers; placing a huge *bull's-eye* on the entire city. U.S. bond drivers rallied for support of the military and the war movement with their propaganda slogan, *From the many, to the few*.

"Catchy, but depressing." Doris said. She got up and changed the station. "Sooner or later they gonna have girls out there fighting."

"Shoot, that's men's work. It looks like everybody's joining up. I say, if that's what they wanna do, then let 'em, because over here,'" Ruthie pointed to her personal space, "No heroes."

"That's a catchy one too. We gotta use that." said Doris.

She found a Big Band station and then noticed Ruthie singing along with pop tune.

'It seems, to me I've heard that song before. It's from an old familiar score.'

Ruthie chimed in singing, "I know it well, that melody." As the song continued she noticed Doris staring at her with a look of befuddlement.

"What?" Ruthie answered the strange look.

"You know this? You like this?" Doris asked, surprised and confused.

"You *don't*? Its number one on the hit parade." Ruthie answered

"You need to find another station, country girl. What they ain't got no good music out there in the sticks. I'm a take you to hear some good music."

"This is good music"

"No. I mean good music like some King Cole, some Mabel Lee, and some Fats Waller. That boogie woogie."

"Like the Andrew Sisters?" Ruthie teased.

Exasperated, Doris answered, "Something like that. Look, we gotta hit the avenue and try to get you hep to the jive."

"OK, but I'm not as square as you think."

"I hope not."

The two spent the rest of the day and all evening talking and catching up.

The next day Ruthie woke with a stretch. Looking around from her makeshift couch/bed, she noticed from across the apartment, that Doris was already up quietly ironing her dress.

83

"I'm off today. So we get to do the Avenue." Doris said.

"Great." Ruthie said yawning. "I'll be ready in a half hour. I'm kind of hungry though."

"Well that's good because I know a good diner."

"Solid."

The Avenue

The walk to the Avenue was nice. The day was like the one before, warm and sunny with a few clouds that guaranteed passing relief by casting shadows of shade. It was early April and mid-morning so the only people on the streets at that time of day were older folks and city workers. The residential side-streets were lined with typical two and three storied, red-bricked row-house flats with alternating wooden, concrete and marble stoops. Automobile traffic was light but heavier toward the main strip. The ladies turned right at the crosswalk onto Pennsylvania Avenue. The avenue hadn't changed much to Ruthie. It was the same hustle and bustle; the same impersonal closeness. A few new businesses had popped up amongst some of the older ones as the ladies walked by a building with a fancy billboard, under which two elegantly dressed female manikins stood behind thick curved glass.

Looking up smiling, Ruthie said, "I see they still got the charm school here."

Doris responded, "Please they ain't going nowhere. Look around. If it's one thing the avenue couldn't do without, it's a charm school."

"Yeah, my momma was gonna send me there, until..."

Ruthie's words tapered off as if recalling something she did not want to.

Sensing her friend's distress, Doris redirected the conversation, "And how is Miss Lil anyway? You know I gotta get up there to see her."
The two walked onto the next block, known as 'The Eatery'; so called for its concentration of bakeries, restaurants and diners.

"In here." Doris directed.
Like most businesses along Pennsylvania Avenue, this diner was just a converted row house. Inside, there were booths full of people that went the length of the building to the right, a walkway in the center and an eating counter with stools to the left. On the other side of the counter worked the waitress and the cooks that prepared food on a long grille and stove. The diner was fairly crowded. All of the tables and most of the stools were taken. As the girls scanned for empty seats, one of the bus boys got their attention.

Holding two fingers in the air, he hollered, "I got two down here on the end."

"Thanks!" the ladies said in unison as they walked hurriedly back to the stools. Sitting down, they grabbed menus and ordered. In less time than Ruthie thought, they were eating their breakfasts.

Nearing the end of their meals, Doris, as if waiting for the right time to speak, finally managed to utter, "Ru Ru..." she struggled, "This might not be the best time, and I know there's a lot happening with the move and all, but we never got the chance to talk."
Ruthie's brow frowned in question. Doris tried to get to the point.

"Look, you're like my sister, and...and..." Her words got caught in her throat. She couldn't speak for what seemed like an eternity. Guessing her friend's thoughts, Ruthie's eye welled up.

With a gentle resolve she managed a smile and simply said, "I know, Dorie. Thanks."
Doris realized that as she was trying to console, she was the one being consoled. It was then that she noticed a maturity and deep strength within the person she thought so naive, just a short time ago. The moment passed. The busboy came to clean the table, followed by waitress who asked them if they wanted coffee. They both declined and asked for the check. As they waited, two plainly dressed young men walked over to their table.

The one wearing a navy blue windbreaker spoke. "Ladies, How y'all doing?"
The girls gave a cynical smile in acknowledgment.

"I'm Mil," then nodding to his partner, "this is Big Joe. We'd be honored if y'all would joint us for a coffee and some pie, our treat."
He made a hand gesture across the diner to the table they occupied. Mil was tall and brown skinned. Big Joe however, was not aptly named as he looked to be less than medium height and of a portly build. The ladies weren't very interested at the moment. They looked at each other.

Doris answered, "No thanks, we just ordered the check."
Just then the waitress walked by handing Ruthie the bill.

"You can pay at the counter. Thanks for stopping by. Come again."
Intercepting it, Mil kindly snatched the bill from the waitress before Ruthie could get it.

"I'll take that. Allow us to get this one, ladies."
Snatch!

Doris had taken the check back, "And I'll take that.
When strange men treat, strange men think you owe."
The men stepped aside, temporarily defeated.

'Nice.' Ruthie thought.

Big Joe persisted, "Ah come on, now. It ain't even
like that. Let me talk to you a minute."
The girls ignored the men's polite protests and pleading
as they walked to the cash register, paid the bill and exited
the store.

Watching the girls walk down the Avenue from the
doorway, Mil, trying to save face, said to them "Ah, nice
talking to y'all. We'll see you ladies later." And then
determined, under his breath he mumbled, "Oh, this ain't
even over."

It was just after noon and the girls had done a little
shopping on the Avenue's commercial district known as
'The Shop'. For her stay, Ruthie had packed a few dresses,
but she and Doris both agreed that she needed to be
brought up to fashion. They went in one dress store for
twenty minutes and another for twice as long. Ruthie had
a little money, carefully budgeted from the small fortune
her uncle had put away for her and her mother; besides,
she was good with numbers and frugalities.

Her uncle had always said, 'The only person who
gotta know you have money, is you.' Ruthie smiled with
that thought, but then reasoned 'Hey, you only live once.
What the hell.'

After a shoe store and two hat shops, the two spent
over and hour trying on dresses in 'Mary Ellen's Beauty

Wear'. Seventy-four dollars later, their clothing purchases were arranged for home delivery. As they left the store, out in front, leaning up against a dusty brown moving truck and looking as handsome as a plainly dressed man could, was Mil. He didn't try to make this second meeting look coincidental; he wanted it known that it was *intentional*. His partner, Big Joe came from around the back of the truck with a sudden smile.

"'Bout time. What was y'all, buying up the whole store?" He looked at Mil chuckling, "Women be shopping."

Mil answered sarcastically, for the benefit of the ladies hearing him, "Evidently not. They came out empty handed." He walked slowly and smoothly toward them; eyes on Ruthie, "But I think we can do something about that."

"Well I think not." Doris said protectively, blocking his path.

Amused and irritated, Mil asked, "What are you, her chaperone? Let her answer for herself."

With equal sass, Ruth confirmed her friend's earlier declaration, "Well *I* think not."
They both began to walk down the sidewalk. Mil looked behind to signal Big Joe who was already moving. Big Joe eased up on the opposite side of Doris mumbling something funny. Whatever it was, worked because Doris was laughing and giving him her full attention. This was Mil's chance.

He walked beside Ruthie, and then blocking her way, he said apologetically, "Wait. I'm sorry. Can we start over? *Please*." He saw a softening in Ruthie's otherwise stoned face, but still she remained silent.

He said extending his right hand, "I'm Milton. Milton Newsome. *Very* pleased to make your acquaintance." Ruthie ignored his hand and stared blankly at him as if waiting in vain to be impressed. That look of mild irritation was the most beautiful thing Mil had ever seen before, in his life.

He said simply, "The poem of your smile has yet to be written, but when it is, I shall author the first line."

Ruthie looking at him blankly, thought, 'Nice.' and then smiled. "A poet eh? You better start writing."

Mil immediately said, "Oh, consider me your personal poet." He suggested, "Look, I know a spot. Music, drinks, whatsay we get together?"

"Sorry, I don't date." she resolutely responded.

"Well maybe if we could…"

"I'm not interested." she cut him off.

She turned to her friend who was still chatting with Big Joe, "Dorie, let's go."

Milton shook his head at Ruthie saying, "Damn, and here I thought *she* was the mean one."
Doris reluctantly broke off conversation with Joe and joined her friend as they walked off down the Avenue.

As the men watched them stride away, Milton, in desperation said, "Well, at least tell me your name."
He was encouraged when she turned back and simply said, "Ruthie."

CHAPTER EIGHT

Officer

The hollering could be heard from down the dank half lit hallway. Two prisoners were being escorted from the police station's main floor, by way of stairs, down to the holding pens in the basement by two officers. One of the prisoners seemed to be dead drunk, hardly being able to stand, let alone walk. The other was just loud.

With voices in echo, the sober prisoner angrily shouted, "This is bullshit officer. How you gon' lock me up for breaking into some store? How you even know it was me?"

"Cause it was you we caught climbing out the back window, idiot." the escorting officer answered, annoyed.

"Just because I was breaking out don't mean I was the one breaking in. Y'all need to get y'all facts straight." The inmate said with comedic contempt. This comment seemed to be the proverbial straw that broke the camel's back.

"I've had just about enough from you boy." the officer yelled back, slamming his prisoner up against the cellblock wall. He continued, "Now you shut your mouth and get in that cell."

The loud inmate stood, cuffed, now in front of the holding cell when he turned to the officer. Eyes blazing, he gritted his teeth.

"I hate you honky, white bread mother fuckers. FU..!"

Before he could yell the whole word out, the thickness of a Billy club found its mark right below its victim's sternum, stealing his breath and his balance. The inmate folded to the ground in full view of the holding cell's occupants who passively observed the predictable outcome. As the floored inmate struggled to his knees, the officers thought the timing was right to teach a lesson of law & order, and respect. They rained down Billy club swings on his side and legs as he cried out from a fetal position.

The officers didn't give a thought to the other inebriated prisoner who just waited, barely cognizant of his surroundings, arms cuffed behind him, half nodding off, half trying to keep his balance. This prisoner was of medium height and build, and smelled of whiskey. After the beating, the officers uncuffed their prisoners, unlocked and slid open the cell door. One of them gave the drunk a wordless nod toward the pen and watched as he stumbled his way through the bared opening, then the two proceeded to grab, drag and toss the beaten man onto the middle of the holding pen's floor. As the cell door clanged shut, the beaten inmate slowly dragged himself to the nearest corner and spent the rest of the night curled up on the floor groaning. The officers locked the bar doors, then walked back up the hallway continuing an earlier conversation.

Once they vanished up the stairwell, the drunk walked to the back of the pen, to a long wooden bench that lined the walls. Few noticed that his stride was no longer clumsy and belabored but now smooth and steady. On the bench was another man, sitting hunched over. Beside him was a man lying on his back, sleep. An old light bulb kept the room dimly lit and quiet conversations between prisoners, kept it from feeling like a total crypt. The quasi-drunk man took a seat on the bench next to the hunched inmate.

Looking down, the hunched man said, "The drunk act, huh. This *must* be urgent. What y'all couldn't wait?"

The sobered drunk, staring forward answered, "It's going down in two days, besides, who knew when you were getting outta here? We need to know which route it's on so we can plan it out." He had morphed from drunkard to strictly business.

"So long as you remember whose idea this was; not to mention my cut." the other reaffirmed.

"Is it still happening, or what?", sounding impatient and annoyed.

"Yeah, yeah, it's still on. Relax." he said defensively.

"When and where?"

"You gonna remember this?"

The fake drunk taped his own temple, "I got it." They spoke just above a whisper; only those in the immediate vicinity would be able to hear.

"It'll be in a Kinsler Brothers bread truck, and the pickup is on the corner of Greenmount and Chase at or around five thirty in the morning. Then, there'll be two more; one on Central and Monument and the last on Gay and Madison. After that, y'all can move on them at any time."

"Good, Good."

"But I got one more thing. I need you to tell Sweets or Foxx, or whoever, they need to get me outta here."

"We 'working on it. You' the one that got yourself in here in the first place."

"You' in here too. How you even gon' get out in time?"

"I'm drunk remember. I'm just here until I dry out. I'll be gone in the morning."

"OK. Just don't forget about me."

The fake drunk grunted, and the rest of the night remained relatively quiet besides faint inmate chatter and footsteps of a periodic pacer. Around three am, those prisoners that finally fell asleep were abruptly awakened by the clang of a Billy club on the cell bars.

"Jones!!" an officer shouted. The startled inmates cleared their heads as they looked around. The prisoner on the back bench, still lying on his back with his hands folded across his chest, woke in a daze and mumbled,

"Jones. 'Right here."

"Get up." the officer said, "You made bail."

The inmate sat upright, wiped his eyes, cleared his throat and stumbled toward the opened bars.

"Lucky bastard." one inmate said under his breath. The rest quickly lost interest and went back to whatever they were doing.

The officer, annoyed at the newly freed prisoner's slow pace, barked, "Hurry up, you. Or you'll find yourself enjoying an extended stay."

The ex-prisoner hurried out the cell and was escorted down the hallway, up the stairwell and onto the main floor of the Eastern Precinct Police Department. At the processing bench there was no awaiting wife or girlfriend, no bail poster of any sort; just a few people waiting for loved ones, scattered police officers and what looked to be a Sargent. He had a grim face and a file in his hand. His name was Sargent Ralph Schmidt, fifteen-year veteran of the BCPD. He turned to face prisoner and escort as if for inspection.

"This Jones?" The Sargent said, looking at the prisoner.

"It is, sir." the officer answered.

He glared at Jones, then growled, "Take this piece of black trash to room three. I got questions." he grunted. The office grabbed his escort by the forearm and shoved him into an office off the main hallway. Jones, after a second, looked around and then sat in a wooden chair that was in front of an old wooden desk full of old files and a metal lamp.

'Classic cop office.' he thought to himself.
About five minutes passed when the door opened. In walked Sargant Schmidt with the half chewed cigar. He silently glared at Jones, then walked around him to his desk and took a seat.

Chewing on the soggy cigar for a few seconds, the old cop broke silence as he asked, "So Ross, what da' ya' got?"

Jones, or now Ross looked up with a wry smile, "I think I got it the information I needed; 'Drops, pickup, times, possible set up; almost everything. 'But one thing, sir?"

"Ask, son."

"Sargent Schmidt, request permission to go along on the bust, sir."

"Request denied."

"But sir…"

Schmidt cut him off, "Denied, Officer Ross. As one of only two colored cops in this district and the only one undercover, you're too important to this case and others related to it. Not to mention future cases."

Ross pleaded his case, "Sir, I don't have to be in on the arrest. I don't have to blow cover. You could even have me arrested along with the others. I just want to be there to make sure we get who we need to get. 'Keep it going perhaps."

"Keep it going, *maybe*. But probably not with you on it, Ross." Schmidt sat back in his creaky chair, peering from behind some files. "This could be big. If this pans out, it could mean promotion, to detective even."

After some thought, Schmidt came to a conclusion, "You're a good cop Ross. Granted they probably won't let you work to your fullest potential; you're good. So I tell you what," Schmidt moved in close from across the desk to give his proposition. "You arrange the sting, set everything up, put all the players in their places, under my badge of course; and when it goes down, you name it, within reason, and it's yours."

Ross set back in his chair and without a thought answered. "Done."

As a Baltimore City Policeman, Officer Fredwin Ross had to be smarter and work harder than his white colleagues. He was amongst the first colored officers in the city, scoring in the top percentile on aptitude and agility tests. His intelligence and determination had gotten him chosen as one of five, out of a Negro hiring class of fifty cadets. Yet these achievements meant nothing in a segregated city's all white police force. It had only been about five years since the Baltimore City Police Department had decided to allow colored people to serve on the force, and only then, the first was a woman.

Someone had once told him, 'Baltimore is a tough place to live, especially if you're a colored man', a reality Officer Ross had learned the hard way. His difficult childhood had shown him on more than one occasion, the harshness of life. Despite this, he had decided to make something of his life and in the process try to improve the lives of others through public service; 'private' public service. Because though they were allowed to serve, colored policemen were forbidden from wearing traditional officers' uniforms. And so it was, that Officer Ross donned his 'plain-clothes' attire as an undercover officer to serve his community; directing a sting operation for BCPD's Eastern Precinct in hopes of promotion and fulfilling greater goals.

CHAPTER NINE

Nightmare

Ruthie stood from her creaking bed. She rubbed her eyes in an attempt to clear her vision from the blur of waking up. She was so tired that she couldn't tell whether or not she had been lying asleep or sitting on the side of her bed, just before standing. There were voices off in the distance, maybe in the next room. She recognized them; warm friendly voices. They sounded like they were playing cards, laughing and talking; things grownups did when children went to bed. Ruthie walked towards her bedroom door in what seemed like a blurry fog. She rubbed her eyes to no avail.

'I'd better sneak out, so momma won't catch me.' she thought.
She noticed that she had her favorite nightgown on and her plats were still tied up to the top of her head, 'Just like momma left it. She hates when I mess it up in my sleep.' Ruthie thought.

As she neared the door she heard a voice that she definitely recognized. It was a man's voice, heavy with slang.

"Uncle Poppy." she whispered excitedly.
She couldn't wait to run down the hallway and through the door to and give her uncle a great big hug. He'd probably hug her and tell her to get back to bed because it's a school night, but not before he gave her a Baby Ruth candy bar, her favorite. When Ruthie turned the knob to

her bedroom door and opened she was suddenly standing outside, in front of a store entrance. Nothing seemed out of the ordinary as she now had a sweater on over her favorite nightgown. It was late evening and nippy out. Her attention was turned to her uncle's familiar voice and she looked in its direction. There he was, now talking to some little boy. The boy had kind sad eyes. She smiled. As she walked toward him to give him his big hug, she became horrified to see another hand, a gun and a flash. *Blamm!*

Ruthie woke up with a gasp. She looked around as she sat up sweating. She found relief as she realized that she was on the makeshift bed of a couch in her best friend Doris' apartment. Her old bedroom; the door; the old storefront, even the gun flash had all been a nightmare; a nightmare of that horrible night all those years ago. Still breathing heavily, Ruthie felt her eyes begin to well; she shifted her thoughts away. That was how she would often deal with her feelings when things became too emotional.

'Bury them deep. The past is the past. I was little. It wasn't my fault. Focus on the now and the future.' That's what she told herself.

Though she knew very little of what transpired in the events of her Uncle Poppy's death, Ruthie felt somewhat responsible for it. She knew that business was sometimes treacherous and the streets were mean, but she felt that if she could have just warned him or pushed him out of the way, things might have been different. She might still have her Uncle Poppy. But those were the ranting's of a girl; a scared child. She was a grown woman now. And grown women must move on. This same inner conflict had been going on for years. Sometime she would act out

98

by secluding herself, most times she would just bury her feelings, but in the end, Ruthie knew that sooner or later, something would have to give. She bit on her bottom lip and lay back down on her pillowed and sheeted couch, then drifted off once more into sleep.

Over the next two weeks Ruthie got herself acclimated back to city life. She and Doris took day trips to different parts of the city. Doris worked at a fabric factory evenings and was usually off on Tuesday and Fridays so most of their traveling was done on those days and late mornings. They traveled and shopped along Gay Street's commercial district in East Baltimore, they visited Doris' friends in the colored community of Turner's Station, but the one thing they hadn't done was strolled along the other parts of the Avenue. They had frequented the shops and eateries along the middle part or 'The Shop' as they called it, but Ruthie had no real interest in visiting the top of the avenue; too traumatic. They hadn't the chance to see 'The Bottom' either. With its movie houses, showroom theaters and jazz clubs, they had loose plans to go there.

Every so often, Doris and Ruthie would run into Big Joe and Mil. While Joe and Doris talked like old friends, Mil was very cordial and cautious with Ruthie, asking how her day was and engaging in polite conversation. Whether his strategy or not, with each encounter she was less cold, chats were of deeper content, and the two became more familiar. And though at first Ruthie resisted, she found herself, more and more, thinking about Mil.

On the Wednesday of her fourth week in town, Ruthie sat on the stoop of Doris' apartment building. It was the beginning of summer and she was enjoying the midmorning breeze. The calm of the day was broken by birds chirping and mild traffic. A dusty brown moving van drove past, southbound and for a split second Ruthie thought she saw the driver looking at her. She shrugged it off as the truck turned right at the next corner. Less than a minute later that same truck pulled up on the intersecting side-street to her left. Driving alone in the truck was Mil. He seemed to be on his way to or from some moving job, but noticed her and decided stop by.

"Hey now, you pretty little thing, beautiful morning." Ruthie didn't say anything but Mil noticed a small smile creep on her face. He took this opportunity to turn off and exit the truck, and then approach her as she sat on the steps staring off in another direction, feigning disinterest. In his hands were two Coke's, one was opened, the other he was saving for himself to drink later. He offered it to her. She gladly accepted. Neither said a word. He sat beside her on stoop enjoying their silent conversation.

Then, after a moment, Mil said, as more of a statement than a question. "Why don't you let me take you out? Show you around, show you off."

She looked at him with tilted head and one eyebrow up, "And why should I let you do that?"

"To be perfectly honest, I don't know. But I like you. Besides, you ain't from around here."

"So?"

"So, that means you're different. And I'm different, we'd probably make a perfect match."

She looked at him with a smirk and her lips turned up, "Is that the best line you got?"

"Did it work?"

She thought for a second then answered nonchalantly, "Yeah, I guess. Hopefully it'll get better."

He jokingly responded, "Well, it's hard to improve on perfection, but I'll try. So, can I call you? What's your phone number?"

"You got something to write it on?"

He pointed at his temple, "Photographic memory."

"You probably need a phonographic memory. But anyway, it's Lafayette-3587. It's house number to our apartment building. Just ask for Doris, she'll come get me."

"You mean the prison guard. Oh God. I guess I'd better make every minute count, then."

They both laughed. Mil looked relieved as if a great weight had been lifted. He then seemed to be having a short conversation with himself, in which he had reached some sort of conclusion.

He asked, "What y'all doing Friday night?"

"I don't know. Nothing planned. Why you ask?" Ruthie responded.

"Well it just so happens that I have acquired four tickets to the show at the Royal that night, and I don't know about Joe and Dorie, but I would love to have you as a date. I'll behave myself. I promise." he said holding his right hand up.

Ruthie looked him up and down and said, "OK. But don't worry; there won't be a reason for you to misbehave. *I* promise."

"Well alright, then!" Mil happily conceded. Numbers were exchanged, arrangements were made and dates were set. The foursome would meet for a double date; the Friday night show, at the Royal Theater.

Double Date

Friday came quick, but not fast enough for Milton. But now the day was here. He had gone out and bought a zoot suit with a matching hat, and now, standing in front of his bedroom mirror, he bore witness to his manly perfection. His dark gray trademark baggy pants, tapered at the ankles, exaggerated his bop. His matching jacket, complete with shoulder pads accentuate his physique. A single button joined his jacket, under which a solid black, collared shirt lay.

"Man, you gon' knock 'em dead." he said to his mirror image.

There was a honk from a car's horn. Looking at his timepiece, he knew it was time to go.

'That must be Joe.' he thought.

He went to the window and looked out. In front of his row-house apartment in a dark brown '38 Chrysler sat Big Joe, looking at his wristwatch.

"Be right out, Joe." Mil hollered. Out the house and into the car Mil went with a few hoots from onlookers. The two slid each other five as the car pulled off. Big Joe sported an exquisitely tailored chocolate zoot suit, dark shoes and a matching brown hat with a small feather that was attached to its cream colored ban. His cream colored shirt gave the ensemble just the right flare.

"Let's be real gone."

"You got it Jack."

The evening had begun and they were off to pick up the ladies. Big Joe had asked Doris to the show, to which she happily accepted. Driving through the Winchester neighborhood, just off the avenue, even at this time of day, it was lively. It seemed that the residential streets were just a little less crowded with people than the main Avenue. People were on their stoops, playing spades at small card tables and walking about. Children played and ran and some people even pulled their floor model radios to their doors or windows so everyone could enjoy the Friday Night Hit Parade.

Minutes later, Big Joe and Mil pulled up on the corner of Doris' apartment. They didn't have to wait because Ruthie, who was sitting by the window, spotted them, gave them a wave then vanished inside. Mil saw the second floor window lights blink out and a minute later Doris and Ruthie walked out of the front doorway, down the stoop and toward the car. The men were happy with what they saw. The ladies were absolutely stunning. They quickly recovered then rushed out of the car to intercept and assist. Doris wore a burgundy one piece, naval-style dress with cream trim and buttons, while Ruth sported a navy blue knee length skirt with a fitted sky blue V-neck silk top with ruffled shoulders. Big Joe and Mil greeted and opened the front and back passenger side doors for their dates.

"Ladies. Beautiful as always." Mil complimented, as he looked Ruthie up and down. "Ain't I the lucky fella."

Ruthie, pleased with the night's start responded, "Likewise. You clean up quite nicely, 'moving man'. You sure look mella'."

The ladies were seated, doors were closed, the gentlemen entered the driver's side front and back and the couples were off to see the show at the Royal Theater. The neighborhood seemed to buzz with excitement; which still paled in comparison to Pennsylvania Avenue. Even with the summer's late evening's, the night life was already jumping. With dusk, the streetlights and billboards flickered on, the low hum of avenue crowds and traffic could be heard a block away and rhythm & blues, jazz and big band flooded out from the various spots along the strip.

"You know we gon' have to park on the side street. It ain't never no parking on the Avenue." Mil suggested from the back seat.

"I know," responded Big Joe, "but I just wanna drive down the Avenue to see the sights, feel the excitement. Look, it's packed out here."
Driving south on Pennsylvania Avenue, they saw it. On their left-hand sides was the most popular of the many movie-house/show theaters on the strip.

The Royal

The Royal Theater; Baltimore's answer to New York's Apollo, Philadelphia's Uptown, Washington D.C.'s Howard and Chicago's Regal. It was a major stop on the Chitlin' Circuit, a collection of clubs and theaters catering to colored performers and audiences alike. It seemed that almost every other night there was a top singer, comedian, dancer or orchestra performing there and tonight was no different. On the brightly lit marquee that extended over the front entrances in black letters was, 'Royal' and on the sides read 'Tonight, Billy Eckstine and his Orchestra'.

Doris said excitedly, "Ooh, I can't wait. Hurry up and park before the show starts."

The line along the theater was a half block long and getting longer and everyone in line was dressed to the

104

nines. Their car turned left on the next intersection and parked nearly three blocks away. The walk back to the theater was a brisk one and they found that once they arrived, the line was almost gone because the doors had been opened. They gave their tickets the walked in through the front lobby. It was draped in deep red velvet curtains that framed ivory colored walls. The ceilings had three inlays in which three exquisite crystal chandeliers hanged. The floors were patterned marble and plaster sculptured figures stared out from every available corner. Ruthie had never been there before, but she had heard the stories, and they all seemed to be true. The Royal Theater had the grandeur that rivaled the Hippodrome or the Towne Theaters downtown. On the back wall of the lobby, two domed entrances served as portals through which entering the showroom was like stepping into a palace. One felt majestic; as if they were, Royal.

The couples took their seats in the center section right, toward the back. They sat boy- girl, girl- boy as the show began. The crowd got quiet as the lights dimmed, and then from behind the stage curtains, the theater's resident emcee stepped to the lone, spot-lit microphone stand.

Embracing it he exclaimed, "Ladies and gentlemen, welcome to the world famous Royal Theater; Entertaining Baltimore since '22. Home to the best seats", the crowd cheered, "the best acts", the crowd cheered, "and the best audience, in the world." he shouted.
Everyone responded with stomps and claps.

"So I ask you, Baltimore, are you ready?" The crowd brimming with excitement and anticipation answered with a roar.

Not satisfied, the emcee asked again, "I said, Baltimore, are you ready?"
The crowd answered with an even louder roar.

He continued, "Well I need you to put your hands together, because coming to the stage is the man you've all been waiting for tonight." The horn section played from behind the opening curtain as the emcee continued, "Introducing Billy Eckstine and his Orchestra!!"
The crowd burst into cheers and applause as the curtains opened to the tall, handsome bandleader/singer. Mil and Joe cheered, Doris screamed, Ruthie swooned. She secretly adored the performer. He had been one of the few colored singers that had filtered through and onto the white suburban radio station's Hit Parade. But she had only heard him, she had never seen him, and now that he was performing in person, she felt as if she was in the clouds. She hid her emotions well, exhibiting only a look of general interest. The band played a mixture of upbeat dance numbers, complete with show girls, and spotlighted crooning ballads in two hour-long sets broken up by intermission and the comedy stylings of Timmie Rogers.

It was an evening of music and laughter no attendee would ever forget. By the end of the three hour show the couples were emotionally exhausted; but not physically. It was a little after ten pm when the theater released its patrons out onto the Avenue. The street in front on the theater was congested from valets pick-ups and heavy spectator traffic. The light from the theater made it look as if the lobby extended to the other side of the street. Most of the theater-goers had mixed into the already crowded foot traffic and filtered into the various clubs and bars that lined the street. Mil and Joe waited in the front lobby for their dates, who had gone to the powder room to 'freshen up'. After a few minutes, Joe impatiently scanned the room for Doris and Ruthie.

Spotting them, he elbow bumped Mil, "There they go. I knew going to the bathroom don't take that long; even for women."

Mil agreed, "I see 'em. Let's go get 'em, so we can get out of here."

They walked towards their dates only to see them chatting with another girl. The girl was dressed in a dark, matching, button-down top and knee length skirt. As the men approached, the ladies, remembering that they had kept them waiting, apologetically introduced them to the girl, perhaps as the reason for the hold up.

Doris apologized, "We are so sorry fellas. We just ran into my cousin," turning and speaking now to the girl, "who I didn't even know was here."

The girl just hunched her shoulders.

"Fellas this is my little cousin Jacks, I mean Shirley. Shirley, meet Mil, and this is Big Joe."

Everyone caught the hint of possession in her the introduction. Joe smiled.

Shirley asked, "What do you mean 'little'? I'm only two years younger than you."

"Decades, in wisdom and beauty, decades." Doris retorted jokingly. Everyone chuckled.

Big Joe asked, "Jacks? How'd you get that name?"

Shirley frowned as Doris answered, "She got it when we was little. The girl could play a mean game of jacks. The name kinda stuck."

Mil, being polite but direct, cut in, "Well while it's nice to meet you Jacks, Shirley, or whichever, the night is young and the Avenue awaits. Ladies." He gestured to the exit.

"Well that's what we were over here talking about." said Ruthie. "Shirley's date had to leave early, but they're supposed to meet up later at the Club Casino in the 1500 block. He works for the guy that owns it. She can get us in."

Big Joe looked at Mil, "Exclusive. You gotta be a big wig to get in there." They were impressed but skeptical.

"You sure you can get us in?" Mil asked doubtfully.

"As long as y'all with me." Shirley answered confidently, then sensing hesitation, she added. "Look, I'm meeting him there either way, y'all going or not?" After quick glances between the foursome, all agreed.

"Alright, I'll meet y'all out front." she said.

Outside, they met in front of a neighboring walk-up apartment that had the misfortune of being right next to the popular theater. For Ruthie, it was her first official night out on the town, and it was off to a magnificent start. Everything was electric and vibrant as the quintet crossed the street, walked two blocks up the Avenue and begin part two of their night out.

CHAPTER TEN

Flooding Back

The Club Casino's oblong rounded diamond-shaped sign hanged, brightly lit, above its tinted glass door. Like most buildings, it was just a wider converted row house that stood near the middle of the west side of Pennsylvania Avenue. People stood to either side of the entrance, which coughed out jazz and smoke with each opening of the door. The couples headed by Shirley, passed through the crowd single file and up to the door. On the other side stood a tall solidly build man, in a dark suit with his arms crossed. The couples figured him for a bouncer as he moved to block their entrance. It was only when he glanced down at the significantly shorter Shirley that he recognized her and his face changed.

"Hey, Big Al. They with me." Shirley said, mentioning to the couples. "Choc here yet?"

"He was. He made a run. He should be back in a few.", the bouncer answered.

Big Al stood aside and let them pass. They spotted a table that was being vacated by customers and took seats as the waiters wiped it off. Their table sat near a roped-off exclusive section with what looked to be important types; politicians, entertainers or maybe gangsters. The quintet ordered drinks and ate appetizers while enjoying a local band belt out song after song. Suddenly, they noticed a man, nicely dressed in a tailored suit, standing behind Shirley's chair, briefly and suspiciously studying them.

Momentarily startled, Shirley turned to recognize the man. "Oh, you're here." She stood from her chair beside the man. "Baby, meet my cousin Dorie and her friend Ruthie and their dates Joe and Mil. Everybody, this is my man, Choc."

The introduction was full of pride, which Choc was obviously used to and lavished in. He was dark complexioned, hence nick name Choc, short for Chocolate, though his moniker could have derived from his given name Charlie or Chuck. Choc radiated importance. With a standoffish, quiet arrogance, he answered the introductions with a polite bow of the head.

"Ladies, pleased to make your acquaintance." Then to the Joe and Mil a slight nod, "Gentlemen."

The gentlemen nodded back. They thought he was more cultured than he looked.

Shirley offered, "You gonna sit with us and have some drinks?"

"I can't right now, something came up; business." he responded

Shirley turned to Choc and quietly complained while the couples pretended not to hear or see.

It was ended by Choc's abrupt, "Hey, what did I say?", which ended the conversation immediately.

His intense stir guided Shirley back down to her seat. She sat angrily but quiet. The ladies were confused but took note. The men were strangely impressed.

'Well I guess he told her.' Joe thought with a chuckle.

After Choc left, the couples persuade Shirley to relax with a couple of drinks. The mood lifted as they talked amongst each other. Ruthie looked over and suddenly noticed that not only did Big Joe still have his hat on, but he'd had it on all night. And more over, she'd noticed that she had never seen him with it off.

After a sip of her Whiskey Sour, she said, "We're having fun, Joe. Relax, take your hat off."
With a small hesitation, Big Joe reached up and removed his hat. To the girl's surprise, his head was completely bald. Everyone chuckled.

Doris, coming to her date's defense, hugged up against Joe and rubbed his head saying, "Oh y'all leave him alone." Her voice was pouty and humorously nurturing. "It takes a confident man to wear it like this."

Ruthie playfully interjected, "I don't think he had a choice."

"Well I like it. I like my 'Joe Baldy'", still running her fingers across Joe's head.
Everyone at the table glanced at each other, stunned at Doris' improvised nickname. Big Joe realized that he wasn't offended; he actually liked the name. Doris had made it sound respectable; made it sound, good.

"Then that settles it." Mil said to the table as he lifted his glass. "Joe Baldy it is."

"Joe Baldy." Everyone answered in unison with a toast.

A while later, the night was winding down. The band had just finished their last set and dancers were making their ways back to their seats from the dance floor. The VIP section, just beside Shirley's guest table, had a party of about three men and about five ladies. The men were talking loudly as the ladies hung on every word. It sounded like they were gangsters; low leveled, but still

111

gangsters. The ladies sitting with them seemed fascinated with their lifestyle and the stories that came along with them; and the men were all too willing to tell them more. Without even noticing, Shirley and the couples found themselves eavesdropping in on the conversations, though they pretended not to. They nursed drinks and had small talk while they struggled to listen. One of the would-be gangsters talked about having an audience at Mayor Jackson's home. Looks of doubt went across the couple's faces. Another gangster spoke about having a direct line of contact to infamous New York gangster Meyer Lanski. He was immediately called out by his partner, citing that if he actually had a direct line, he would never be able to speak of it. They had gotten into a good-natured argument and anyone who may have been listening would have lost interest. By then the bragging and one-upmanship had become quite pathetic. Big Joe and Mil joked around and Doris and Shirley quietly started to chit chat. Ruthie just looked around. She saw the bartender pointing a drunken patron out to a bouncer. She watched that bouncer grab the drunk and shoved him out the door. Then, by the front window, she saw a woman whose face looked out of place there. The woman quickly looked in the other direction. Her face was pretty, but old. Also worn; but not so much from age, but more from hard living.

'Poor lady', Ruthie sympathized as her attention shifted.
She was in a state of boredom, that's when she heard it. That name. It could have been the same name for a different person but the name was enough to jolt her back from a daydream.

"My momma's cousin used to be a big man 'Up Top'. 'Worked under that nigga Pop." a man said.
The table of braggarts behind her was still involved in a game of one-upmanship. Stunned she listened further as they talked amongst each other.

"I remember him. He used to be a legend up there. He took over when the old dude, um, uh, Goldie, left. Man, that was a short reign on the throne, jack."

"Yeah, but don't nobody know what happened."

"Oh I know, cat-daddy, dig this."
Ruthie, facing Mil and the others with her ear in the direction of the braggarts, fell into a state of shock when she heard the man say,

"My boss' boss was the one that pulled the trigger."
Ruthie's heart dropped, and she silently gasped for air.

The man continued, "Shot him right in the chest. And get this, walked off like it wasn't nothing. From then on, he was a fucking legend."
For a moment Ruthie didn't breathe. Her fist clinched as she looked to her lap. She hated what she had just heard. The memories all flooded back. Only Doris, who casually glanced Ruthie's way, noticed her anxiety and began eaves dropping on the braggarts again.

One of the ladies at the gangsters' table interjected, "Hold up. I seen ya boss' boss. He looks too young to have been out there doing stuff like that."

The man explained, "Well that's just it. He *was*. He was *real* young; but how you think he got his name? He was only **sixteen** when he shot that nigga. And when people was asking, 'Who shot Pops 'Up Top'?, they was like, 'little man, he sixteen'. I guess it kind of stuck."
Everyone sat in quiet amazement for a second.

113

"What a fucking story. Nigga, you win." His partner exclaimed.

The whole table laughed as this bit of street lore elevated the teller to the top of their hierarchy.

"He never got locked up for that?" a second lady asked.

"You see where he at now?" the man answered. "The cops ain't messing with him. Shoot, for all we know, they probably had something to do with it."

Ruthie exhaled. Instinctively, Doris, upon hearing and piecing together their conversation, understood and gently grabbed her friend's hand for support. By then Mil, Big Joe and Shirley had noticed that something was wrong. Ruthie pulled away from Doris, got up from the table and traversed through the crowded bar area, out the front door. Doris immediately got up to follow only to be passively blocked by Mil's fore arm.

"Relax," he told her. "I'll see what's going on. Don't worry, I'll take care of her."

Normally Doris would have ignored him and brush pass to help her friend, but something in his eyes and the way he said, "I'll take care of her." made her feel that he *could* handle it. She was impressed, but she was going to wait a few minutes and follow them out anyway. The Club Casino, near the middle of the block, sat one row house from a small alleyway. In that alleyway paced Ruthie, arms crossed, from one side to another. It was well lit, but only wide enough for pedestrian traffic. Further down the alley, alongside the wall and some trashcans, a few couples were quietly doing whatever they were doing.

Ruthie's mind was racing. 'That night, that night. Uncle Poppy is dead.' she thought to herself. 'They shot him. They killed him. That boy. Uncky didn't have the gun. They did it, *he* did it. I'm sorry Uncle Poppy. I'm sorry.'

For a brief moment Ruthie felt as if she was outside herself; watching herself. She was losing it. All those memories, all the fear, all the hurt, all the pain, all the anger, all the rage... all the loss, came rushing back like a tidal wave, almost drowning her in a torrent of her own emotions. Tears streamed down her face as she found herself leaning up against the building's dirty brick sidewall. She finally found the strength to breathe when she felt a familiar presence and noticed an arm pull her in a protective embrace. Ruthie looked up to see Mil's gentle concerned eyes staring down at her.

"Ruthie? Baby, what's wrong? How can I help?" he asked softly but sternly.

Frantically, 'I'm going crazy. Those men, in there, killed my uncle in front of me when I was twelve, and now they bragging about it; laughing. And I feel so helpless and afraid, but I hate 'em and I want 'em all to die. I just wanna go home'. That was in Ruthie's mind, that was what she wanted to say, that is what she thought she was saying, but that was not what she said. She didn't say anything. She just closed her eyes. After another moment she inhaled, then exhaled slowly through her nose.

Calm, she opened her eyes to see a worried Mil asking her, "What can I do?"

She just shook her head as if to say nothing, as she look from his face to the ground.

115

Mil crouched slightly and said, "You know if you need me, I'm here. If you ever need to talk, just tell me, alright?"

Ruthie managed a frail smile for a 'yes' as he pulled her close. She hugged back as she laid her head on his chest. Just then, Doris came into the alley.

Relieved, she said, "I *was* gonna ask, was you OK, but I see you're in good hands."

Still hugging Mil, Ruthie answered, "I'm alright. 'Must've been that Whiskey Sour. I'll be fine."

"Alright then, let's go back in." Mil said. They walked back towards the club.

Reading Ruthie's face, Doris cut in, "We'd, rather go someplace else. I already told Big Joe and Shirley. He's settling up, now."

A moment later, they all gathered outside Club Casino and decided to hit a spot one block up and across the street. It was almost one o'clock in the morning, yet the street traffic, pedestrian and vehicular, was as if it was four o'clock in the afternoon. The next hole-in-the-wall club had a gambling room in the back and a dance floor but for the rest of the night, the couples were content with just drinks and listening to the band. On the surface, Ruthie's mood lifted but she spoke very little as she held Mil's hand close. Choc made an appearance at the club. He had a drink with the party, then after a short time, he and Shirley left together. At the end of the night, Big Joe and Mil, drove and escorted the ladies to the front stoop of their apartment building.

"Ladies, thank you for a beautiful evening. It was a gas." said Big Joe.

"The pleasure was all ours Big Joe Baldy" sang Doris, playfully offering her hand for Big Joe to kiss, which he most assuredly did.

As Ruthie walked up the stoop, Mil grabbed her arm turning her toward him. She was now face to face, at eye level with him. She shot him a wry look, making sure he kept his earlier promise of keeping his hands to himself.

Then her face softened as she said, "Thanks, for everything. I had a good time. I really did."

"Well then, I did my job." he responded. "And I hope to *keep* doing my job. See you soon?"

Ruthie stood on the balls of her feet, softly kissed his bowed forehead and said, "Sooner than you think, Milton Newsome. Good night."

CHAPTER ELEVEN

Satin Club

Two small time hoods stood alongside a multileveled green felt, wood trimmed craps table. The stickman dressed in a white button-up and dark vest used a bent-ended metal rod to scrape a set of dice toward him.

"Your roll." he said as he picked them up and handed them to one of the hoods.

"Ain't nothing but a thang, baby. I'm a roll these bones and take all you chumps' money." he said overconfidently.

With a short shake of his hands, the hood threw the dice on the table with a, "Baby need shoes, but daddy need a zoot suit."

The dice rolled down the middle of the table almost in slow motion. They seemed to hesitate as if they were undecided on which way to land. Teetering, the dice leaned in favor the hoodlum, but suddenly fell opposite. A chorus of "Oohs!!", went around the table which had now crowded with spectators.

Temporarily defeated the hood said, "Like I said before, t'ain't nothing but a thang."

His friend patted his shoulder to console him, "Cool baby, it's only money."

It was a nightly situation happening at the Sphinx Club, one of the hottest spots on the The Avenue, Up Top; popular with local rollers. It was housed in two combined row houses with a front facade that resembled a diner.

The inside boasted two bars lining opposite walls with tables in between. To the wall in the back was a short walkway that opened up into an extended exclusive room. This is where the gambling took place. This back room, like the front, had a classy appeal; some crap tables and a few others for Black Jack and Poker. The staff was all exquisitely dressed and the place was professionally run. The Sphinx Club had reputation for attracting high-rollers and big spenders, providing relaxation in relative safety. To the patrons and employees, it was something of a status symbol. To the boss who ran it, it was just another place where people dropped off money. The right people were paid off so that operations could remain running uninterrupted. Gamblers big and small, were made to feel like VIPs; all the while losing their shirts.

"Man, I'm going ta get a taste. I'll cover you." the hood said leaving the table.

"Solid, jack." his friend accepted, as he followed him through the crowd. They exited the back gambling room, headed straight for two empty stools in the front area.

As they took seats at the bar one of the men laughed to the other, "Man, you know I just dropped seven big ones back there. Whew! Just imagine if I had a real job."

"I'd rather not." the other responded, then mentioned to the bartender, "Ay, barkeep, I need something strong. You got any white lightening back there?"

The tender responded irritated, "We don't sell that back woods shit in here! You should know that. You in here almost every night."

"Easy, baby. One can dream, right."

"Well this place ain't for dreaming; it's for drinking. Now what'll it be?"

"Alright, alright." one hood said as the two gave their drink orders, "Two Cognacs, straight."

"That's more like it." the bartender said as he turned to make the drinks.

A few moments of relative peace was broken by a, "Lawd have mercy."
One of the hoods who was facing the middle of the crowded room, nudged his associate.

"Lookie-lookie-lookie, at this white sugar cookie." The associate turned to face the object of his friends affection. She was white, medium height, with dark hair and olive skin. Her face was a narrow oval shape with kitten-like eyes and the body type of a colored woman. Basking in the attention they got, was her portly escort.

Upon seeing her, the other hood teased, "Jack, you got about as much chance with her, as I got with Eleanor Roosevelt; not that I would want her. That white girl wouldn't even notice you."

Still in a trance, his friend simply responded, "Like you said earlier, one can dream, right?"

They continued to stare at the woman and her date as their coats were checked. It wasn't uncommon to see white faces at the main clubs 'Up Top', but this one was certainly a standout. From the look of her escort's neatly tailored suit, he looked to be a banker or a downtown investor. Most looked in admiration, but a few, from the shadows looked at him for what he was; the latest chump. After about fifteen minutes of having drinks at one of the VIP tables, the woman whispered in her date's ear. Apparently wrapped around her finger, he chuckled, got up, pulled out her chair and escorted her back to the gambling room. As the couple walked by, one of the hoods noticed the woman's slight smile and a nod in the direction of some big shot off to the side. Just before entering the back room, she noticing that she was being watched. She looked directly at the hood, and with the same knowing smile, she winked. He thought his heart dropped. But just as suddenly as the excitement of her presence filled the room, it was gone the next instant. The two hoods as if released from a spell, turned back to the bar and nursed their drinks.

In the back gambling room, the woman and her escort settled at a Black-Jack table, then to the crap table, and then Poker. After a while, he had grown even more impressed with himself. His skill and luck had earned him a nice winning streak, but he felt he had only won chump change. He wrestled with the thought of upping his wagers but his conscience quickly objected. And then that voice; that voice and those lips.

"Do it. I like it when you play, hard."

From over his shoulder she encouraged him, brushing her body close to his, "I love a man confident man."

"Why's that, honey?" he asked.

She seductively whispered, "Because, when you win big, you win BIG."

The man nervously swallowed, and then, resolve thrown to the wind, he placed a huge wager on the table. Unbelievably, his streak continued.

"Yeesss! I can't be stopped. Next bet."

His date at his side and the crowd cheering him on, the man started to spread his small fortune around the room. Ten minutes later he had five thousand dollars in winnings, twenty minutes after that, he was fifteen large in the hole. He was flat broke. The reserve cash he carried in his billfold was just enough to cover his debt and buy him a much needed cognac on his way out. He was so upset and embarrassed that he didn't notice or didn't bother to look for his absentee date. With tail between legs, the man moped out the Satin Club's front door and into a waiting limousine. From the shaded second story window, two shadowy figures looked down at the departing limo. As the vehicle below skirted off, two shot glasses met in the darkness, with a toast.

Detective

"This is your desk. A Captain Warren will be in to give you rundown of operations. Any supplies you need, put an order in with the clerk if you can't find it in the closet. I'm Lt. Murphy, welcome to Western Precinct." the chubby lieutenant said as a matter of course; probably repeated to a hundred cadets, a hundred different times. He spoke as if he was reading off of a new recruit manual's check-list.

Detective Fredwin Ross graciously accepted the information and the welcome with a stiff salute and a, "Yes sir, thank you, sir."
The lieutenant just looked at him blankly and walked away shaking his head. Ross looked down at his new desk, which was off to the side of the main office area, on the wall in between two tall file cabinets. It was unclear whether this positioning was a space issue or a racial one. It didn't matter, either way he was happy with the promotion to detective and the transfer to Western Precinct. He felt he was finally in a position to do some real good and maybe resolve a few personal issues in the process. He had just come off of a successful narcotics

and racketeering bust on the city's east side while working out of the Eastern Precinct. His orchestration and undercover work garnered him accolades with the brass, but the nature of his work forbade him public praise or notoriety in the press. His fellow officers regarded him as little more than a colored cop at best; nigger competition at worst. Never the less, here he was, at the famed Western Precinct; straightening and arranging his desk, gathering supplies and preparing for his orientation. After about a half hour of waiting, Ross, somewhat irritated, stood from his desk preparing to walk towards the room's entrance to find this Captain Warren. As he stood the office room door opened. A portly officer with captain's bars walked through.

He looked in Ross' direction, "Ross." he said as more of a statement than a question. "Good, they got you squared away. I'm Captain Warren, Follow me."

Ross managed to get out a "Yes sir." before hastily tagging along behind the captain like a toddler.

He couldn't figure out why he struggled to keep pace with someone shorter and stouter than he. An explanation for Ross' long wait never came; it wasn't even an issue for the captain. Ross shrugged it off. Down the hall and up a stairwell they went, not a word uttered between. His brief walk through the police station was met with stirs and grumbles. Though colored faces were more than common outside the station, it was rare to see one on the inside that wasn't wearing shackles or posting bail. Ross wore his novelty like a badge of honor and though he was the first, he would make sure, at least by example, that he wasn't the last. He was dressed in street clothes but was sure to carry himself in a manner which set himself apart from

123

any civilian, colored or white. On the second floor they entered a private office that had a door window of opaque glass.

"Sit down." the captain said without looking or gesturing.

The room was wood themed, very neat and trimmed with awards, trophies and certificates. There was an oak desk with one comfortable looking chair behind it. Ross closed the door behind him and took a seat as the captain lit a half smoked cigar and fingered through a file he pulled from his drawer.

After the quick scan, he said, "Impressive Detective. I guess times are changing."

Ross assumed the file was of him. "How's that, sir?"

"Your assignment there, your new placement here. You made a hell of an impression on somebody."

"I had good support, sir. I just did my job."

"'Looks like you did more than that. You left a good man, over there. Schmidt, your last boss, we came through the academy together."

Ross felt somewhat relieved.

Captain Warren continued, "'Worked on a lot of difficult cases, me and him. And people say *I'm* tough, but he's a *real* hard ass. Still, you came highly recommended."

"I won't disappoint you, sir."

The captain sat in his chair, chewed a little on his cigar, then looking down at a city grid map he'd spread across his desk, he started.

"OK Ross, this western district, as you know. This," pointing at a smaller section of the map, "is the western precinct, in one of the city's main colored sections. The main thoroughfare is Pennsylvania Avenue."

Ross nodded.

Warren continued, "The entertainment and nightlife here attracts a certain element. This element has festered within the neighborhoods adjacent to it; and quite simply, we mean to eradicate it."

Ross thought of his own experiences, then his own objectives. They were, at least in part, of one accord with the captain's.

"Over the years, we have attempted to disrupt, disperse and destroy any and all organized criminal activity along this section of the district with little to no result. Aside from the occasional raid, bust or low-level street arrest, there is no discernible affect from our efforts. Oh, there have been a few close calls, but somehow the big boys remain just beyond our reach, always a step ahead. Frankly, they can see us coming a mile away. That's where you come in."

Ross, understanding the situation, listened patiently. Captain Warren reached over to the right side of his desk, and fingered through his opened drawer of files.

Pulling one out, he handed it to Ross, "I'm guessing you'd fare a little better down there, so I'm starting you on *this*, your first case."

As Ross took the file and skimmed through it, the captain further briefed him.

"There's a warehouse over on Etting Street. It used to be a stable or something. Now it's used it as a depot, or some sort of base of operations. You get in close, watch the place, and ask questions. See what you can dig up. It's an open investigation and we got a contact from Central in the mix, so work your magic kid. Everything you need is in that file, case specifics, suspects, informants. Study it. Know it."

The captain leaned in toward Ross and spoke in a low tone, "Now listen kid, this is very important. The brass got questions, in-house and out, so I'm playing this close to the vest. Now you got the freedom to do what you do, so you act rank and file, but you report directly to me and me only with the dirt. Got it?"

"Got it?"

With that, Captain Warren rose from his chair signifying the end of the meeting. Detective Ross rushed to stand up first, saluting his superior. The captain looked him up and down, nodding approval, and then returned his gesture.

"Firm salute, but it looks kind of funny in plain clothes. So, at least to me, no uniform, no salute."

"Right sir, sorry sir." Ross said, standing at ease but looking straight.

The captain sat back down nonchalantly straightening papers on his desk and said, "Excused, Detective Ross."

CHAPTER TWELVE

Sting

About two blocks east, off Pennsylvania Avenue, on the corner of Etting and Lafayette, Detective Ross stood, smoking a cigarette. His dark pork-pie hat, navy blue fall jacket and khakis blended him well into his surroundings. It was now late summer and the unseasonably chilly wind gust of the early evening blew his cigarette smoke back into his face. Whatever he waited or looked for had not yet happened or shown up. Wanting to remain inconspicuous, he flicked his cigarette to the ground, mashed it with his feet and walked east to the next corner.

His research and investigation, based on Captain Warren's file, led him to this corner. He did not have a full picture of events, but everything pointed to this place and time. He had utilized the captain's briefing in addition to second hand information from vague questioning and eaves dropping. Ross realized that this would be his first and only chance to do truly undercover work, for afterwards, his face would surely be well known. It had been about a month since he had been transferred to Western Precinct, and word was starting to leak about a new colored officer working the area; though most expected one in full uniform.

Ross thought to himself, 'I'd better make this one count'.

On the next corner stood two men, engaging in a quiet conversation. Ross' pace slowed as he went into the

127

corner phone booth to make a quick call. He left the booth door opened as the men talked.

"What do you mean Amos can't come? He's gonna mess everything up." one man said.

"Hey, I'm just the messenger. Don't get sore at me. I'm here. Don't that count for nothing?" replied his associated.

"Yeah, but that man said he needs three men. If he don't see three, he gonna find somebody else. And boom, we out twenty bucks a piece. Twenty bucks, just for unloading a couple of trucks in a warehouse."

His associate thought for a second and then suggested, "Does it matter who? He don't know Amos, he never saw him. We could get anybody to help out; for a smaller cut, of course."

"Now ya talking, more for us. But who?"

Glancing around, his associate mumbled, "What about this guy?" nodding to Ross who was exiting the phone booth.
The other quickly nodded in agreement.

Turning to Ross the man asked, "Hey you, come here, let me talk to you."
Hearing most of the conversation and matching the information with his investigation, Ross instinctively saw a way in. He went over to the men.

"Me and my partner got a proposition for you. You come with us, you help us unload a couple of trucks, quick job, you make ten bucks. Whatayasay?" the man said, talking fast.

Ross feigned a look of uncertainty on his face, then accepted, "For ten dollars? I'm in."

The man said, "Good. And if anybody asks, you're Amos. Let's go."

The trio crossed the intersection, walked back west on Lafayette, then turned up the small alley-street, Etting Street. In a city full of row houses, this block was peculiar in that it had none, just an old schoolhouse and a couple of storehouses, one of which sat across the narrow street from the rest. This storehouse had the look of an old barn, with a hoisting pole and pulley atop the wide double doorway; probably used during slavery as part of some farm before the city rose up around it. The building looked desolate and unused, but intact. The men walked up the building's side walkway to the back where they were met by a heavy-set man, blocking the back door, with a pipe in his hands; obviously a lookout or some form of security.

One of Ross' associates approached first, saying, "'Here to see John-boy."

The heavy-set man turned to the side and let them pass into the back of the barn. Ross, with his concealed service revolver and badge under his jacket, was relieved that they were not searched for weapons. Two covered moving trucks pulled in the, now opened, front barn doors. Waiting for the trucks and the off-loaders was John-boy; a very dark, hard looking man. He wore his hair conked back, sported a gold tooth and had a cut under his left eye; a real tough-guy and obviously the one in charge.

Clapping his hand, he said, "Alright, alright, perfect timing. Everybody's here."

He turned to Ross and his associates, "You guys can get started off-loading those trucks. After that, stack 'em in the cellar."

He turned and walked away. Ross noticed that the truck's occupants were white. The drivers remained in their trucks as a passenger from one exited and walked toward John-boy. He was quickly joined by another older white man, who had walked in through the opened barn doors. A handshake and a smile indicated that they knew each other. The first man, named Hawkins, took the lead as they engaged John-boy in quiet conversation; apparently to settle up for the transaction. Ross and his associates got busy off-loading the first truck. The boxes were containers of some sort, but the sending address caught Ross' attention. The manifests read 'PORCELAIN PIGGY BANKS'; OAXACA, MEXICO; matching the wording and location from Captain Warren's briefing. Add to that, the barn boss' name, John-boy, Ross knew he was in the right place. As he worked, he kept his eye on John-boy, Hawkins and the older white man. Hawkins looked to be middle management; definitely connected. But it was something about, the older white man that made Ross take notice. Perhaps it was a straightness of the back, or a more than usual un-comfortableness. Ross was not alone in this assessment. One of his fellow off-loaders was also staring intently at the uncomfortable looking, older white man.

"You know, that pecker-wood looks awfully familiar." he said accusingly.

"How can you tell? They all look alike to me." his friend chuckled.

"Naw, I'm dead serious. I can't put my finger on it, but I know his face from somewhere."

His friend replied, "It's your eyes, man. Your blind ass probably need to go to the eye doc."

It was something in that phrase that triggered a memory deep in the other, because he thought for a second, and then glared back over to the taller white man, who was still conversing with the others.

"Doc." he mumbled. And then mumbled again as if he were deciphering a puzzle. "The Doc, doc, the **docks**!" It came to him. "He's a cop." he said with quiet venom. "That muva fuka's a cop!" he hollered angrily across the barn.

Before Ross could react to the man's declaration, all hell broke loose. Guns were pulled, people shouted orders at each other. A pistol was pulled off of the accused older white man. The two white drivers exited their trucks with shotguns aimed. It was a Mexican standoff, and as if the situation wasn't tense enough, suddenly a siren went off from the outside. For a second the whole barn-house was frozen in fear and confusion.

A bullhorn sounded, "This is the Baltimore City Police Department. We have this building surrounded. Lay down your weapons and come out with your hands up."

Beyond the barn doors were policemen with weapons drawn behind squad cars, light polls and walls. Expletives could be heard around the barn as men ducked for cover and waited for a signal of what to do. John-boy and his immediate party ducked into a small office that offered some cover from the police.

"You bring a cop to my place of business?" John-boy growled.

Equally angry, Hawkins argued, "What are you, nuts? We' done business before. You know me!"

John-boy answered, "I do. But I *don't* know your boy. Did you check him out before you got here?"

"My boy?" Hawkins asked, confused, "I thought he was with *you*."

In that instant, Ross knew that the older white man was Captain Warren's inside contact; an inside contact with guns trained on him. He was in deep trouble; life or death. Ross had to act.

John-boy hollered out to his men, "Everybody git down, nobody make a move until I say. Looks like we might have a little hostage insurance." looking at the older man. He cupped his hands to his mouth and called to the officers outside, "Hey coppers. Looks like you got the drop on me. I think I wanna negotiate."

Through the bullhorn, the officer in charge answered back, "We know who you are John Riggs, and we got your rap sheet. You're in no position to bargain. You're looking at fifteen years, hard labor, minimum."

John-boy looked at his entourage, then at his would-be hostage and said to him, "You know, I don't even think they know you're in here."

Ross had come to the same conclusion.

Thoughtfully, John-boy continued, "But he's right you know. No matter how I come out, I go *in*; for a long time. The thing is, if I gotta go, it's gonna be for a good reason. You, on your knees, Now!"

The older man's face went pale.

132

Grabbing a revolver from a henchman, John-boy stood over his new hostage, cocked the trigger and said, "I guess *you* gotta be that reason."
BANG!!!
Some turned away, some blinked, but in the split second they expected to see the hostage with a bullet in his head, they saw John-boy's limp body fall to the ground.
BANG! BANG!
Straight from a prayer, the hostage opened his eyes to see two other armed men in the office drop lifelessly to the floor, before being pushed on the ground himself. After another moment of confusion he realized that one of the truck off-loaders was holding a gun, the obvious shooter.

The other off-loader stared, baffled, "Amos, what the hell?"

Patting him and the others down, with gun in hand, Ross said, "My name ain't Amos, genius. Sit down and shut up." After securing the office, he stood by the door and addressed the men out in the barn, "This is Detective Ross of the Baltimore City Police Department, Western. Once again, we have the barn surrounded. If you don't comply, we will use lethal force. Lay down your weapons, place your hands behind your heads, and walk slowly out the front doors. I *will* not ask again."

A moment later, to Ross' relief, men, hands above heads, started filing out the barn doors. Policemen came in and secured the whole building, recovering guns, fifteen thousand dollars in cash and two hundred cocaine filled porcelain piggy-banks worth over one hundred thousand dollars; the biggest bust in the western precinct to date. Ross helped the older man off the floor, as the others were hand cuffed and escorted to paddy wagons.

"Captain Warren's inside contact, I presume.", Ross said with a salute.

The man just stared at him, then gave a hearty handshake.

"I don't know what to say. I owe you big time Detective."

Ross saw a flash of emotions in the contact; sincere, but prohibited by protocol.

An underling's voice alerted from behind, "Lieutenant, Central Office Commander Grimes, respectfully requesting a briefing, sir."

"Of course, of course." the Lieutenant answered over his shoulder, then turning to Ross, "Uh, I can't thank you enough, son. Ross, is it?"

Solemnly shaking his head with gratitude, respect and a salute, he said walking away. "See you around."

Shirley

Shirley sat in front of her family's floor-modeled radio listening to WCAO's Afternoon Hit Parade. It was close to the Rhythm & Blues Hour, when they played the more grittier tunes. She had been waiting for about a half hour and her patience was rewarded with the song They Raided The Joint by Vanita Smythe. It was a song about a young woman caught up in a house party's police raid. Shirley imagined herself in that situation; it seemed glamorous and dangerously romantic, like in the gangster movies. Being Choc's girlfriend, she had seen her fair share of street life, but it was mostly the shiny polished side. He never had her around the gambling spots and the card games. He bought her nice things and took her to nice places, though far less frequently, and recently, she was beginning to feel like she was just eye candy; his trophy girl.

She frowned at the notion, then thought of her situation, 'Some girls have real problems. Who the hell could be mad at this?'

As she began to once again lose herself in the song, she remembered she was supposed to pick up her dress from Hendin's Clothier. It was a special order placed by Choc. She was sure he was planning something special for them soon. He was good to her mostly, but sometimes he would snap at her, be impatient, meaner. Most times she chalked it up as job stress.

'Just so long as he didn't cross the line.' she thought to herself.

As she freshened up, her mother appeared in the bathroom doorway. She was a heavyset woman with a floral print housedress that hanged just below her knees.

"Leaving?" her mother asked

"Yeah, ma."

"Hanging out with your big cousin Dorie?" she asked optimistically, "You probably should more often. She got a job, her own apartment, maybe she can rub off on you."

"Naw, not today." Shirley answered nonchalantly. Her mother just looked at her. She sighed as she remembered the days when her daughter was just a little girl, playing jacks on the marble stoop. She had been one of the best jacks players on the block, so much so, it had become her nickname to a few, Jacks.

"My baby, my baby Jacks."

Shirley complained, "Ma, I'm not eleven anymore, can you please not call me that."

"I'm sorry baby, that's all I have of my little Shirley-Jacks. You're so serious now, so grown up."

"That's because I am grown up, ma."

Shirley looked at her mother, whose face showed traces of hurt.

She cracked a wry smile as she gave a hug, "I'm sorry ma, but you know I'll always be your... Jacks. I gotta go now."

Her mother's tone changed with a thought, "I hope you ain't going to meet up with that boy. I told you, I just don't get a good feeling about him; what little I seen of him, anyway."

Exasperated, Shirley turned to her mother rolling her eyes, "Ma, how many times we gotta talk about this. Choc might be a little quiet sometimes, but that don't make him bad."

"The few times he came around he barely acknowledged me." her mother shot back. "He won't even look me in the eyes, Shirl. Any man that won't look you in the eyes just can't be trusted."

Shirley gently grabbed her mother's hands.

With a smile she assured, "I'm-a be alright. Momma didn't raise no punk."

Her mother's concerned eyes looked back, "Baby. I just don't want you to go through what I went through with your fa..."

"Ma." Shirley cut her off. "I can take care of myself." she said in a stern, calm tone. "Trust me."

"OK." Her mother conceded.

She kissed her daughter on the forehead then walked down the hallway to her bedroom. Shirley grabbed her keys and her purse, threw on a jacket and out the front door she went.

The Avenue hummed with its usual afternoon traffic. Shirley crossed Pennsylvania Avenue with her destination in site. Hendin's was a high-end women's clothing store that boasted Hollywood and New York fashions. As she entered the store the sales lady recognized her and immediately came to her.

"Hello, young miss. And welcome back to Hendin's. How can we assist you today?"

"Well, I'm her to pick up my dress. It's the cream satin, with the brown ribbon." Shirley took an order ticket from her purse and read, "Order number 921."

"Right away."

The sales lady took the ticket and gave it her coworker, who ran to the store's back room.

"Can we offer you something while you wait? Tea, some cookies perhaps?"

"No thanks." Shirley answered.

Those polite manners were a far cry from what she received her first time at the store. On her first visit, she was confronted by a snobbish sales lady who didn't allow her to try on clothes and only showed her the cheapest out fits.

"What, you don't think I can afford anything in here? I probably got more money than you." Shirley responded as she peeled off a wad of dollars, much to the snob's surprise. Of course she had gotten the money from her new boyfriend, Choc, but that was her business. That day Shirley had ended up spending close to thirty dollars in

Hendin's; commission, of course going to another sales lady. She was now a preferred customer.

"Here we are." the sales lady said as she handed Shirley the new dress in paper covering. "Will that be all?"

"Yeah, that's it. Thank you." Shirley answered and left the store.

As she walked up the avenue she saw people going about their daily task. She saw men in uniform walking about.

'Sailors. Poor guys. Off to war soon, better have all the fun you can.' she thought.

She walked pass avenue businesses. She noticed a man cutting fish in a fish market, a man buying tools in a warehouse and a woman trying on a hat in some hat store. Shirley had not gotten more than three steps pass that hat store before she had realized that the woman trying on the hat was facing a man that looked like Choc. She backtracked until she stood at the entrance of the store. Upon closer inspection, Shirley saw that the man was indeed Choc. She stormed in the store, still carrying her new dress flung over her shoulder and stood right in front of the couple.

"Chuckie, who the hell is this?!"

Her anger was offset by the confusion in noticing that Choc didn't look guilty *or* nervous; he didn't even look concerned. He just wore a small grin, as if Shirley wasn't there.

"Chuckie! Did you hear me? I said who is this?"

Choc barely looked her way, "You know I go by Choc, and don't you worry about who she is." he said coldly.

The other woman just stood quietly as if she expected Choc to 'handle' this annoyance. By then a few patrons were starting to take notice.

"Well *Choc*, if you don't tell me who this bitch is, I'm a git her, then I'm a git you." Shirley threatened.
But almost as soon as she finished the statement Choc had her by the throat. With a quiet fury, he pulled her close. Everything in the store got quiet; tension was high.

"Who 'you think you talking to? You don't keep tabs on me, I keep tabs on you. I do what I wanna do, when I wanna do it. And if you try this again, I'll kill you, **got it**."

Shirley could barely breathe, less answer. With that, Choc pushed her into a manikin stand and to the floor. As she gasped for air she looked up to see Choc pay for the hat and walked with his female companion out the store. He never even looked back. The sales lady helped Shirley to her feet, asked how she was and offered her a drink of water. Shirley, staring off in the distance, dusted herself off, declined the drink and walked out. She left her new dress on the floor.

CHAPTER THIRTEEN

Ruthie sat thumbing through the latest issue of Stardom Magazine. Gary Cooper shared the cover with her favorite actress, Barbara Stanwick. From across the room, Doris saw that though Ruthie stared down at the magazine, her mind was elsewhere. Since the incident at the Club Casino, Ruthie seemed quieter, more focused; on what, Doris did not know, but she did notice a change.

In an attempt to lighten the mood Doris started, "Oh, and I just talked to Big Joe. He 'been talking to Mil. We' double-dating again."

"Dag, do I get a say?" Ruthie said sarcastically. "Where we goin'?"

"Joe said they got tickets to The Carver this time; the Lionel Hampton show."

"Ooh, that show been sold out for weeks, where they keep getting these 'hard-to-get' tickets?"

"Friend of a friend I guess. You know how they are, wannabe big shots. One foot in the game, one foot out." Doris thought for a moment then asked, "So, you and Mil getting kind of serious, eh?"

Nudged out of her daze, "I guess." Ruthie answered thoughtfully, "But it's new, you know. I just gotta figure what's next."

"Well you better figure it out quick. A fine looking man like that, you better marry him before he gets drafted; get some of that G.I. wife money." Doris teased.

"Girl, I don't know what I'm gonna do with you." Ruthie said laughing, "I'm bored. Let's go get some milkshakes."

The ladies gathered jackets and pocketbooks and ended up in front of a diner in the 'Eatery'. It was a typical sunny day, mild in the sun, and cool in the shade; autumn was nearing. The Avenue was crowded as usual. Pushing through the shop's thick glass doors the ladies sat on some stools at the counter. The counter was 'L' shaped against the left and back walls. Square tables dotted the open floor space and along the right wall.

The soda-hop approached, "What can I get y'all?"

Looking at the over grill menu, Doris ordered, "I'll have a root beer float, and.."

Ruthie cut in, "And I'll have the banana split." Turning to Doris she said, "Girl hold my seat, I'm going to the ladies room."

As Ruthie left, Doris waited patiently for the desserts to arrive. Casually scanning the sitting area, she noticed a woman, sitting alone at a table on the opposite side of the shop. She noted that the woman had a pretty face but looked a little old, but not from age, more from hard living. She would've been hardly noticeable except that she was staring in the direction that Ruthie had gone in. Her stare wasn't an overly obvious one, but it was long enough to be noticed; to seem uncomfortable.

'What the hell?' Doris thought. 'I know she wasn't... I'll see if she's still staring when Ru comes out the bathroom, before I slap the taste out of this wench's mouth.'

"One Split, and one Float." the soda-hop said placing the girls' orders on the counter.

141

"Thank you." Doris answered turning around.

"Yeah, I'm about to tear this Banana Split up."
Doris looked over her shoulder to see Ruthie focused on
her ice cream.

"That was quick."

"What did you expect, I just went to pee. You
thought I was in there staring at the wall."

"No. But speaking of staring, that woman over there
was just staring at you like she got a problem."

"At me? Who." Ruthie asked.

"The one over there at that table. She watched you go
all the way to the bath..."
To Doris' astonishment, the table of which she spoke was
now empty. Ruthie looked at Doris for an answer she
didn't have.

She just conceded, shaking her head saying, "There
was a lady over there, but now she's gone. I don't know."

"Anyway," Ruthie said changing the subject, "How's
work?"

Doris sighed, then said, "I'm getting laid off in two
weeks. Word is, they just got a new government contract
for army combat uniforms; rapid expansion. The whole
garment shop is being converted to Uncle Sam's own
private men's store. They're supposed to be hiring more
people by the end of the month with the reorganization."

"Well, that should be a good thing, right?"

"You would think. The thing is, 'first dib' jobs are
going to G.I. wives; white G.I. wives. Which leaves
colored women out in the cold."

"Damn. So are you OK with money?" Ruthie asked
concerned.

"For the time being. But I guess I'll have to start looking again, soon after.?"

"Well don't worry too much, 'cause you know I got a few stashed away. And if I'm good, you're good." Ruthie assured.

"Thanks." Doris said. "What about you, Ru. How you holding up?"

"Eh. After the other night, those men at Club, bragging." she shook her head then sighed, "Maybe I just need to get my mind off of it. I be trying, but I heard names, I remember faces. It all keeps flooding back."

"I wish there was something I could do?" Doris sympathized.

"I know, but I guess it's just something I gotta deal with."

"At least we going to the show, maybe that'll take you mind off of it."

"Hopefully."

The Game

It was a great show. Lionel Hampton and his orchestra belted out all the big band covers as well their original pieces, but he blew the roof of the house when they played their new hit "Flying Home". The Carver Theater was comparatively smaller than other Avenue theaters, but that made for a more intimate sound. Hampton's xylophone resonated throughout the room. It was like he was playing for each person, individually. Mil & Ruthie, along with Big Joe & Doris felt like this was a better show than they saw weeks before. After the show they were amped up for more nightlife. They found themselves, once again, on Pennsylvania Avenue when the night was young.

"Any suggestions?" Mil asked.

"I don't know. We went to those spots down 'The Bottom' last time." Doris answered, "How about something different. 'Anybody been to the Satin Club?" she asked with excitement.

The girls noticed the guys exchanged a look.

"I don't know." Mil said in an evasive manner.

Ruthie immediately teased, "Oh, what the big tough guys can't handle the Satin Club?"

"Oh we can handle it. And we got the dough." Joe shot in, "We just rather go to our own spot."

Doris looked at Joe skeptically, "Y'all got a spot?"

"Well, kind of." Mil explained, "We know the guy that runs it."

"Yeah it's solid. We was supposed to meet him there later tonight, but I guess we could make it a little earlier. We should go there." Joe suggested.

"Y'all trying to get us to go to some shabby juke joint?" Ruthie asked.

"Don't worry. It's safe." Mil said.

"It's a gambling spot!" complained Doris.

"And the Satin Club ain't?" Joe argued, and then continued, "It's the same thing… just less classy. Come on, whadoyasay?"

The girls looked at each other and reluctantly agreed.

Walking toward the spot, each couple arm in arm, Doris sassily joked to Joe, "Ok, but you get us killed, I'm-a kick your ass."

The stairs creaked with every step. Paint chips hung jaggedly off the walls. It was dark and old and nobody in their right mind would want to be in this building. It was a semi-abandoned tenement, four blocks off of Pennsylvania Avenue, on one of the side streets. It looked like squatters had set up residence on the ground floor with the second floor remaining empty. Big Joe & Doris followed by Mil & Ruthie came to the top of the third floor staircase to a hallway. Muffled music and light from an apartment's open door spilled into the hallway. There was a party going on.

Standing in front of the door, Joe snickered, "Here we are ladies. Follow my lead and act like y'all *been* somewhere before. I'm an important guy."

"Yeah right." the other three answered with smiles as they walked in.

They were greeted at that door by a man named Tiddy and entered into the apartment's dining area. The apartment had a homey feel to it, like a poor, elderly couple lived there. There was a low hanging ceiling lamp, under which four men sat at a table playing spades. The couples were hardly even noticed. The dining area was sectioned off by a wide arching entrance leading into the living room. In it, was an old two piece living room set and a coffee table with an old radio on it. Two other couples sat on the couch while one couple danced to the music. As Joe and Tiddy spoke, Mil got the ladies drinks and guided them to the living-room area. The ladies were pleased to see that Joe was in fact an important, or in the very least, a well-liked man at the card game, evident by the level of respect he was shown. Mil watched the game from across the room and Doris sat listening to the music, but she couldn't help but notice Ruthie secretly watching everything that happened in the apartment while pretending to nurse her drink. She decided to follow Ruthie's line of sight, and every time she did, she found something interesting at the other end. In one direction stood a lone gentleman. He didn't drink or speak to anyone; most likely some kind of security. In another direction was a man trying to get one of the ladies to go into the bathroom with him.

'Pigs.' she thought to herself.

In yet another direction she noticed the front door open and two men step in and to either side. An older man with the look of ferocious importance made his entrance. He was obviously somebody's boss' boss, because the men at the table, including Joe greeted him with reverence.

"Big," one of the men said, "thanks for coming down. It's an honor to have you come through personally."

"Eh, every now and the I like to come out, inspect the new talent. It ain't nothing." the old man answered.

'Who the hell is this?' Doris thought to herself. 'He coming in here like he Paul Muni or something.'

The old man turned to Tiddy, who was already humbly approaching.

He waited a second and then impatiently said, "What, I gotta ask?"

Tiddy nervously shot a look at Joe, who in turn signaled one of the men from the party. That man went to the kitchenette, then came back with large stuffed envelope. One of the old man's goons transferred its contents into a briefcase. Doris, who was inconspicuously staring from across the room recognized the situation. It was a payoff, tribute, protection money. Functionally, to keep random thugs from robbing the card-games, but essentially a reason to skim money off of the top of neighborhood operations. Doris was excited to see that side of the game. That excitement was interrupted by a crushing sensation on her hand.

"Owww." she whispered.

Ruthie, who had grabbed her hand, was staring in the old man's direction, and it seemed the longer she stared, the more her grip tightened. Doris tried to pull her arm away. Ruthie released her grip, then looked to the floor. Doris couldn't be sure whether Ruthie's action was shame or anger, but she decided to offer her hand back to her childhood friend. After a minute, the old man and his henchmen were gone, the party seemed to be simmering down and Mil and Joe walked over to Ruthie and Doris. Joe was answering a question Mil had asked him on the way over.

"Oh that was just Tiddy's boss Big Shot. 'Told him he had to start paying him double starting next week." Doris thought she recognized that boss' name. It sounded like someone important on the avenue. She rubbed her still aching hand suddenly remembering the connection between that name and her best friend.

"That's messed up. Big keep treating his people bad like that, one of them gonna hurt him." Mil responded.

"Shucks, the only way you can hurt that greedy bastard is in the pockets. That's all he cares about is money." Joe said.

Sitting quietly, Ruthie's eyebrow went up, 'Oh really?' she thought.

That night and many more after were sleepless for Ruthie. It had seemed that just as she would settle from one horrible memory, flashback or experience, another would pop up in front of her. She had come back to the city for a much needed change of pace, but had run into staggering psychological and emotional roadblocks. Ruthie was beginning to think that she had made a misjudgment in returning to the Avenue.

One night, weeks later while lying in bed, she had come to a conclusion and made a decision to go back home to 'The Hill'. Back to her real home, where she had refuge, love and relative peace. But the peace was just that, relative. The nightmares, memories and flashbacks would still be there; they would follow her wherever she went. She would suffer for the rest of her life. But the people, those responsible for her uncle's murder and the reason for her anguish, those people wouldn't. They would go on with their lives. They would experience happiness, sadness, joy, failure, perhaps even triumph. They would live; whether they remembered who her uncle was or not. This was unacceptable to Ruthie. Why should they get to go on as if nothing happened? Why should they get to experience the sweetness and opportunities of life? Why should they not suffer the consequences of their actions? Something subtle in Ruthie snapped. As if a once dormant side of her had suddenly awaken. A dozen different paths of retribution appeared before her. At this point she was unsure of which she would take but her ultimate focus remained clear. Those who had taken from her had to pay, and whatever needed to happen, she would make happen. She would somehow figure a way to disrupt businesses or ruin lives. And if it

148

came to it, some would have to pay the ultimate price. Oddly enough, this line of thought gave her the peace of mind she needed to finally drift off to sleep. It was the best sleep she had in weeks, there would be a few more in the nights to come, but those would be the last good night's sleep she would have for months,

An Idea

"'You serious? You mean rob it?"

"Yeah, I think we should."

"Kinda 'out of the blue', don't you think?"

"Kinda, but that's what'll make it work."

"You don't even need the money, Ru."

"It ain't always about money Dorie. There are more important things..."

It was morning, a week later. Ruthie and Doris sat at their kitchen table.

"This is about something else, ain't it?" Doris asked. Ruthie sat silent.

"Mister Uncle Poppy, right?"

Ruthie remained silent, but looked up.

"Ruthie." Doris reasoned, "You can't go putting yourself, and me, in harm's way for revenge."

"I'm not! I mean... I don't know. I-I have to do something. If I don't, I'll go crazy."

"Me along with you." Doris added with reluctance.

"Dorie, you're my best friend. I would never ask you to do anything extreme. But *this*, this is absolutely fool-proof. You' seen them card games with your own eyes. They're lax; no security, no look outs, they're just asking to be taken."

Dorie eye brow went up, "I see you been thinkin'?"

"I been plannin' a little bit."

"I don't know. What if somebody suspects us?"

"We're girls. Girls don't rob card games. Besides, we'll wear big clothes, dress in all black, look like boys. Who's gonna even think to look our way."

Doris puzzled, "OK, but card-games?"

"Well that's where the money is; their money. Besides, I feel like I wanna shake things up. Plus, how else are we gonna finance it."

Looking across the table at her friend in amazement, Doris said, "Huh. This whole time, I thought you was the hick and I was the city girl."
They shared a chuckle.

"It's one thing I'm still trying figure out, though. Guns. We can't do it without 'em, but I don't know how to even get none."
Ruthie saw Doris' light bulb go off.

"What is it?" she asked.

Doris answered, "Well, you know the washing machine in the basement? About two months ago I was washing some clothes. I just so happened to look behind the machine and saw a balled up shirt. I figured I had dropped it there, so I picked it up to throw it in the wash with the rest of the clothes. When I did, out of the shirt dropped three guns. 'Scared me half to death. Someone had stashed them there. It took about an hour for me to put them back the way I found them and after that I was even scared to look back there, for a while. Anyway, last week when I was down there washing clothes again, I suddenly built up the courage to give it another look. What do I see? You guessed it, the shirt bundle of guns. They were still there and they're still there now. Who ever they belong to either forgot 'em or don't need em. But we do."

"Yesss. This is too good to be true," Ruthie said. "Everything is falling into line. That solves one problem, but what about coverage? We need somebody to lead it, to get the money and to watch the door."
They sat thinking about possibilities, contingencies and logistics.

Coming to some conclusion of thought, Doris said, "It'll be too hard for just us two. We need a third person, somebody we can trust."

After a moment of thought, Ruthie suggested, "What about your cousin, Shirley?"

CHAPTER FOURTEEN

Sixteen

People moved out of his way when he walked down the side walk. Even those who didn't know who he was stepped aside. It may have been because of reputation, it may have been a copying instinct, but to most it was probably because of the dark cloud that surrounded him. He was the infamous gangster nick-named Sixteen; a top player in the Pennsylvania Avenue crime syndicate. He had worked his way up from child street hustler, to hit man, to his boss' Big Shot's third in command. He was of medium height and build, with an average face and no discernible features save a split left earlobe. How he got it was steeped in Avenue lore. He was making one of his rare day-time appearances and being a man of obvious power and influence, he walked with only two associates; neither of which was a bodyguard. He was so respected and feared that he didn't feel the need for security, which he regarded as a sign of paranoia and weakness. He actually believed in his own invulnerability.

One of the men beside him, his operations man, Gene, went over business with him, while his money man, Scratch, held open the door of a bakery he owned. Through the glass door and straight to the back the trio went. When they got to the back supply room, they were met by a man dress in a tailored suit. His name was Maxwell, a top man in the Gay Street organization on the east-side. The back door to the alley was opened as uniformed bread deliverymen hauled baking supplies to and from a truck parked in the alley.

"Thanks for meeting on such short notice." said Maxwell with sarcasm.

He was gracious but brimming with contempt.

"I try." answered Sixteen with a sneer.

"Evidently not hard enough. I've been trying to meet with you for over a week. You have something for me and I don't like to be kept waiting."

"Well sometimes we don't have a choice." Sixteen shot back.

Maxwell noticed Scratch's brief case, "Is that the payment?"

Scratch nodded. It was then that Sixteen noticed one of the delivery men move quickly to close and guard the front entrance to the back room. Two more pulled revolvers and positioned themselves behind Sixteen and his men. A fourth stood by the back door. Sixteen's face tightened.

Maxwell started, "Look, I'll be quick and to the point as I have other dealings. You," pointing to Sixteen, "are an arrogant little bastard. Now, I *know* about your little rep, but honestly, you're bad for business and you got-ta go."

Calmly defiant, Sixteen exhaled, and then asked, "Just one question, who's decision is this?"

"Mine and mine alone. I've no need to confer. I'm on the come-up. Concerning *you* though, let's just say, it was time for new management." Maxwell said with a grin.

In a monotone voice, Sixteen responded, "Funny, I was thinking the same thing."

Just then, the guns that were trained on Sixteen were now trained on Maxwell. Maxwell's eyes popped wide open a second before they were filled with bullet rounds. He fell dead.

Scratch nonchalantly stepped around the body and walked to the store's front, placed a call on the telephone.

When the person on the other end picked up, he 'matter of factly' said, "He's gone. Congratulations on your promotion and a fruitful new partnership."

He hung the phone up then turned to his boss Sixteen, who was emerging from the back with Gene.

Scratch said in a plain tone, "It's done. Breakfast anyone?"

"Calling, available officers to the twenty-hundred block of Brunt Street. Possible shots fired. Be advised." Detective Ross' police radio crackled the message from inside of his unmarked police-issued vehicle.

"Detective Ross, en route." he answered into his radio receiver as he drove down the Avenue. Making a left onto Presstman Street, he looked north up the first alley and saw men standing, looking around, security guard style. Ordinarily this would arouse no suspicion, but these men were in full bread deliverymen attire; aprons and all. Ross parked his vehicle and then strolled casually up the alley to a delivery truck parked in back of a bakery. Something still seemed odd because the deliverymen tensed and then reached for weapons when they saw him.

Ross immediately pulled his service revolver and badge.

"BCPD! Drop your weapons and reach!"

The deliverymen hesitated then complied. Ross secured the men and the area and then began a sight investigation. He noticed wet ground forming a path from the bakery's back door to the truck. The moisture was lightly tainted with some red fluid, like the water was being used to wash something away. He backtracked the wet path to the truck where on the back step-lift the tainted red fluid looked thicker, darker; like blood. Something bloody was in the back of that truck.

'Uh oh.' Ross thought.

Just then two BCPD squad cars pulled up. Exiting the cars were a Sargent and an Officer. Ross recognized them from the precinct. The Sargent approached him as the Officer inspected and frisked the deliverymen.

Stating the obvious, he said, "Ross, right?" The Sargent exuded some authority, but oddly, he looked around nervously. "Good work, we'll take it from here."

Ross protested, "But Sir.."

"I said,... we'll take it from here, Officer." the Sargent interrupted.

This time he had a more decisive tone and a serious look in his eye. Ross knew to back off.

"We'll investigate the area and process all necessary paper work Detective. Carry on."

"Yes sir." Ross responded.

He reluctantly walked back to his vehicle and resumed plainclothes patrol, forcing himself to believe that the case would be properly processed. Deep down inside, something was telling him it wouldn't.

The muffled sounds of footsteps, and music could be heard from above as Gene and Sixteen rose from a large oak table. It had been a few hours since the ruckus at the bakery and they had just closed another meeting with

Tuck, the manager of the establishment above. General security concerns and generated income were discussed. As workers moved bags to an awaiting car in the back alley, Sixteen, Gene, Tuck and his associate decided to join the festivities upstairs, and have a drink. The air was filled with the sounds of jazz, celebration and smoke. People drank until they were drunk, gambled until they were broke and partied until they were exhausted. And yet with all this excitement, this was just another ordinary early evening on Pennsylvania Avenue at the Sphinx Club.

Sixteen was given his due respect and acknowledgement as he made his way around the gambling floor. Never placing one bet, he lavished in his fearsome aura. Women threw themselves at him constantly; some caught, some thrown back, all appreciated. Sixteen's party of four found themselves at the VIP table in the lounge area. They were enjoying a batch of fried chicken wings along with their drinks when they saw a couple enter the club. The man, was an older white gentleman.

'Some lawyer coming uptown for some colored nightlife' Sixteen thought.

With the man was what Sixteen thought was some exotic queen. She was white, but not like any of the white women he had ever seen. Her skin was olive, her lips were thick and her hips were wide. Sixteen's one thought was, 'I likes.'

Upon noticing the Sixteen's party, the couple made their way over to their VIP table. Tuck stood.

Extending his hand he said, "Your Honor, how ya doin'. Thanks for coming by. Let me introduce some friends of mine."
Each introduction was met with a polite nod.

"You know my colleague, Marshall. And this is Mr. Rogers and his associate Gene Mack.

"Benning. The Honorable Judge Benning. 'Pleased to meet you. And this is the lady Ms. Lisa..."

"Vallis." the judge's date cut in.
She gave his hand a caress, signaling him leave.

The Judge nodded, "Gentlemen." excusing themselves, and the two vanished down the back hallway and onto the gambling floor. But just as they left, within a microsecond, Sixteen could have sworn he saw the lady, Miss Vallis giving Tuck, the club manager, a look; one of familiarity. After about a half hour of small talk, Tuck and his associate excused themselves and walked off to other parts of the club. Sensing their night's festivities were coming to an end, Gene leaned in to recap the day's business and to remind of upcoming meetings and talks.

"I think that thing over East should work out real good. The setup is nice, and could lead us to bigger and better things."
Gene talked over the clubs noise. Sixteen gave a silent nod.

Preparing his briefcase to go Gene wearily suggested, "I was thinking maybe we get some men to hang around. Some security."
Sixteen shot a glare.

Gene cautiously explain, "Six, we go way back. I know what you're thinking, but hear me out. With this new deal, we getting a lot of money, but with the new transition we got some new enemies too, I've been hearing some things. We gotta be safe, we need a buffer from the drama."

Sixteen thought for a second then conceded, "Security detail, huh. I must be doing better than I thought. OK, do it."

Gene noticed that Six seemed more tense than usual; his mind was definitely elsewhere.

As he got up from the table Sixteen grabbed his arm, "This Ms. Vallis,"

"Yeah boss?"

"Arrange a meeting."

With that request, Gene got the answer to his concerns,

'Six likes the white chick.' he thought with a smile, then responded, "I'll get somebody on it." and walked out of the club.

Amateurs

"Nigga, didn't I tell you to have the drinks and the chicken wings ready?"

"I got the drinks right here, I just gotta set 'em up. And Russell coming with the wings right now. His momma fried 'em."

"Alright. We got some high-rollers in here tonight, I need you to be 'Johnny-on-the-spot' with the liquor and the food. Got it?"

"Got it."

"I'll be at the table doing my thing."

Eric, a low level hustler from the Winchester neighborhood, barked his last order to his cousin Mook, then stood by a kitchen table converted for gambling, already occupied by four hustlers. The game was spades and the men talked trash as they partnered up. Eric was in charge of this particular gambling spot, which was just another row house flat off of the Avenue. It also served as a cash pick up spot, and though he ran the place, its proprietor was a man further up the food chain.

Everyone knew who that man was though most didn't mention the name. His reputation was enough to ward off any shady plots. Eric checked his watch, waiting for more gamblers to show. From the door came a knock then it opened. Eric was disappointed at the same time delighted to see his old friend Murray with his partner and four ladies. They went straight to the dining room area and sat around a saloon styled stand-up piano. Murray's friend began to play a few Fats Waller tunes. The ladies loved it. A few minutes later, another knock came at the door. In walked one couple and two men they all acknowledged each other and joined the piano party or waited for the next opening at the card table. Behind them came Russell carrying a grease stained cardboard box. The spot seemed to get louder as the partiers cheered at the making of plates. Eric did his job, making sure everyone was situated and comfortable. Table gamblers laughed, joked and complained about losing. A young man served chicken on napkins and filled empty glasses when needed. Everyone was having a good time, but no one noticed when the entrance doorknob turned and three masked assailants rushed in aiming guns.

Everyone was stunned but quickly realized what was happening. The robbers were dressed in all black sweaters and trousers that looked too big for them and moved quickly to cover all parts of the living space. None of the robbers spoke, and the partygoers were forced to guess at their weird game of charades. They were noticeably nervous and to the partiers and gamblers, seemed a little uncoordinated. They communicated through head nods and gestures and bumped into each other; one even dropped a gun on the floor. No one dared interfered and everyone cooperated. Agitating amateurs could result in nervous bullets. One robber collected from the table, and then aimed a gun at Eric, who pointed to a small closed cupboard near a back room door, another robber went to retrieve the goods. Inside the cupboard was two small-sized bags, ready for transport; convenient. None of the partiers were robbed, and under three minutes the robbers were out the door. Eric stood in disbelief.

He said, almost to himself, "That was the raggediest ass stick-up I ever seen in my life."
The people were still in shock and were no longer in the partying mood.

Mook came over to Eric and asked, "What we gon' do, boss?"

Eric looked over at his cousin, "I guess I'm gonna have to tell the man. We got robbed."

Days later Detective Ross sat at his desk preparing for an upcoming investigation. He thought for a second about a feeling he got from that arresting Sargent at the bakery and wondered the status of the perps. He would investigate. Through his inquiries, Ross found the bakery and a few names associated with it. One stood out; Melvin Rogers. It was a name he had known, though he had known him better by his street name, Sixteen. It was common knowledge that Mr. Rogers had been mixed up in all kinds if shady dealings, but on file he was basically invisible; rarely ever seen. His street rap sheet was long but he only recorded one arrest in the Western Precinct.

'In all those years, one arrest. Interesting.' Ross thought.

Rogers was a third of an owner of the bakery, so *that* was a red flag. Ross checked the policeman's log and arrests sheet for that day and saw no record of an arrest, suspect or an investigation. Ross was disappointed though not surprised, but he had known better than to express his concerns as it might disrupt his other investigations. He suspected this situation to be a part of Captain Warren's 'in-house' investigation, alluded to in his orientation briefing. He knew no file or case could be muffled or could 'vanish' unless it was cleared from the top. Just then Captain Warren walked passed his desk. Ross noticed the captain checking his vicinity for eaves droppers and waited for what looked to be important news.

Captain Warren simply said in a low voice, "Our man downtown has taken a shine to you. 'Still making impression, eh? Anyways, he's with Internal Affairs. 'Says to look for his call in a few days."
Surprised, the confused, then delighted, Ross responded, "I will sir. Thank you, sir."

CHAPTER FIFTEEN

Stick-up Girls

"Owww! You wrapping it too tight. Why we gotta do this anyway?'

"You already know the answer, now hold still." Ruthie pulled an ace bandage tightly around Shirley's chest.

"For this little bit of discomfort, the payoff is great. I gotta make you look like a boy and we all gotta do it. Now stop whining you big baby, and breathe deep." Shirley inhaled deeply. Once the wrapping was done she breathed out. Doris stood in her apartment's kitchen as the other two finished.

"We gotta practice. That last time was too clumsy. Something bad could've happened." Doris said.

"What is this, a dance troupe?" Shirley joked.

"She's right." Ruthie agreed. "Our movements need to be second nature. You never know. If a situation comes up, we gotta know how to improvise."

"The only thing we need to know, is get in, get the money, and get out." answered Shirley.

"And what about if things don't go to plan?" asked Doris.

"Then we do what we gotta." Shirley replied simply. Ruthie and Doris shared a glance.

Shirley continued aggressively as if it was directed at another, "I'm serious. If we gonna do this I think we should really do it, all the way."

Doris face went from a smile to concerned.

"Jacks, is everything alright? Is there something you're not telling us?"

Regaining her focus, Shirley focused on her cousin, "Don't call me that. I'm not twelve anymore. Besides, I'm fine. It's nothing."

Doris' eyes thinned in curiosity, "I' known you all your life, you think I can't tell?" Then after a second of thought, "It's that damn Choc ain't it? What did he do? When Shirley sat silent, Doris asked again, louder. "Shirley what did he do to you?"

Shirley answered, "Nothing. Nothing I can't handle."

Doris came to kneel in front of her and asked firm but calmly, "What- did- he- do?"

Shirley relented, "He didn't hit me. He just, choked me. He choked me and threw me on the floor."
She looked up to see Ruthie now beside Doris, both with concerned, sympathetic looks on their faces.

Shirley continued, "I was on the avenue, I saw him in the hat shop. He was with some hussy." Her eyes welled somewhere between anger and sadness. "He didn't even *try* to hide, 'didn't try get out of it or nothing. It was like he didn't care one way or another. And that's when *I* loss it. And that's when *he* grabbed me by the neck."

Doris recoiled angrily, "Ooh! I wish I was a man. I would bang him right in his face. 'Matter of fact, I'm-a call Big Joe, he'll teach him about puttin' his hands on girls."

Shirley calmly raise her hand in protest, "Don't." she said. "Don't get Joe involved, don't get Mil involved, don't even mention it to nobody. It's done, I'll deal with it."

"Yeah, It's a lot of that going around." Doris said sarcastically, pointing at Ruthie and Shirley, "Both of y'all go issues."

Giving Doris the 'this is not the time and place' look, Ruthie then turned to Shirley and sighed, "Ok, but just know, we're ya girls. When you need us...."

"Thanks." Shirley said as they hugged. "Now, back to the plan. I think it needs to be straight forward."

"She's right." Ruthie added, getting back on track. "We focus on the goal: check the surroundings, get in, get the money, get out."

"What about surprises? How do we deal with them? Do we pistol whip?" Shirley asked in jest.

"No, that's too close up on people. I don't wanna get into any scuffles." answered Ruthie. "What if they trying to be tough? What then, a warning shot? A leg shot?"

"Well if you have to, yeah, but in that order. And if it's the leg, at least it's non-lethal. 'Lets them know we mean business."

"Ok what about if they ain't cooperating after that or coming at me? We should be able to shoot them."

"If a warning and a leg shot don't learn 'em, then you might *need* to shoot em in the face." Doris said jokingly.

Ruthie cut in, "No. No kill shots. And definitely no face shootin'. The cops may not look for card game robbers, but they will look for killers."

"Killers," Shirley said to herself, "I like the sound of that."

The other two looked down at her and said in unison, "You got issues."

165

A stolen dark gray 1936 Dodge sedan crept slowly on to a side street pulling in just beyond a small alleyway. It was early November and seasonably cold. At this late hour, the street itself was dimly lit and desolate. Engine off, Ruthie and Doris took off their overcoats, revealing their oversized outfits of all black. From under the passenger seat, the three old .38 caliber revolver were pulled for use. Folding their overcoats on the car floor, they put on black ski masks, waited until the street was empty then exited the car. Up the block they went until they came to an alley street. It too was empty. From a small pathway leading from the street to the back of the row houses stood a third figure, dressed in black; It was Shirley. She was dropped off minutes earlier to case the area. The block, though presently desolate, was a more populated area and they didn't want to take the risk of late-comers or passersby stumbling in on the heist, so Shirley would guard the front of the house so they wouldn't get trapped on the inside with a bunch of unsavory characters. When she saw Ruthie and Doris she gave the 'all clear' signal and all three headed to the second house from the corner.

This house was just supposed to be a simple gambling spot, no stash and no parties. Standing on the front steps, Ruthie pulled a revolver from her side, gave a silent three-count with her fingers and then casually turned the knob and walked in. Doris followed and Shirley stood watch. The men in the gambling spot went through the gambit of emotions; first shock, then fear, then anger, then acceptance. Doris took the lead once Ruthie secured the first floor. Doris noticed that the gamblers were slow to take direction from hand signals alone, so she decided to speak, but in a low, raspy voice. Ruthie was shocked and impressed at this improvisation.

"Stick 'em up." she said pointing her two guns out from either side of her. "No heroes."
Ruthie went about gathering the table's winnings. Looking at the men's faces, she could tell that they were angry at the fact that they were getting robbed but impressed with how smoothly it was happening. Just as quickly as it had started, it ended. The ladies stood waiting by the front door, loot bags in one hand, guns pointed in the other, waiting for Shirley who was still standing post, to give another 'all-clear'.

When that signal came, Doris waved her gun, rasping, "Don't follow."

They walked quickly down the stoop and onto the alley-street, with Shirley walking sideways to cover the rear. When she saw a man peek his head out of the front door of the gambling spot, she fired a shot in the air over the house. The head quickly pulled back in, along with any eyes peeking through shades. Around the corner to the side-street and to their awaiting vehicle they walked swiftly. The streets were still clear as they entered the car, took off their mask and slipped back into their overcoats. They knew that the gangsters from the game and the police, if someone even bothered to call them, would be searching for three men dressed in all black, not three pretty ladies. The '36 Dodge sedan pulled off drove a few blocks and then merged onto Fremont Avenue traffic.

From the back seat Shirley said excitedly, "Now that was smooth. I even got to shoot."

"I guess you had to do it this time, but don't get carried away." Ruthie said for the front passenger's seat.

"I won't, I won't. How'd it go on the inside? I couldn't tell when I was looking out."

"Smooth like butter. And did you see all the money? This might be our biggest take." Doris answered excitedly.

"I *like* this. It's like a rush. I want to be on the inside next time." Shirley suggested

"There may be a 'next time' but that 'next time might be the last." Ruthie said.

"Hold up, hold up. The last *time*? You serious? Y'all gettin' all this money and just gonna stop? Naw, I don't think so."
Doris and Ruthie shot disapproving looks.

From the back seat, Shirley continued, pointing to Doris and then to Ruthie, "Whether you in it for the money, or for something personal, which is probably the case, or even like me, you in it for the excitement, *this* ain't the last one and this *ain't* gonna stop until we get what we *all* want from it."
The two were impressed and surprised to see how much insight Shirley had on their motivations.

"Me personally, I love it. I love the dangerous street life. I wish I could find a way to get famous from it; without getting lock up, of course."

"Look at James Cagney back there." Ruthie teased as they drove. "You should probably get a alias."

Shirley responded, "I might."

"Uhm, a woman that knows what she wants." Doris said. "That's kinda weird."

"Stranger things have happened." Shirley answered.
The ladies transferred the stolen money into brown paper grocery bags, ditched the Dodge on Fulton, across North

Avenue and took a Sun Cab to Doris' apartment. There, they divided up the night's earnings and planned for the next job.

A jazz spot's muffled hum could be heard out on the Avenue, however this was not one of a standup bass solo, but the hum of excitement, of anticipation. This particular club, Gamby's, was almost to capacity and the hum was its patrons crowding themselves in. Gamby's owner Mr. Mack was a former boxer on the amateur circuit in the twenties and had wisely invested his winnings in the night club. In those early years he had been eager to get foot traffic into his business and from time to time let unknown acts perform. One of the acts, a singer, had been hanging around the club, cleaning and waiting tables. She was a scrawny underage girl from the east side, but Mr. Mack had grown quite fond of her and became sort of a father figure to her; protecting her from the advances of the older patrons and the dangers of Avenue street life.

She had been going through some problems at home and it was Mr. Mack who financed the young singer's move to Harlem, New York where she pursued her singing career. The singer became famous and took the name Billie Holliday. She would come back to her roots on Pennsylvania Avenue and sing at Gamby's for Mr. Mack every so often; though with her increasing popularity, the visits had lessened. Recently, Mr. Mack had been boasting of Lady Day's return, and it was for this reason that so many people had come to his establishment. People stood around the bar area, acting like they weren't waiting for Billie to show, but after a while they started gradually enjoying themselves.

Amongst the merry-makers were Big Joe and Mil who were sitting at a table near the middle of the bar's floor space. Gamby's was their spot to blow off steam after whatever jobs they had finished. This night, they were there on business. Big Joe had been contacted by a representative of Tiddy's boss. They were told to meet there to discuss their futures. Joe suspected promotion. He was excited. Where Mil's reserved demeanor relegated him to lower, mid management, Joe's toughness and enthusiasm got him recognized. Mr. Mack himself brought over the two shots of whiskey.

Placing them on the table he gave an approving nod. "I hear you boys did good with the Biggs. I heard he was real impressed."

"Damn Mr. Mack. How the hell you know?" Mil asked

"You youngins is something else. How you think I stay around so long. I know people too."

"We know that. But that information is pretty high up on the chain, I'm thinkin'" said Joe.

"Yeah, you must be connected." Mil added.

"I ain't said nothing. But one day I'll teach you young bucks how it's done."

"You got it, Jack."

"Stick around. I might introduce you to Billie."

"Solid, Mr. Mack."

As Mack walked off toward the bar, a chain reaction of heads began to turn in the direction of the front entrance. The crowd seemed to buzz with excitement, Billie Holliday would soon be there. But to everyone's disappointment, the parted crowd only produced a man name Ray. Black Ray, who was followed by Tiddy. Once spotted, they joined Joe and Mil at their table.

"You guys hung around." Tiddy said.

"Why would we not?" Joe answered. "This might turn out to be a beautiful night."

"Maybe." Ray added as they took their seats opposite Mil and Joe.
He signaled a waitress over and ordered two shots for him and Tiddy.

He started, "I'll get right into it. You guys have been doing real good with the spot and the pickups." Referring to Tiddy, "Your man right here impressed the big boss. 'Like y'all operation. So much so, he got tapped."
Though it was said to sound impactful, it was not. Tiddy had known for a few days and had already told the men the news, swearing them to secrecy. Mil and Joe acted somewhat surprised at the news and offered their thanks.

"With his promotion comes opportunities for his people." Black Ray said
Mil slightly recoiled. He had never considered himself apart of anybody's organization. Sure he had helped with a few jobs and was privy to some inside information, but mostly his hanging around was a result of his friendship with Big Joe; though he would never turn down any of the perks of being 'connected'. Joe was a different story.

Ever since he could remember he was fascinated with the Avenue life. Growing up just off of it, it was a part of his everyday experience and, more importantly, how he'd met his best friend. Young Joe and a few of his ruffian friends would venture east across the avenue to terrorize the children residing on the other side. One of these excursions led them to an alley where they had

171

surrounded a scrawny young Milton. As Milton desperately clutched his grocery store money, Joe, the ringleader, threatened a thorough beating if the dough wasn't given up. Young Mil resisted and just as they pounced, two beat cops arrived swinging clubs. As the crowd scattered the police managed to capture only two, Joe and Mil. When they ask Mil what had happened they noticed he looked a little frightened. One of the cops assured Mil that he would be safe if he spoke up, because they would take his accused assailant for a ride. Everyone knew 'a ride' meant they would take you to the rail yards for a brutal beating, sometimes resulting in bruises and broken bones, and on rare occasions, death. When asked was Joe and his friends attacking him, Mil swallowed and told the police that he and Joe were in fact friends and that the boys were chasing the two of them. He had saved Joe from a severe and possible fatal beating, and Joe knew it. As the police let them go, the boys walked out of the alley and down the street side by side. The police watched the boys from afar, and when they reached the corner and saw that Joe's gang of thugs were waiting, Young Mil got ready to fight for his life only to hear Joe tell the thugs,

"No. He took up for me back there. You hit him, you gotta hit me."
The two had been like brothers ever since. And now the 'brothers' sat at one of Gamby's tables to get the news they waited patiently to hear.

"Y'all three work good together. It's been recognized." Ray said, "And now that Tiddy's in, he needs a team to help him out. Y'all." He pointed to Mil and Joe. "I'm sure it's something y'all already figured but, now it's official. It'll be a little better than before, but at least now

you can use the boss' name and influence. Get with Tiddy tomorrow, he'll let you know what you'll be doing. Remember, there's a lot of room to move up."
Everyone seemed pleased with the news and concluded the meeting with a toast.

"Oh, and one more thing, and this is probably the most important thing, you shouldn't, but if y'all have any problems on the routes from the cops, mention this man's name," referring to Tiddy, "they on the payroll and that should be enough to get you off the hook. Got it?"

"Got it." Joe and Mil answered.
Without a word Ray downed his drink and got up from the table. Shadowed by Tiddy, he mixed into the crowd and was gone. Mil and Joe sat for a moment before speaking.

"So, what do you think?"

"It looks like we're in. We can finally get off of those trucks, start making some real money."

"Hopefully."

Just then, there was a commotion coming from the front end of the bar. There were some murmurs, a few yelps and a crack, followed by a crowd of gasps, but it was so smoky and dim that Mil and Joe could not tell what was happening. They both figured that the famous Billie Holiday had just made an entrance and people were just clamoring to see her. From where they stood the commotion didn't seem to be a ruckus.

Mil, stretching his neck in an attempt to see over the crowd said, "They don't seem to be letting her through. I'm curious. Let's go see what's going on up there. Old man Mack said he was going to give us a personal introduction anyway."

The house band had just taken their fifteen-minute break as the two walked toward the front of the thickening crowd. Mil's height advantage showed him a hole in the crowd just a few feet in front of him. He guessed it must be Ms. Holiday, signing autographs or something. But upon reaching the edge of the crowd's circular opening, they saw one of the biggest, toughest looking brutes they'd ever seen; only he was lying on the floor in the fetal position. Before they knew what to make of it, a foot kicked the brute's head back with a thump. He was now flat on his back, unconscious with a vicious, bloody head gash. To Mil and Joe's surprise, standing over the man, and flanked by two smaller, but impressively built thugs, was a young woman of medium build and height sporting a 'bob' hairstyle. In her hand was a thick glass liquor bottle. Its edge was dripping with blood; presumably the brute's blood. The bottle was so thick that it had not broken upon impact. The crowd was stunned. The young woman gave a head-nod command and to everyone's surprise the men cleared a path to the front entrance and then followed her out. Just as she left out of the front door Mil caught a glimpse of her face.

"Hey Joe," he asked, "ain't that your girl's little cousin?"

The brute was taken to nearby Provident Hospital, and the crowd went back to normal. Billie Holiday never showed.

CHAPTER SIXTEEN

Love in the City

It was a chilly December day and the avenue was decked in the tradition of the holidays. Christmas was just three weeks away and shoppers lined the sidewalks of 'The Shop'. Behind store windows were manikins dressed in brightly colored, festive sweaters. Bows and ribbons hung in every possible place and ten different Christmas tunes played in ten different stores. Ruthie, who had just come out of a knick-knack store, looked around for the next stop on her shopping spree. She missed this time of year on the avenue. Some of her best memories were her childhood at Christmas, even in the midst of the depression. She stopped to take in the scenes. Right in front of her, near the curb stood a Salvation Army Santa Claus. As he rang his bell, Ruthie chuckled at how thin he was. Up the street she saw a man carrying a little girl on his shoulders, beside him smiling was a woman, presumably his wife. She sighed. She loved love. Across the street she saw a couple strolling up the block looking as if they had no particular place to go, but from the looks on their faces she could tell it didn't matter; as long as they were together.

"I love this time of year." she said.

It had been less than two minutes since she came out of the store, thinking about the holidays and love when she looked to her left. Down the street was a man staring at her as if he was a buyer, appreciating fine art. For a split-second she felt uncomfortable until she saw that the man staring at her was none other than Mil. He himself had just come out of the barbershop. Freshly groomed in his long overcoat Mil was a tall handsome figure to behold. Ruthie gave Mil the 'are you gonna come here?' look, to which he popped out of his trance and started toward her.

"Hey Ru. How' you?"

"Alright. Where you gonna stand over there and stare all day?"

"Naw," Mil seemed stuck and at a loss for words. "I was just..."

"You was just what?" she interrupted.

"I was just... never mind." he didn't want to explain. "I was going down by the Royal, walk with me."

"And how you know I ain't doing nothing." she said.

"But you are, you're walking with me."

'Clever' she thought, "Let's go."

They crossed the street at Wilson and walked down the Avenue. The sidewalk was full but there was enough room for couples to walk side by side. 'Sounds from the heavy traffic was enough to create a barrier around conversing parties.

Mil asked, "So Ru, we been going out for a while right? It's something I always wanted to ask you."

Ruthie braced herself for some difficult question. "Go 'head, ask."

"What's your story?"

"What do you mean?"

"I mean, your story? You're so secretive."

"You know almost everything about me." she argued.

"Eh, I wouldn't say *everything*."

"There's not much more. I'm boring. Maybe I'm just a boring type of gal."

"It certainly seems that way; most of the time. But I've noticed, every so often, you're like a different person. It happens in a flash, but it does happen."

"Well, I don't know what you're talking about. I'm the way I am, all the time."

"Naw," he rejected, "Sometimes overly cautious, sometimes feisty, sometimes sad."
She turned to him and gave him a look like he should've known better.

"We all got a story Milton."
She used his full given name; usually when she was serious with him. He liked to hear her say his name.

"I suppose, so I go back to my original question, what's your story? Why would somebody from the county want to come to this hell hole?" he asked.

"Hell hole? What do you mean? People from all over the country want to come to Pennsylvania Avenue." she advocated.

"That's because they only see the glamorous side. The lights, the action. They don't see the heroin addicts, the whores, the stick-up men." Mil reasoned.
Ruthie tripped her steps. For a second she had actually thought Mil was referring to her. 'Did he suspect anything? Naw.'

She quickly came to her senses, saying, "Some people just need a change of scenery."

"Well, I can't relate." Mil took Ruthie by the hand and turned her to face him. He looked down into her brown eyes. "When I saw you in front of that store back there, my heart stopped. You were the most beautiful thing I had ever seen and I didn't want the moment to end. I could've looked at you forever."

She bashfully looked back at him, "I *guess* that's a good of reason as any to stare."

"Yeah, but all I really wanted was this." He tilted her head and gently kissed her lips, and amidst the crowded Pennsylvania Avenue sidewalk, they were all alone.

Seconds later when the fog of passion lifted, Ruthie said in a wispy voice, "That's what I wanted, too."

"Well then I guess that's one *more* thing about you that I know. But there's still so much more, hard things I'm guessing." Mil, coming to some realization, gave her a curious look. "You know, you make me wanna take care of you; protect you."

Ruthie indulged him, "*Protect* me, from what?"

"I don't know. But I do know this, from now on, I *will* be here for you."

Ruthie just rested her head on Mil's arm and held on to his arm as they spend the rest of the early evening walking down and up the other side of the Avenue. They listened to carolers; stopped for a bite to eat and stopped pass the photographer studio to have their photographs taken together. They decided against seeing a movie or a show and just enjoyed their time walking and talking together. They held hands all the way.

Comeuppance

"You sure you don't wanna stay the night, baby?"

"I told you I had business to take care of. You think you're more important than money?"

"You so crazy." a young lady giggled as if the question was asked in jest.

In all actuality the question was very much a serious one; one that the asker knew the answer to. Choc waited as his female passenger exited his parked '43 Cadillac. Her additional comments were unheard as the car pulled off. Choc was on his way to an important meeting this evening. He was charged with negotiating new territorial boundaries. His boss had faith in him; gave him this responsibility, and Choc accepted it in his climb to the top of the organization. He was well liked amongst the street soldiers and had a well-earned reputation of quiet ferocity; he was also a good earner who carried himself in a regal manner. He felt that there were only a few people on his level. His peers, along with the bosses, were the only ones to be respected, everyone else didn't matter, unless they could be of use. The drive from Riggs Avenue up Gilmore was a short one. He admired the tall three storied row homes and marble steps that accented them. He thought they were stately, well-kept and looked financially well off. It was now close to the Christmas holiday and a trace of snow from two days before lined the sidewalks and gutters. Bows and holly hung on some doors, reefs hung on others.

Looking around, Choc thought to himself, 'This ain't even the rich part. I gotta figure out a way to get some money out of these people.'

His car pulled up to house on an alley-street. It was only one of three houses on the block; the rest were an abandoned storehouse and an empty lot. It was dark and desolate but Choc didn't bother to look around, even though he was alone. This was pretty much his territory, or soon would be. He was well known, feared and respected. No one would dare accost him; it would mean their lives. As he crossed the snow-dusted lot and small alley to enter through the back entrance of the last the row house, he noticed the second floor windows were lit. Someone was already there.

'Good, the party's already started. They should be there for the meeting, waiting for me.' he thought.

He entered the building, up to the second floor and into the party room; which was basically a card game; his card game. His gambling spot. His place of business. When Choc walked through the door, he received his due acknowledgements. One of his underlings, Doug who actually ran the spot, quickly approached, took Choc's jacket and escorted him to a back room; the one he used for meetings. Upon entering the room, Choc saw the two men he was meeting with. One was from the Baker Street Organization, the other represented the Mosher Street gang. Individually, these territories were wild and a general nuisance, but consolidated, could mean a bigger market, more personnel and more overall power, and that would definitely get Choc the prestige he felt he deserved. The men were simply dressed in blazers and slacks.

Extending hand in greeting, one of them spoke. "Choc, how ya doin'? Thanks for having us."

Shaking each hand, Choc responded, "No problem. My pleasure. I assume you're being treated well?"

"Very much so. 'Nice set up you got over here. Looks like you guys are cleaning up." the man said.

His associated added, "Yeah. Booze, broads, gambling; if this is how your organization is run, this meeting may be a done deal."

"Thank you gentlemen," Choc said, "Now let's get to business, shall we?"

The three smoked cigarettes as they negotiated the terms of a deal that would expand the territory for one party and the profits of the other. Choc was given the authority to close the deals but had to work out a few small issues first. It was then that he noticed the noises from the party had stop. There was still music playing, but there was no longer the low-pitched mumbles from the partygoers. The one thing he did manage to hear was the muffled phrase or someone saying,

"No heroes."

'No heroes? What the hell?' Choc thought, but before he could get up to investigate, the door flung open. In rushed someone with at robber's mask on, pointing a revolver. Choc was more shocked than anything.

'Could this be true? Could someone actually have the nerve to rob my spot?' he thought.

The robber at first seemed stunned, and then made a gesture with his gun, directing Choc and his business associates out of the back room into the main gambling area. They all complied, but Choc was the last one out. When he did enter the main room he noticed everyone, hands held high, while two other robbers gathered the money from the table and stashes in the kitchen. From the looks of their bags they had gotten most, if not all of the house winnings too.

"Son of bitch." he said. Looking at his underling Doug as if the robbery was his fault. "What the hell is going on out here?"

The answer came in the form of a thirty- two revolver shoved under his chin. The masked assailant stared at him for a moment then move to face the men.

"Y'all know who game this is? It belongs to me."
Choc said. The anger in his voice was commanding to a
point where it startled even the armed assailants.

He continued, raising his voice, "This is
disrespectful. Y'all niggas *betta* enjoy this, cause when I
find out who y'all is, it's curtains."
The rage in his voice shook the room, and no one made
eye contact except for the robber who now pointed the
gun at him.

Still in an angry rant, he yelled at the robber, "Point
that shit somewhere else! I'm Choc nigga. You know who
the fuck I am?"
The robber simply nodded yes, pointed the gun at his face
and pulled the trigger.
Two ladies at the party yelped, the gamblers gasped and
the robbers left quickly as Choc's body hit the floor. He
was no more.

Briefing

In downtown Baltimore at the City Police Central
office building, Lieutenant Wright walked back to his
office with a freshly poured cup of coffee. It was close to
mid shift and he'd figured he would gather a few things
before going out on a pending investigation. Being and
office jockey was more to his aptitude than his early days
working the beat in the Western precinct. He figured he
had paid his dues on the street, suffering through years of
fruitless arrest and blown cases. He had seen first hand
the favoritism and corruption, and longed for the day
where he could truly make a difference; hence his transfer
to Central, six years prior and his subsequent acceptance
into the Department of Internal Investigations. He was

not, however, above getting his hands dirty from time to time as evident in his recent involvement in a warehouse sting in his old district.

'Just a part of the job.' he thought.

On his way out, an underling approach him, "Lieutenant Sir, Commander wants to see you in his office, sir."

Wright nodded. 'Perfect. Just when I'm on my way out.' he thought.

The Commander's office was just down the hallway.

When Wright gave a knock on his opened door he was greeted with a, "Come in, have a seat Lieutenant." Commander Grimes was tall and thin with a head of steely gray hair; he had the looks of an old-school cop.

"Yes sir." Wright sat in the empty chair at the commander's desk.

Looking at some files, Grimes started. "How's your injuries coming along?"

"Almost like new, Sir. 'Just a couple of bruises, it was nothing really."

"Nothing really is right, and I'm glad it was just, 'nothing really'; thanks to that colored officer up there in western. He saved your ass and the case."

"He did sir." Wright said with a knowing chuckle. The commander looked up at Wright.

"Your investigation, and the recent turn of events, didn't get us to our goal, obviously."

"No sir."

"But it seems that Lady Luck has shined her light our way." Grimes said with delight.

Wright listened more intently.

183

Grimes continued, "Second hand information tells us there's an upcoming meeting, a big one. Possibly the one we need; both criminal element and one of ours. No one knows where, but we have special units keeping the pressure on the street, so our targets will bypass their usual meeting places and more likely use one of the unorthodox ones. That makes it easier for us to get someone in as a plant, it also give our criminal friends a sense of perceived safety."

"Yes sir. And theoretically, we can guess location by the lack of deployment in a specific area, at a specific time. But we would need an insider for that information, no?" Wright added.

Grimes shrugged, "Lieutenant, you know the nature of this situation. It's serious. You served under Western's commander and you know what 'son of a bitch' he is. So take extra caution. We're getting close, but we don't know who is who over there; where loyalties lie. No one else is privy to this investigation. Understand?"

"Understood, sir."

"I've pulled the few people I had, off the case, so now it's just you, me and who ever else you pull in. This is our chance to take that corrupt bastard down, once and for all."

Wright breathed deep at the gravity of the situation before him.

"Any ideas on who you might need?" Grimes asked, ending the discussion.

Wright thought for a moment, then answered, "As a matter of fact, yeah. I do know a guy. I'll give him a call."

A three-storied row house flat on Calhoun Street was more than its residential shell. Music and voice muffled onto the street and the occasional couple entered or exited the home. It was rare for a 'spot' to be on a residential street, but this particular game was run by Lil' Man, nephew of Cleveland Black, the last of the old bosses. The direct connection to Black was enough to deter any ill-intent. The inside of this row house was typical with its dark wallpaper and old furniture. It was neat and clean and the proprietors were sure to keep it that way as they were just day-renting from the actual renters. A record player mounted on a floor modeled radio played the newest in rhythm & blues hits as a mixture of gamblers and partiers schmoozed.

Ruthie and Doris sat in a corner of the dining room nursing their drinks and rejecting the occasional suitor. Doris had investigated and mentally worked out the floor plan of the row house's first floor, including blind spots and exits. Ruthie had smiled in the face of one of the men who ran this spot who, half high, was bragging valuable information to her; information that was duly noted. Now, as the ladies realized that their presence here no longer served their purpose, they decided it was time to leave. As they rose and made their way to the front door, someone put on Andy Kirk's new record 'Take It And Git', the modest crowd went wild. Most danced, those who didn't rocked with the music. It was a good time. Then, like something from the movies, the front door flew open. Policemen from the Western Precinct poured into the already crowded house.

"Raid! Every body sit down and get your hand on your heads. Now!!!" an officer yelled.

185

The officers streamed through the length of the house occupying each room, yelling and ordering. People panicked, some tried to run, most just sat as if 'going through the motions'. The Andy Kirk record was screeched off as the mumbles of the soon-to-be arrested now filled the air.

'Caught in a damn raid.' thought Ruthie.
This was the last thing that they needed.

"Stay close." Ruthie whispered to Doris as she quietly led in the opposite direction of the crowd, toward the back door. In the kitchen, three men were getting frisked by officers. Pre-occupation and distraction. Doris felt a glimmer of hope, seeing the back door only about ten feet away. It seemed like they were almost invisible because of all the commotion. The closer to the door they got, the more nervous and happy the ladies became. And then the bottom fell out.

"What about these two?" an intercepting officer asked. "They should be out front, right?"

His superior officer briefly looked at the ladies then said, "Eh. There's a wagon out back too. Put 'em in that one."

Ruthie and Doris' hearts dropped. They were going to jail. And what's worst was that they were going to jail for absolutely nothing; being at the wrong place at the wrong time. The irony. As they fell in line with the other arrestees and marched off to an awaiting police wagon, Ruthie bowed her head. Out through the back yard and into the alley they filed. Ruthie raised her head only once, and when she did, she saw him, looking at her. It was that colored cop; the one that everyone along the Avenue was talking about.

She immediately looked down again, but then though to herself, 'That face. Familiar.'
Suddenly, a hand grabbed her and Doris' arms, pulling them out of the line.

Before the closest officer could respond, the colored cop cleared it with them, "I got these two. I'm gonna question them. See what they know."
Not waiting for a response, the colored cop directed the ladies to the alley up from the house.

"What are y'all doing in there?" he asked as if they knew they weren't supposed to be there.
The ladies looked at each other, answerless.

Not waiting for an answer anyway, he said, "It's your lucky day. Take a walk.
The ladies looked at him strange, like they couldn't believe what he said.

He interrupted, "Hey! You heard what I said. Y'all two. Get outta here."
Doris and Ruthie walked quickly and quietly down the alleyway and off into the night.

CHAPTER SEVENTEEN

Enticed

Lisa Vallis sat in the lobby of 'Nick's', one of the Avenue's smaller night spots. Usually she would be in one of the glitzy, better known establishments, on the arm of some politician or businessman, but tonight, this much-needed change was welcomed. Tonight she lounged at a place that bore much more of personal attachment. 'Nick's' was a bar known for its very attractive staff, both men and women, and its likelihood of standard music singers to stop by to sharpen their chops with the house band. Though it had mixed patronage, its anonymous owners catered mainly to whites who craved a grittier uptown experience. It was a real up-scale hole in the wall, but within its walls could be seen, everyone from Lena Horne to Fats Waller to Peggy Lee. It was said that some skinny crooner named Sinatra sang there a few times in the early days.

"A phone call for you Miss Vallis." a waiter said.

"Thank you." she said as she walked to the phone near the bar area.

Like most of the businesses on the Avenue, Nick's was narrow, but long; bar in front, lounge in the middle and stage area to the rear.

She picked up the receiver. "Hello."
(caller)

"Yeah".
(caller)

188

"I made sure everything is to your specifications."
(caller)

"Yes the bar is running smoothly, we ran out of peanuts but the new batch is coming in tomorrow."
(caller)

"I gotta go."
(caller)

"I know you worry, you shouldn't. I'm a big girl, I can take care of myself. Besides, I'm not doing anything 'dishonorable'."
(caller)

"OK. I'll think about it."
(caller)

"No, I haven't seen her."
(caller)

"I'll let her know to call you."
(caller)

"OK, bye."

Lisa gave the receiver to the bar manager and then waited in the lounge area near the stage. An unknown white singer belted out a ballad with the house band as Lisa lit a cigarette. She took a long hale, then softly blew it out. Through her cigarette's smoke she saw a conservatively dressed colored woman approaching her table. Without uttering a word, the woman mentioned permission to sit at her table. Sensing she was important or connected to someone important, Lisa nodded to an empty chair. The woman sat.

After a moment she spoke, "Greetings Ms. Vallis, I'm an associate of Mr. Rogers. In case you don't recall, he was in the company of Mr. Tucker nights ago, at the Sphinx."

189

The woman was well spoken and polished, more like an English professor. She carried herself like a Wall Street power broker.

Taking another puff from her cigarette, Lisa stared in the direction of the band, "Go on."

The woman continued, "Mr. Rogers has taken quite an interest in you and would be honored if you would join him as a special guest at The Carver for a showing of 'Pride of the Yankees'."

Lisa flicked the ashes off your cigarette. "Business aside, whites and coloreds don't mix in Baltimore."

"Business aside, this ain't Baltimore, this is Pennsylvania Avenue." the woman replied.

Lisa responded with raised eyebrow, "I'm flattered, but all this, just for a date to the movies?"

"Mr. Rogers' actions are very cautious and deliberate. He knows what he likes and he pursues."

Lisa thought diplomatically, and then said, "While the offer is, enticing, I will have to decline. My," looking around the bar, "business and my pleasures must be agreeable."

The woman nodded, then rose from her seat.

Smiling, she politely spoke, "Mr. Rogers thanks you for your time and offers a small gift. No strings attached of course."

Without waiting for an answer, the woman placed a small box on the table, bid her farewell, and left. Lisa opened the box to find a pair of pearl earrings.

'Interesting.' she thought.

Nephew

It was the last week of the year and being done with the holidays, people prepared for the New Year. Nineteen forty-three promised to be a transitional year. News of the war had gotten worse on both fronts, and the Avenue seemed to be getting just as violent. Among other things, there was a string of sporadic robberies along the Avenue neighborhoods, one even resulting in murder. This concerned Detective Ross, even if it was the hoodlums that were getting hurt. He walked through a residential block just east of the Avenue receiving many a strange look. As a matter of protocol, he briefly scanned the faces he encountered. Most had heard of his exploits at the warehouse months earlier. Some were outright oppositional, some were weary, some were delighted. There were even a few who thought they recognized him. He had made it a point to stop and talk with the older folks who sat on their front steps and even played a few games of crate ball with neighborhood youngsters. He had also become acquainted with most of the neighborhood merchants and professionals.

It was close to eleven o'clock and Ross' hunger pains had started to kick in. Since he hadn't a good home cooked meal since dining at his mother's house a few months before, he felt it was time to visit the nearest greasy spoon. He had been to a few restaurants along the Avenue, but this one in particular, Bernice's Kitchen, had grown to be his favorite. The service was homey, the food was delicious and the ambiance was quiet and intimate. It had dark, rich wallpaper and furniture, with a dimly lit dining area and soft jazz selections that catered mostly to the avenue's post nightlife.

It was relatively early, but Ross was at the end of his shift and felt that this was the perfect way to wind his night down. He walked through the restaurant doors, greeting some staff before he took his usual seat at the end of the counter. Without having to order, the waitress guessed his 'usual' from the menu and brought him a newspaper. A half hour later Ross was finishing his meal of candied yams, collard greens and fried fish. A quick glance around the dimness of the room showed him a few couples quietly talking over their meals and a few more singles eating. He continued reading his paper by the dim counter lights when his brain registered something that happened seconds before. It was almost like an intuition. It felt like someone was watching him. He casually looked over his right shoulder.

Across the room, in a booth by the back, a young lady sat alone. She wore a forward tilted, wide-brimmed dark hat that draped her face in shadow. Ross could barely make out her features. He couldn't tell if she was staring at him, but she was definitely looking in his direction. He turned in his stool to face the lady just as a waiter approached her booth and placed two filled shot glasses on her table. After a few seconds when she was sure he was looking at her, the lady pushed one of the drinks into the empty space at the table, opposite her. Ross took this as an invite.

He walked over and stood in front of the booth, "Anybody sitting here?"

"Just you." the lady responded.

He sat across from her.

Referring to the drink in front of him, he asked, "'This for me?"

192

"If you want it."

"I don't drink on duty."

"You get off in twenty minutes. Wait a few, you might need it."

Ross was now intrigued, answered, "Impressive. You know my shift. So you know who I am."
For the first time the lady's face came out of the shadows, staring at his.

After a second she sat back and answered, "Yeah, I do. I'm sure now."
Seeing her face, he recognized her.

"OK. You're the lady from the raid the other night. Glad to see you made it out. But other than that, do I know you?"

The lady looked out into the dining area and said, "No. But I know who you are, who you *were*."
Ross sat back with a grin.

"It's a little late for riddles, don't you think? Just who do you think I am?"
Still staring out of shadow, the young lady calmly said five words that almost made him forget where he was.

"You're June Newsome's nephew, Freddy."
Ross stopped breathing for a second, his eyes widened, his pulse quickened. He looked at the lady in horrified amazement.

"How- how do you know that name?"

"It belonged to someone my uncle loved."

Even more confused, he asked, "Who *are* you?"

The lady answered, "Someone who wants the same answers as you do."
Ross was still in shock, mind still racing. He became defensive.

In an aggressive hushed voice he asked, "How do you know me?"

The lady then looked at his face, then down and solemnly said, "You have the same eyes as you did when you were fourteen. Some things don't change."

Ross felt suddenly vulnerable. Control and command of this situation had quickly shifted away from him. He stared off, reliving a night in his past. A night that almost no one should know about; only this strange lady did.

She continued, "You ran to a man on the avenue the night you found out your uncle was killed."

He gasped. A memory from the past, replayed; and then the revelation of its aftermath.

After a moment, Ross regained his composure.

He struggled with words but managed a stuttered, "H-How, how do you know all of this?"

Replaying the memories in her own mind, the young lady answered, "'Cause, I saw it. I was there."

Ross downed his drink in one gulp.

CHAPTER EIGHTEEN

New Blood

They were mad at her and she knew it. They didn't
say anything, they hardly even showed it aside from the
initial scolding that came after the incident, but she knew.
They talked less and sometimes seemed a little
apprehensive about speaking in front of her. This was the
pits. Then again, maybe it was all in her mind. Maybe she
was overreacting; maybe it was her own guilty conscious.
Not *because* the incident happened, but *how* it happened.
Was it too careless? Was it too brutal? Maybe. But it
couldn't be helped. It had to be done. It was the perfect
time and place, that opportunity would never come again,
and no one would ever know it was them either way. Plus,
the timing couldn't be better. Besides, that bastard had to
go. But they were still mad. They would just have to get
over it; and now they acted like they wanted to stop. They
must be out of their minds.

'They can stop all they want. For me,' Shirley thought
to herself, 'this is the life.'
As she sat in the passenger's side of a '40 Buick, she
thought about recent events and the perceived tension
they caused between her and Doris and Ruthie.
It had been about three weeks since 'the incident' and now
she and Willie Dumps were on their way to a store on
Greene Street to pick up a package. The 'package', a box
of flip knives and switchblades were acquired through a
favor for a favor. And Willie, from all outward

195

appearances, looked like a driver or bodyguard. He was and he was not.

Willie Dumps was a tough guy from down around west Biddle and George Streets. Raised by an aged grandmother, young Willie took to the streets and fell in with a neighborhood gang called the Gents, The George Street Gents. They did small-time extorting and sometimes pulled robberies, but most times they sharpened their skills fighting in the streets. Being one of the gangs from a neighborhood not directly off of Pennsylvania Avenue, The Gents were constantly being tested. Rival thugs regarded them as doormats and often tried to trespass without fear or respect. This changed one Friday evening when boys from the Avenue came to see some girls that lived around George Street. After a heated exchange a brawl was planned for the following Sunday. What was unknown at the time was that the trespassers were from two different neighborhoods along the avenue. The boys from George Street had inadvertently set up the fights on the same day, but weren't about to back down. On Sunday the three sides met on an empty baseball field and by the end of the day, the Gents were legends. They had handily fought and beaten two rival gangs at the same time. News of the brawl had echoed all along the Avenue and it was known that George Street was to be respected.

With no particular vice to profit from, through the years The Gents were eventually employed as collectors or outside enforcers. The toughest of the Gents, Willie and his friends Pep and Duck, secretly graduated to 'doing hits for hire'. They were only hired by elite clientele and were very discreet. That clientele was usually high-level mobsters, who had sensitive cases; ones that couldn't be handled out in the 'underworld' open. One of these assignments was on a man named Damon. Damon was the 'numbers' man to a lieutenant of the Cleveland Black organization. The lieutenant, himself, was a man not to be trifled with, but somehow Damon had slighted or wronged someone, probably within the same organization, and was contracted to be hit. The Gents were efficient and the job was completed, but days later there were rumblings that Damon's boss, the lieutenant, was out for revenge. This lieutenant was known to be resourceful and had a fierce reputation. It would be only a matter of time before he used his influence to find out who did Damon's hit. This was unacceptable to Willie; he would have to strike first.

For weeks he tailed the lieutenant, studying routes and habits, even company. That's when Willie first saw her, the girl on the lieutenant's arm. She looked like a colored cupie-doll and Willie felt his heart drop.

'This idiot, her 'boyfriend', barely looked at her, as beautiful as she was.' Willie thought.
If she were on his arm, he would never stop staring at her. He would be hypnotized and fully under her control. But that's a lot of ifs. She probably wouldn't even look his way, he thought. In fact, he shouldn't even be focused on her, he should be focused on this lieutenant; what's his name, Choc. After a few weeks more, Willie figured the best time to hit Choc would be on his way to or from one of his card games.

One winter night, when all of the conditions were right, Willie waited for Choc near his main gambling-house. It was a row house facing the adjacent street, that sat with its back to an abandoned field. He sat in his car, across the small street under a tree in shadow. A half hour later he saw Choc walk casually across the empty snow-dusted lot and then vanish into the back entrance of one of the row houses. Why an important guy like that would sneak into his own spot, Willie couldn't say.

"Precautions are precautions I guess." he said to himself.

He would be patient. These things mustn't be rushed. This target was far too dangerous and smart to be careless. He would wait until his target left the game, then he would take him in the abandoned lot. Minutes passed as Willie strategized in his mind his approach and execution, and then something caught his eye. Through his peripheral, he spotted three figures in black sneaking across the empty lot. The figures wore dark masks and moved in the shadows. They trailed along the alley paths and then vanished into the same row house as Choc.

'Interesting', Willie thought.

He sat recalculating and re-planning, even thinking of canceling the hit. And then suddenly, 'POP'. A single gunshot came from the card-game row house.

'Oh shit!' Willie said in a hushed voice.

A moment later the same three darkly dressed figures ran, in an orderly fashion, out from the back of the row-house and across the field, one behind another.

"Why 'you shoot him? What's wrong with you?" the middle one asked the last, in a hushed voice.

Willie could barely hear them but quickly gathered that the last one of the trio was the shooter. They all carried bags in one hand with guns in the other.

He could hear the first one say, "Not now. We gotta split up!"

The first two turned left on the side street, ran to the corner and then walked in opposite directions. The last one's jog slowed to a quick walk towards Willie's parked car, mask on and gun in hand. Willie turned his body so he could slump backwards into the car's shadow and out of view. To him, this was better than watching a cliffhanger matinee. And true to form, he would receive the shock of his life when the figure coming toward him, oblivious to his presence, pulled his mask up revealing himself to be a *her*. And what was more shocking was that the *her*, was the same one he had been awestruck with weeks before; the same one that was with this Choc cat. She was gone around the corner. Before he could fully figure out what was happening a commotion spilled out of the card game row house. People hollered and yelled, some cried.

"Somebody call the police." someone said.

"Yeah, those niggas got my money." another said.

"Well you got off lucky. That nigga Choc got shot in the face. He dead than a muv." a man answered.

"Daammnn!" a woman yelled.

'What the...?' Willie thought, 'Could this be real? Did that chic, Choc's own girlfriend, just shoot him? Did she do my job for me?' He chuckled to himself.

"So*lid*. Oh, this is too good to be true. Beautiful and deadly. That's the woman of my dreams." he said aloud. He said it as a joke to himself but soon realized that he meant it. However he looked at her at first, it was now amplified and multiplied. If he liked her before, he was in love with her now. Willie started his car, turned on his front lights and pulled off of the side street and into main street traffic, before the cops came.

It took Willie another three weeks to track down his lady killer. He hung near every hair salon, had been to every beauty supply store, and frequented everywhere he thought a lady might be.

But then he thought, 'Would a lady killer really be in those places? I need to think more practical.'
With the best luck in the world, the next place he went, there she was. It was a Saturday Night Fish Fry in his own neighborhood, in one of the rare non-connected row-houses. This one had a front and side yard, with a small alley. Willie saw her in the crowd leaning up against a radiator. He couldn't tell if she was alone or not. He wanted to run up and exclaim his love, but froze when he got closer. Suddenly she got up and walked to the basement of the house. The basement is where the hard-core gamblers were. It was dark and dank and the perfect place to make whatever move he planned. He followed inconspicuously. Once in the basement he waited until she was alone and far enough away for bystanders not to interfere. She walked from the craps room, down a short hall to the basement exit. To Willie it almost looked like she had been casing the place.

"Oh I *really* love her, now." he grinned.
After a moment, she walked back in from the exit and up the empty corridor when he approached her from behind.

"Stick 'em up." he said in a low voice.
She felt what probably was a gun on her back. She looked over her shoulder and glared at him. For a split second he was hurt and offended. She should know that he would never hurt her, he couldn't. Why was she giving him the evil eye? And then he remembered, 'Oh, 'cause I got a gun in her back. Oh well, it would work itself out. He'd tell

her the who story, he'd make her believe, no matter what it took. He guided her to the back door and out to the back yard. It was eerily quiet and peaceful, almost like a graveyard. They walked to and up the alley a few houses up from the card-game.

"Alright, stop right here." They stopped. "Turn around."

When she turned fully around to face him, she seemed prepared for something, like she had made her peace with whatever outcome. What she saw when she faced him didn't particularly impress her. To her, he looked a little battle-worn with eyes that weren't easily read. But the thing that stood out the most was his height. He was probably around six-one, but his huge hands and massive head made him look much taller.

'He would be alright if he wasn't trying to kill me.' she though. He gave a cautious look around. She just glared.

He spoke, "This is not what you think. I know who you are, and I know you killed that nigga Choc. I saw you coming from it."

She gasped.

He continued, "Don't worry though. I ain't gonna snitch, you did me a solid. If you wouldn't'a got 'em, I would'a... or he woulda got me. Here."

To her surprise, he reversed the position of his gun and offered it to her handle first. Shocked, she took the gun and without missing a beat, she stepped back, aimed it at his throat and cocked the hammer. She deduced that since he was the only one that knew who she was, he was the only one who could connect her to the robberies and the murder. She looked around, then at the revolvers barrel. It was loaded. She could blow his brains out and no one would know she had done it.

"If I was gonna tell, why would I let you know, then give you a loaded gun?" he said calmly, not even offering a defensive stance.

A gut feeling and circumstance made her believe him. After a thought she uncocked the hammer of the gun.

"I don't wanna get you in trouble." he said with sincere confidence.

"Well what *do* you want?" she asked stone faced.

Too shy to share his amorous feelings toward her, Willie kept it business, and simply said, "I ain't never seent no lady like you before. You're like some kinda pistol packin' momma. I wanna follow you to the top." She hesitantly lowered the gun and raised an eyebrow trying to get a read on his intent. She deducted that he could grow to be trusted and noted how valuable a tool he could be to her ambitions. She smirked, as if acknowledging an answer to a prayer.

"So." Willie said, as if waiting for an answer that should have been already answered. "You gonna tell me ya' name?"

She looked him right in his un-telling eyes and said, "My name is Shirley. You can call me, Jacks."

CHAPTER NINETEEN

Within an Inch

The start of the New Year was much like the end of the old one, though in some ways 1943 hinted at being a little worse. The U.S. military still struggled to get a foothold on the European Continent, while suffering massive naval losses in the Atlantic and Pacific Oceans. Internment of Japanese citizens had begun in response to the decisive defeats and inevitable invasion of the west coast by the Empire of Japan. The government, in support of the war effort, also enacted food and gas rationing in the form of ration tickets. Of course organized crime found a way to take advantage of the situation, trading and selling the tickets to their profit. The military draft had picked up pace as able-bodied men began receiving their notices of induction. Periodic air-raid siren test were more and more common and the blackouts that accompanied them, had even affected Pennsylvania Avenue. More than usual, people were on edge.

The drive up the Avenue was slower than usual. There looked to be some kind of blockage a half block ahead; crowds of people intermingle with the evening traffic.

"Goddamn shoppers. The holiday is gone. I thought this shit would over with by now." said the impatient driver of the 1940 Pontiac Sedan.

"It happens. No rush. Don't worry about it." answered the backseat passenger, a man called Greene, as he waited patiently in the back seat.

Greene was no stranger to the Avenue. He had grown up and still resided in one of the neighborhoods downtown by the port. He'd been employed by certain people on the Avenue over the years, although very few could or would recognize him. In certain circles he was known as a problem solver, and his specialty had grown to be a sort of detective work; detective work for gangsters. This particular time he was hired by the 'Boss Down Bottom' and charged with finding the men behind the card game robberies. Too much money and respect had been lost and extreme measures had to be taken. Greene had been randomly and discreetly dropping by different card games in the neighborhood, but he always seemed to be one step behind. The robberies themselves had been sporadic, occurring with no rhyme, reason or pattern, so this night there was no real expectations of any unfortunate occurrences. He had been instructed to stop the robbers by any and all means and if possible make the cruelest of examples of them, for all to fear. At this, Greene was well versed.

As the Pontiac pulled onto the alley-street and stopped in front of a row house gambling spot, Greene exited the car.

"I'm gonna end the night out, here. Go home, I'll take a cab later."

"Much obliged." his 'mob supplied' driver said and pulled off.

Greene casually approached two men conversing on the house's marble steps. They looked to be front security for the gambling spot.

"Jack, I just got my papers in the mail the other day. Ain't no way I'm going out in the middle of no ocean to fight no Japs." one said.

"You ain't got no choice. It's either the Japs or jail." the other responded.

"Well send me to jail. It's too dangerous out there."

"Out there? It's just as, if not more dangerous around the Avenue."

"What, you talkin' 'bout, those stick-ups? Man, it ain't that bad. Besides that one thing with that Choc cat, it don't seem that dangerous."

"It's a card game stick-up, genius. It's going to be dangerous. I know. I was at one of them."

"Naw, you serious? I didn't know, what happened? Were you scared?"

"Eh, not really. Its kinda weird though; like, while it's happening, everything is moving slow. But afterwards, you can't even remember nothing."

"Damn. Nothing?"

"Well, it was this one thing one of them said. I remember because that was some weird shit to say, plus his voice was different, kind of like a sissy or a girl."

"Well, what was it?"

"That nigga busted in like Bogart and said something like, '**No heroes**, like somebody dumb enough to jump in front of a bullet for some money."

"No heroes, huh? Were *you* thinking about being a hero?"

"I'm still here talking to *you*, ain't I."

205

The men chuckled and continued talking about another matter. Greene stood off to the side half listening; taking mental notes. He checked his watch then up and into the house he went.

The smell of reefer was rank as people hung in the upstairs hallway of the spot. The gruesome characters that lined the hallway paid no particular attention to Greene. His destination, the back room, was crowded with men in a large circle, playing craps on the floor. It was lit by a single shadeless lamp. Off to the side of the room, watching the others, was a man named Chester. He ran the spot and it was his game. He recognized Greene and was not particularly happy about seeing him there. Chester felt he could manage the affairs of his own spot without outside intervention sanctioned from the top. Greene could feel the 'cold shoulder' but he didn't care. He was here to do a job; besides he felt if they could do it, he wouldn't be there in the first place.

Greene pieced together in his mind, the bits of information he had gathered since he was hired. To him, these heists were too perfect; almost like an inside job. He would look for tell tale signs and act if necessary. After small talk and a few questions Greene resumed his inspection, checking the other rooms and returning to the downstairs gambling area. He passed a few young ladies talking at the base of the stairwell and made his way to the kitchen. There was nothing out of the ordinary, so he decided to take a smoke in the back yard. Standing by the back door, he heard it. Someone said that phrase, **No heroes**.

He was shocked, but sure. Stranger though, was that the voice of the speaker was, to put it short, feminine.

Greene quickly processed the information and the situation, and deducted only one possible outcome. It clicked. Whoever said 'No Heroes' was connected to the stick-ups. And the only people that were speaking in that immediately vicinity a second ago, were the two ladies that were at the base of the stairs, and *they* were now walking out the front door. Instinctively Greene turned to walk towards them only to be impeded by partygoers and gamblers. By the time he got to the front door, one of the ladies he saw was getting into a car that was already pulling off. A quick look up the street showed the other lady walking briskly toward the main street. He'd get the other one at a later time. Without drawing too much attention, he engaged in rapid pursuit. Quiet as a cat, he walked quickly and caught up to the lady just as she crossed an alley. Just as they were shoulder-to-shoulder Greene pushed the lady into the alley, covering her mouth and dragging her back into the yard of an abandoned house. The alley lamppost was blinking in and out as the lady tried to scream. The scream was muffled by a punch to the stomach. She doubled over in pain, when her eyes finally met his she was horrified to see this stranger, almost grinning with his index finger in front of his lips.

"No heroes! No heroes!" he said manically in a hushed shout. "I heard that was only said by some niggas at a stick-up!"
With that, he threw her into a set of trashcans. The lady felt her leg and elbow smash up against the tin cans. As she tried to get to her feet, she felt a kick to her ribs that knocked her back to the ground.

Greene continued, "'Thing is, the dude that heard it, said it sounded like a faggot, or a *bitch*!"

He kneeled over her, "So that leads me to conclude that since you said the same shit, then it must be you or someone you know. Personally, I hope it's you."
He open hand smacked her across the face three times. He was a big man so when she tried to fight back, kicking a punching, she was quickly subdued. He managed to hold her hands down and when she tried to sit up, he head butted her back down to the yards cement ground. This dazed her.

Greene chuckled, "Here, all this time, these dumb ass niggas was getting robbed by a bunch of bitches! Who you working for?" he hollered as he shook her.

"Nobody." she uttered.

"Then who you working with? Tell me, now!"

"Nobody. I don't know what you talking about. Please let me go." she cried through a bloody mouth. Mildly frustrated, he beat her for almost a half-minute, then thought for a moment.

He said, "You know, I got a place for young girls like you. Y'all don't like to talk outside," he said mockingly, "Oh, but once I get y'all back to the place, sometimes I can't shut y'all up."
The lady was just half conscious, but she was aware enough to hear and be horrified by what he said. Still dazed she cried and pleaded.

"Just let me go. I just wanted to get him back. He killed my Uncle. He killed my Uncle Poppy."
Greene stopped in mid swing. He was now intrigued. This was getting interesting.

"Who?" he asked angrily.

"Big Shot. He killed my uncle. I just wanna get him back." the lady said, now half conscious with her hands over her battered face.

Greene was stunned for a second, but as he put things together in his mind, he laughed. He laughed not only at the fact that he had most likely discovered and broken up the card game stick-up heist, and that the robbers were actually girls, but he laughed at the fact that one of the girls had a vendetta against the boss who had her uncle killed; the same boss that hired him to find her in the first place.

"What the hell did I get myself into?" he chuckled to himself. "When I bring you in, they're gonna make me a millionaire."

He looked down at the young lady's seemingly unconscious body. That's when a more sinister side of him started to come out.

He scanned her body with a grin, "Maybe I need to take you back to my place first," He tried to whisper softly in her ear, "...have a little fun."

Just then he felt a biting sensation on his ear. He yelled in pain as he yanked his bloody ear lobe from the lady's gritted teeth. He formed his mouth to curse as she spit a mouthful of his and her blood back into his face. He was now enraged. All bets were off.

Greene grabbed her throat and began to strangle her to death. As he choked her, she struggled less and less. She was now unconscious, but he would finish the job. He felt like he could break her neck. In the alley in front of him, there was a rustling of leaves. He looked up from his fury to see an alley cat scampering along, and then continued in his rage. Then he felt a presence behind him.

Easing his stranglers grip, Greene looked over his shoulder to see a revolver cocked at his temple. When he looked beyond the barrel, he saw that the holder was a woman. Her face was vaguely familiar. He then came to a horrible realization.

Green and the woman, both said in unison, "You." A second later, she pulled the trigger. His body slumped to his side and collapsed dead on the concrete.

Spiral

The sound of a siren prompted Big Joe to pull his '38 Chrysler over to the sidewalk. He and Mil were on their way from a card game and had plans on relaxing for the rest of the evening. It seemed to Mil that they were ending their six day work-week and such a stretch should culminate with their ladies, dinner and a perhaps, a movie. That good feeling was disrupted now as they waited for the officer that pulled them over. As the officer walked up to the driver's side, Joe tensed, then after a glance in his rearview mirror, relaxed. In the squad car behind him he saw the unmistakable figure of the Commander of the Western Precinct. The Commander's fierce reputation had been well known along the Avenue for years even by those who had never seen him, but Joe had. This encounter would have been a dreadful experience, but for the knowledge that further up the hierarchy, there was some sort of 'partnership' or in the very least an 'arrangement' between the 'top brass' of the mob and the law. Joe was assured of this by connected gangster, Ray, months before, and since the organization seemed to operate almost with impunity, he figured it was true. The police tapped on the car door and asked for license and registration. Upon receiving it, he examined it and then asked Joe to step outside of the car.

Joe looked to Mil saying, "It's cool." before he exited the car.

Mil sat patiently in the driver's side, nervously switching glances between Joe, the cop and the commander in the squad car behind them. It seemed Joe's conversation was getting heated as Mil heard the officer mumble something about 'the trunk' and 'confiscating'.

'Uh oh.' Mil thought to himself. 'Not only is the trunk where we keep the take from the games, but now the commander is getting out of the squad car.'

Mil listened intently as the commander approached Joe.

"Look, I'm just the driver. I'm with Tiddy, who works for Big Shot. They said everything is cool." Joe explained.

With a nod from the Commander, the cop thrusted his Billy club into Joe's midsection. Joe bent to one knee.

Mil immediately got out his side of the car to help.

"Joe!"

This startled the cop who drew his weapon on Mil. Thinking his friend was about to get shot, Joe grabbed the cop's arm and wrestled his aim skyward. A shot went off as the two wrestled to the ground struggling for possession of the gun. The Commander pulled his revolver, looking at Mil then at the two on the ground.

"Run Mil, run!!" Joe yelled as he struggled.

As Mil backed around the front of the car he heard a POP, POP. He stumbled as he turned. This stumble saved his life as three more pops came his way. The Commander had shot Joe and was now aiming at him. Most of the surrounding row house windows and shades, slid close, though some remained cracked.

POP, POP-POP!

Mil thought he felt a bullet buzz pass his right ear. He zigzagged up the block to the closest alley, which he dove in and was off into the night. He assumed his best friend was dead; died trying to save *his* life and now *he* was likely now a fugitive on the run.

'All because of a 'shake down' double-cross by them stinkin' police.' he thought.

Over the next few hours Mil would go to his and Joe's stash-houses to gather cash and clothes; he was getting off the Avenue, out of town. Jail was not an option. But where would he go? Where could he go? The Avenue was all he had known. He'd spent his whole life there and now *that* was FUBAR and his friend was gone. In Big Joe's apartment, he found a moment to shed a tear over an old photograph of the two of them together. He was then off to his own rented room. From street to street he walked quickly, ducking from time to time, into alleys. Paranoia was getting the best of him. Police squad cars raced past him in the opposite direction, going toward the scene of the crime he had just witnessed; a scene he would undoubtedly be blamed for.

His block was relatively quietly. There were a few older residents playing cards on a table outside one of the row houses. Without his usual greetings and small talk, he walked quickly passed them and to his residence. Once in his rented room he rummaged through his dresser drawers for personals, and then he remembered something. At the top, in the back of his closet, in an old shoebox was some money, a few grand, some of his personal information and a photograph. It was of him and Ruthie. He sighed at it, kissed it then put it in his shirt pocket next to his heart.

As he gathered the last of his essentials, Mil started thinking, 'Wait. Those cops don't really know me. I mean they barely saw my face. They heard my nickname, but I'm still kind of anonymous. 'Still got a little time.' Suddenly, it came to him from a radio announcement. The news alert talked about the slow progress of the Pacific Fleet and the low naval enlistments.

'I could join the navy, get as far away from here as possible. They don't let colored men fight or use guns anyway. I'd rather cook and clean than go to jail any day.' He once again reached for the photograph that he and Ruthie had taken on Avenue at Christmas time.

With welled eyes he whispered, "Oh, my Ru Ru. I can't even say good-bye. I hope you're alright. I'll send word once I'm in."

In the early morning hours, Milton Newsome, clad in a long coat and fedora, with bag in hand, walked from alley to alley downtown, headed for the nearest Naval Induction center.

CHAPTER TWENTY

Revelations

'Darkness. No, I see something. I see light. Soft, gentle, warm. I go toward it. I must be... Wait a minute. Am I dead?! No!!'

'Oh. My eyes are opening. Not dead. I see faint light from a cracked door coming in to focus. Where am I? In a bed, in some bedroom. In his bedroom!'
Panic begins.

'He brought me here. What did he do to me. What is he gonna do? I gotta get up! I gotta get outta here!'
Attempting to sit up.

"Owww!"

'Agonizing pain shooting down my body. My face. My side. My legs. They all ache. They all hurt. What did he do to me? I can't remember. No, wait. I do. He was choking me, strangling me. I was fading out, and then that shadow, the one behind him. Then that pop. That flash of light. Like the light from that door, only shorter. Wait. That door's light, getting bigger. It's opening.'
Focusing.

'A blurry silhouette standing at the door; coming towards me. It's him! Oh my god, I'm about to die. I can feel tears streaming down my face, bracing for the worst. He's standing right over me.'
Tensing.

'I gotta be brave. I try to blink the tears away, focus my eyes. But wait, the shadowy face now standing over

214

me, it ain't his. It's someone else, some lady. I'm relieved. She seems kind, familiar.'

"Who are you?" Ruthie grumbled.

"Oh, you're back. 'Coming out of it, eh?" the woman said. "Rest now, I'm taking care of you. We can talk later."

'Something in her voice says she was to be trusted. I fade out.'

Ruthie awoke the next day with less pain. The woman from earlier entered the room followed by a man. She was older, light brown complexioned and thin with classic matinee idle features. He was an olive skinned, rotund white man. They stood bed-side looking down at Ruthie.

"You gave us a scare there, Hon'. the man said. Then referring to the woman he continued, "You should thank your stars she was there to save your ass."

Groggy, Ruthie looked around, then at the woman, "Thank you. I'm sorry. I gotta get home."
She tried to get up, but was stifled with pain.

The man chuckled, "Looks like your stuck here with us; a little while anyway. Don't worry kid, you're among friends."
The woman just stared at Ruthie with her arms crossed.

After a moment she said to the man, "Amazing. She looks just like him. Same nose, same mouth."

The man added, "Yeah, scary."

Ruthie was perplexed, "Who are you?"

The woman spoke, "My name is Elsie. I was a friend of your Uncle Poppy's."

Ignoring her pain this time, Ruthie sat up, looking at Elsie.

"You're the woman. The one he was working with before he... But you were dead. Everybody said you were dead."

Elsie looked down solemnly and said, "I was."

The man quickly interjected, "You've been out for a couple of days, hon. Why don't you get freshened up and come down for supper. You gotta be hungry and there's lots to talk about."

Ruthie nodded in agreement.

After a quick shower, Ruthie dressed and came down to the dining room. The smell of baked chicken filled the house. At a long table, there were already two full plates, one in front of the man, the other in front of the empty chair in which Ruthie sat. The two ate in silence while Elsie just smoked a cigarette and stared off into nowhere.

Toward the end of the meal, as if she couldn't wait, Ruthie asked, "Why am I here? Why did you help me? How did you even know who I am?"

Elsie stared at Ruthie with understanding eyes, exhaled and then answered, "A few months back, at the Club Casino, I was in the back having a drink. There were some guys bragging about someone being murdered years ago. I knew from the conversation that it was about Poppy. I was upset, I was angry, but then I noticed *you*. I saw your reaction; and then I saw your face and I knew. It was the same face from the picture he kept in his wallet. Still, you were older and I wasn't quite sure. I would see you here and there on the avenue, but I never knew how to approach you; or even if I should."

Processing the story, Ruthie reasoned, "Well that explains why you were in that alley. Were you following me then?"

Elsie nodded no. She thought, exhaled once again, this time more belabored, and then continued.

"Bear with me. A few years ago, a young lady was leaving her mother's house to meet up with a business associate. It was early morning and she had just stopped in the drug store. Crossing an alley street, a man shoved her into it and threatened her with a switchblade. The young lady believed that she was just getting mugged but was knocked unconscious. When she woke up, she was hand cuffed to a radiator in the basement of an old row house where she was beaten, drugged and tortured for three months. Her kidnapper wore a green hat and a green trench coat. He told her that it wasn't personal, that the kidnapping was just a job. He even explained how he was hired to get her off the streets while her partners were being killed off, and that afterwards he would have his way with her before he strangled her to death.

He was a sadistic bastard. She was in that basement alone sometimes for days. One of those stretches, the young lady had managed to unscrew a part of the radiator that she was cuffed to. She escaped. She escaped only to find that her two best friends were dead and what family she had was gone. Overcome by grief and despair, she wondered the streets in a drugged out fog; a shell of her former self. She became an addict to bury the pain, spending a few years on the fringes of society, until a chance meeting with an old friend. That friend's generosity helped her to get clean, and a renewed purpose in life. This purpose gave her focus. The focus gave her

the strength to eventually track down her assailant. It led her to that gambling spot, and then to the nearby alley, where she saw him kneeling over a another young girl, beating her senseless; until she blew his brains out."
She fell silent and sat back in her chair. Room was silent. Ruthie felt the gravity of the story.

"That was you. The shadow behind that man, and that story was yours. But why do you refer to yourself as 'that young lady'?"

"I only told that story one time before today. It was like another lifetime, like another person that lived though it. That man's end was my beginning. A new me."
Elsie's peaceful face looked as if it had gotten younger with that explanation.

"Whew, that was deep." Ruthie said. She looked over to the man. "The old friend she talked about, was that you?"

The man nodded yes, "Nikos. This is my safe-house."

"Thanks for bringing me here. Nikos." Ruthie said, "Nikos, sounds Greek. 'You connected to the Greeks?"

Elsie and Nikos gave each other glances, then back to Ruthie, who bashfully answered, "Oh. Sorry." She got the hint.

"Did you know my Uncle Poppy?"

"I did. Me and your uncle, 'P' I called him, were in Boys Town lockup together. He saved my ass once, and we were good friends from then on."
Ruthie's brow frowed in anger and confusion.

In the most diplomatic tone, she asked, "With all due respect sir, if you were such good friends then why you couldn't you help him in the first place? And why didn't you go after the people who killed him?"

218

Barely restraining his shock and anger, Nikos slapped the table, "Hey! It wasn't that simple." He calmed himself, "I didn't know about the plot to get P. I didn't find out until later, but when I did, believe me, I was on my way over there with a crew of guys. Thinking it would disrupt their money stream, the east side bosses, including my own, stopped me and I was forbidden from getting involved in the Avenue's internal conflicts. My hands were tied. Still are."

"Well mine aren't." Ruthie said defiantly. "And I'm not going to stop until.."

"Until what? You get your face blown off? Do you even know who you're looking for?" said Elsie.

"I'm-a start with anybody I hear bragging about it." Ruthie shot back.

"And get yourself killed by a bunch of nobodies. Meanwhile, the ones that did it get off scot-free."

"Well I gotta start somewhere." said Ruthie at wit's end.

"If you gotta start somewhere, you start here. I think we know a little more of the story than you." added Nikos.

Ruthie sat back in her chair, "What do I need to know?"

She saw Elsie's eyes go back in memory to a night all those years ago. As if narrating from a movie that only she could see, Elsie started.

"It's all so clear. It was a party, Goldie's birthday party; back in '34. We had gotten there about midway through so it was already crowded. Your uncle and June had just come down from their meeting with the boss, Goldie. It was the night he found out he was going to inherit the whole thing; the night he found out he would be taking over as boss. We were all at a table, me and Nicky included. I noticed your uncle looking at a table towards the front. It was Big Shot from down 'The Bottom'. He wasn't boss back then, just a lieutenant, but he was a menace just the same. In the middle of our conversation, Pop just walks off towards that table. As usual June was right behind him. I didn't get a good feeling about that confrontation so decided to wait patiently. I was on the numbers side of the organization anyway. From my seat, I did manage to see who else was at the table. It was Bigg's second in charge, a guy named 'House' and two floozies. Bigg was arrogant even then. I didn't like him. I think he was behind what happened to his boss 'Showtime'. You see, Show' conveniently got sent up the river for seventy years for possession of ten pounds of heroin in his truck. I couldn't hear, but even from across the room, I could tell the discussion was heated.

But by the time they got back to our table his whole attitude had changed. Strange. He was like that though, never letting things get to him, at least never letting it show. 'Great poker face. So much so, I thought the thing with Bigg was nothing. So I dropped it. I figured he would tell me later. He did, they both did, and we started preparing; preparing for the worst, but I guess we were so busy with the transition, after a while we lost track. Everything went back to normal. Everything got quiet, safe. Next thing you know… I was kidnapped. And they, they were both dead."
The room sat in silence once again.

Elsie finished, "We lost so much after that. We all did. And baby, trust me when I tell you," she grabbed Ruthie's hand, "We want what *you* want, but we don't wanna lose you getting it. You're all we have of him." Ruthie looked silently at the table, nodding her head yes. They would be of one accord.

For the next few hours, the three of them sat at the table talking and reminiscing about Poppy; the good times and the bad, the ups and the down, the possibilities and plans. Ruthie told them about her encounter with June's nephew, the detective. They gave her information that could help him as well. It was late by the time they decided to turn in. Nikos was preparing to leave for home; Elsie would stay at the safe house to watch over Ruthie.

"You should be well enough to go home by morning. As far as the Avenue, I know your Uncle P taught you a lot, you would do well to start applying it soon. We got work to do." Nikos said. "You ladies sleep tight, eh."

"Give my best to Rhea. Nik" Elsie offered. Ruthie said, "Mr. Nikos, before you leave, one more thing. What we talked about, I got ideas, but I don't know if I can get close enough."

Nikos thought for a second and then suggested as he walked out the door, "I think maybe I could help with that. Let me make a call."

CHAPTER TWENTY ONE

Next?

A cab pulled up in front of the corner brownstone-converted apartment building on West Laurens Street. Ruthie stepped out, looked around and slow-walked into the building. There was a limp in her walk and a few minor bruises and scraps could be seen if stared at directly, but otherwise she looked normal. When she reached the second floor and knocked on the door of her and Doris' shared apartment, she fought to suppress the anxiety that came with the flashbacks of a week before. A second later the door opened. Doris stood there with a relieved look on her face. Without saying a word, she hugged Ruthie tight, careful not to hurt her still aching body.

A day after Ruthie's assault Doris had been contacted by Elsie and told what had happened. She was told Ruthie was amongst friends and instructed not to speak of it, to anyone. Only the mention of her uncle and mother's real names proved authenticity. For a week, Doris had waited patiently but worried herself to death, and now her emotions had poured out. She had seen Ruthie a minute before the incident and felt a sting of guilt at not being there for her best friend during her time of need. After a long hug, Ruthie made herself comfortable on the couch, while Doris prepared them something to eat. Ruthie told her everything that happened the night she was attacked; how she woke up in an east side safe house, and who her rescuers were to her. Expecting anger and fear, Doris was surprised to find a calmer, more focused Ruthie.

Doris went to the kitchen drawer pulled out a letter and returned to the couch. She presented it to Ruthie. It was an anonymous letter inviting her to a brunch at Rice's Delicatessen with a date and time attached. Ruthie was afraid and then confused, until she saw the signature on the back. The letter was signed, 'Nephew'.

A few hours later, there was a knock on the apartment door. When Doris opened it, in came Shirley. Without acknowledging her older cousin, she went directly over to Ruthie who was still recuperating on her couch/bed. Instead of a nurturing or even a sympathetic approach, Shirley stood over Ruthie, seething on the edge of rage.

She studied Ruthie's healing scrapes and bruises then asked, "Who the fuck did this?"

Ruthie turned to Doris, who responded with hunched shoulders and a look as if to say, 'I had to tell her, she's one of us.'

She turned back to Shirley and was surprised to see a tear of anger run down Shirley's cheek. She was barely holding it together. Ruthie reached for Shirley's hand, but she snatched it away.

"Answer me. Who did it?"

Ruthie managed to grab Shirley's hand. "Don't worry about that. Just sit down so I can..."

Shirley interrupted, "What you mean, 'just sit down', what you mean, 'don't worry about it?' We just gonna let whoever did this, get away with it?"

By now Shirley was ready to lash out and attack any reasonable target.

"Ain't nobody gettin' away with this." she yelled. Ruthie pulled Shirley down next to her on the couch and said intently, "Jacks, don't worry about it." She gestured to her face, "This is not an issue anymore."
Ruthie's tone was commanding. It made Shirley know. The situation *was* or was *being* handled.

Shirley sat down pouting, then after a moment asked, "Was it about the card games?"

Ruthie nodded, "More or less."

"So what's next? Them games is done. 'Can't do that no more, people gonna be looking for us, or somebody that look like us." Shirley complained.

"Naw, I think the man that did this to me was the only one that knew. It was like he was just putting it together when he pushed me in the alley, and he's gone now. Either way, we got enough from the other card games to do what we need to."
Ruthie was talking more to Doris than Shirley.

Shirley looked at them both, "Y'all ain't got to keep secrets. I know about y'all little scheme. I was there at Club Casino that night too, ain't nobody dumb. Plus I'm out either way, I got some other things lined up."

"I bet you do." Doris added. "Where you been for the last couple of days anyway?"

"I been busy, 'met some people."

Doris just looked at Shirley, "Never mind. I don't even want to know."
They giggled. Doris stretched her arms out.

"I think I need a night out on the town."

Ruthie replied jokingly, "You haven't *been*, I figured you'd partying the whole time."

Doris answered, "Girl, how am I gonna go out, when I was worried sick about you. Besides, I ain't seen Big Joe. He told me he might be getting' some new position or something. He must've gotten it. And he must be busy, 'cause he ain't been around here.

"Speaking of…" Ruthie said pointing at her face, "Big Joe or Mil can't know about this. Promise me."

"I promise, girl. You can hardly tell, you're almost healed. We just gotta stay away a few more days."

"Absence makes the heart grow fonder."

"I hope so because we gonna make those hearts buys us dinner."

Doris and Ruthie both laugh, but at the same time notice Shirley looking sadly at them. Buy the look on her face they knew something was horribly wrong.

"What is it?" Doris asked not really wanting an answer.

Shirley looked at them, looked down, and then back to them.

"Mil and Joe," she said solemnly, "something really bad happened."

Rice's Delicatessen was located on the Avenue 'Up Top' one block off of North Avenue. The patrons were a mixed crowd, but mostly white because of its proximity to the neighborhoods to the north. Here one was less likely to be recognized. It was in-between the morning and lunch rush when Ruthie walked through the Deli's doors. She had gotten there a few minutes earlier than the letter requested only to find Ross already seated. Seeing her, he signaled her over to sit.

"Detective." Ruthie greeted as she sat. "Keepin' busy?"

Ross answered, "Lately it seems I don't have a choice." He noticed her scrapes and bruises and asked, "'Something I can help you with?"
She nodded no.

He added curiously, "'About a week back, man was found dead in some yard over in Sandtown; a hole in his head." he looked thoughtfully at her, then shrugged, "Eh, he probably deserved it. Anyway, I wanted to talk to you."

"I'm all ears, Detective." Ruthie answered in a 'matter of factly' kind of way.

"'Can' the 'detective'. When it's you and me, call me Freddy." he said as he sipped his coffee. Then looking over his cup, he added, "Besides, based on what you told me, we're practically cousins."
They laughed. The joke served as an icebreaker.

"OK, Freddy. But before you start, I never got a chance to thank you for pulling us out of the raid that night. I, we appreciate it."

"It wasn't nothing."
Ross had pre-ordered two corned-beef sandwiches on rye and just then, the waiter placed the orders in front of them. As he walked off, Ross noticed Ruthie looking down at her sandwich.

"Is everything OK?" he asked.

"I have news. I mean more news; about your uncle." She had a serious look on her face. "I was gone for a while. Where I was, I met some people. People that knows stuff, I found out a little more."

Ross took a breath, "OK, Give it to me straight."

She started, "The official report from the BCPD said that your uncle was shot by rival gangsters in a territorial dispute. Truth is, he died in a squad car; up in Druid Hill Park. His hands were cuffed behind him. He was executed."

Ross took the news gravely.

"Executed huh? How do they know this?"

"Those people I met, 'friends of our uncles. Got it on good authority."

"Well, do they know who exactly did it?"

Ruthie nodded yes, "Mackey. The commander of the Western Precinct."

Ross sat back speechless.

After a moment he said almost to himself, "Son of a bitch. All this time I was looking in the wrong direction, when the answer was literally fifty feet from my desk."

"Sorry." Ruthie said in consolation.

"Oh don't be. I'm glad I know." He chuckled at the irony. "Funny how things work out, though. This plays right into what I asked you here for."

"I'm listening."

"Well, in a semi unrelated case, an element of distrust has erupted between Western's Commander and his associate from the Avenue. And I have a plan to justify it and exploit it. To put it frankly, He's going down. And I need your help to make it happen. You in?"

"Yup."

"OK, here's what I need you to do."

Lieutenant Wright's face was not recognizable in the neighborhood, however it did stand out. Most white faces that weren't in uniform didn't exactly mix right in. Wright had been weary since having his cover blown and nearly being killed in an undercover sting. Now he walked to meet up with the colored detective who saved his life months earlier. This detective, however *was* recognized around the neighborhood, but he and Wright had been creative. They had disguise themselves as common winos and they needed to get into this stack house. Collective investigation had given them the when and where, but this location was most likely being watched by eyes that would see them coming from a mile away. If entrance were to be gained, it would have to be gradual and cleverly done. They were under no illusion of the gravity of this investigation. And so, a day before what promised to be an important meeting in the side-street stack house, two filthy bums, one colored, one white staggered onto the block, sharing what appeared to be, a bottle of wine. They mumbled amongst each other and argued over wine before eventually taking refuge in the nearest domicile. This building was empty and would have been well lit if not for the boarded up ceiling and roof openings. Now, it was dusty and mostly in shadow. The bums quietly staggered around the stack house. They made their way to the rafters near the roof, and waiting for the events of the next day, as they drifted off to sleep.

Mount and Riggs St.

Officer Pete Wagner sat at his desk finishing up a report. He had been put on administrative leave pending an investigation for an incident involving a fugitive on the run and the killing of a colored man just weeks before. It had been ruled a justifiable homicide because the deceased had reportedly lunged at Officer Wagner in an attempt to get possession of his service revolver. During the struggle for the weapon, Officer Wagner had managed to get his Commanding Officer's revolver, shooting his assailant. It was a life or death situation; an open and shut case. The official police report was little more than a formality. The only thing was, that though he understood why, Wagner didn't like the fact that he had to take blame for the shooting. The Commander had pulled the trigger, and had even shot at the other colored man who fled the scene.

He pouted and griped to himself and after a while realized that it was just the way things went. He figured he had to pay his dues if he ever wanted to get anywhere in the department. Besides, his comeuppance was his birthright. He was the son of the Commander's oldest friend on the force. Those two had come through the academy together and Wagner felt honored to follow in his now retired father's footsteps.

Now finished his report, Wagner straightened his files and headed to the second floor to place it on the desk of Commander Mackey. It was late morning just before lunch shift. The Western Precinct station was of normal mid-day foot traffic; beat cops on their way in and out, lawyers briefing their clients and families waiting for incarcerated loved ones. From his peripheral, he saw his old partner, Wilkes, a beat cop with whom he patrolled Fulton Avenue. Wagner walked over for a handshake just as Wilkes was approached by a young colored girl. She had just entered the station and look to be upset about something. She was petite and wore her hair in a 'bob' hairstyle. The look on Wilkes' face was one of someone being interrupted from a more important task. This look amused Wagner who went over to razz his old partner.

As he approached he overheard the upset young lady utter, "I- I don't know where else to go. He crazy. My boyfriend, he crazy."
She seemed bold but nervous, constantly looking around for someone.

In a dry attempt to console her, the officer said, "Alright missy, we'll try to help you. Just relax and tell me what happened."

The young lady took a breath, then spoke, "I don't know, he just snapped. One minute we were sitting on the couch listening to WCAO and the next he sayin' he was gonna be gone on Sunday. He was supposed to be spendin' that day wit' me, so I said 'where? and who you goin' with?'. Then he hit me, and don't nobody hit me but my daddy. 'Talkin' 'bout some damn meetin'. 'Don't nobody care about no meetin', you s'posed to be wit' me and he worrying about some nigga named Mack."
Officer Wilkes, only half listening, was relieved that she had finally stopped talking. However Wagner, who was now standing amongst the two, was alarmed. Had the girl really said what she *said*? Wagner was no longer interested in the well being of the young lady.

He inquired, "Did you say something about someone named Mack, and some meeting?"

The lady seemed exhausted from talking. She sat with her head in her hands.

"I don't know, Mack, Mackey, somebody. My boyfriend said he had a meeting to set up for, or setting up a meeting, or setting up Mack."

'Setting up Mackey? A meeting? Could this be *the* meeting?' Wagner thought.

He had only known about an upcoming meeting with Commander Mackey, because he was basically shadowing him. But what was this, that the colored girl was ranting about. A meeting, a set up, Mack. She had pretty-much mentioned him by name. All these factors were too much to be a coincidence. He would take this to the Commander himself. He would get stripes for this, definitely.

He said to Wilkes, "Say, you look beat Wilkey. Why don't you let me take care of this one."

"You're a good egg, Wag. I owe you one." Wilkes responded gladly as he walked off avoiding extra paperwork.

Wagner looked down at the young lady and said, "Follow me hon."

The two walked back through the lobby down the hallway and up the stairwell. On the second floor in the third office down was the Commander's office. Wagner knocked. A moment later, Commander Mackey opened the door and acknowledged him. He was a bit put-off when he saw Wagner's colored companion.

"I see we have company. This better be important officer." he grumbled.

"I promise, it is Sir."

"Come in." Mackey said reluctantly.

The young lady was directed to a chair in front of his desk in which she timidly sat.

"Well, let's have it. My time is precious." Mackey barked.

Wagner simply looked at the young lady and said, "Tell him, what you told me."

The young lady frowned in confusion, "OK. My boyfriend hit me because…"
Wagner cut her off.

"No. Not about that, about the other thing."

She thought for a second, "Ah, 'he said he had to go to some meeting?' That part?"

"Yeah," he said, "Tell us that part."

The lady breathed deep and started, "Well, after he hit me, he told me about that meeting Sunday, on our day." And then, thinking back she continued, "Yeah, either something about setting up the meeting for Mack or Mackey, or setting Mackey or Mackel up for the meeting. I don't know."
The Commander's eyes widened then narrowed, when he heard his name. She had his full attention now.

"Then he mentioned 'shot' or 'big shot' or something." Then, as if coming to some realization, she said, "The more I think about it, the more it sounds like they setting somebody up, the bastards. You never know with those people he be hangin' out with. They shady. Either way I sure hate to be this Mack guy. Oww, 'hurt my damn shoulder." She rubbed her shoulder, changing and ending her conversation as quickly as a child would.

Wagner and Mackey looked at each other, and then back to the young lady who sassily interjected, "Then after he hit me again, I got lose ran out the house and I came here."

With a signal from Mackey, Wagner gathered himself, then shaking her hand he said, "Thank you, Ms..."

"Jackson." she said.

"Ms. Jackson, thank you for your cooperation. We have everything we need for our investigation in this matter. I promise, we're gonna get that bastard, and someone's gonna pay. Now if you could please follow me. I'll escort you out of the station."

She stood and walked to the door, "Oh one last thing, he said something about it being some stack-house 'down the bottom'.

"Thank you, Ms. Jackson." Mackey said grimly. After the young lady was escorted out, Wagner returned to Mackey's office. He waited for a moment then spoke.

"Well what do ya think, sir?"
Mackey was now sitting behind his desk in contemplation.

He threw the question back, "What do *you* think?"

"I think we got lucky. We got tipped off without our boy 'Down the Bottom' even knowing about it. 'Definitely Big Shot though. But let me ask you, do you think this set-up is revenge for the 'take' the other night?"

Mackey thought for a second, then said gravely, "It doesn't matter. The fact that he even planned it makes him a dead man. Office Wagner, I do believe it is time for a change in partnership."

"Yes sir." Wagner responded.

CHAPTER TWENTY TWO

Settling up

Big Shot sat in his office silently going over numbers, payoffs and meetings in his head. It was the simple office of a clerk on the second floor of an old drug store. The window shades were drawn and he sat in virtual darkness save a single small lamp that sat across the room. This form of sensory deprivation was conducive to the way he operated and planned. He had long ago learned this skill, which was an important one to have in a world where paper work could be used as proof to land you in prison. He was legendarily known for his air-tight memory and ruthless tactics, and also as a master strategist. With the latter skill he had become adept in spotting plots and schemes against him, cleverly averting and often times reversing them. Over the years, the subversions increased in boldness and complexity; each time thwarted by Big Shot who grew in wisdom and power. But with that growth came arrogance; an arrogance that viewed small threats as insignificant, if ever noticed at all. Such is the cycle of power and war; to survive the battlefield only to succumb to a common cold. In the meantime Big Shot would bask in power's glory.

He went over a few mental notes in preparation for an upcoming meeting. The meeting was a relatively random one and its location was just settled on days before. This was a security measure taken to throw off any higher-level law enforcement investigations. The lower level cops were taken care of already; in fact they were part of the deal, part of the meeting. Not the whole department, not even some, just a few; an important few. A few with whom, a lucrative arrangement had been forged years before. Goods and services had been exchanged in a power grab that put Big Shot on top and made him Boss of Bosses on Pennsylvania Avenue. He and a tiny circle had been privy to the knowledge that in his plot to gain the top spot, he had to strike a deal with the then Sargent of the Western Precinct, Mackey.

Mackey had been instrumental in the set-up of Bigg's old rival, distracting him and making sure his young assassin was free to do the hit without pursuit or police investigation. Mackey also had a direct hand in the luring, kidnapping and execution of the second in command of Bigg's rival. For his part Mackey got a small percentage of the drug, prostitution and gambling take. That minuscule percentage would quietly make Mackey a wealthy man. The hit man Greene was hired to get the girl that worked with the rivals, out of the way before the hits went down. Bigg was content with himself and marveled at how masterfully perfect his plan was executed all those years ago.

He chuckled to himself, 'Even Greene, with his stupid green trench coats was good. But he still managed to get himself killed a few weeks back, idiot.'
The chuckle was surreal, because it revealed the realization that times where indeed changing. Friends and associates were getting arrested and killed and now his longtime partner and protection, Commander Mackey himself, had seemed to rob one of his pick up routes. 'What the hell is goin' on?' he thought to himself.

Just then there was a knock on his office door.

"Yeah, Come in." Big hollered.

Through the door came Bigg's second in command, Millhouse Jenkins. People called him 'House' for short, he'd liked the name and it stuck. House was tall and thin and the two together had almost a Laurel & Hardy appeal, though much more ferocious and calculating. He had been with Bigg under the old-time boss 'Showtime' in the late twenties and made the transition with Bigg when he took over. House' strength was that he was more reserved and liked playing the background; definitely the architect behind the scene.

"The spot's ready. We've had eyes on it since three this morning. It's secure."

"Good. We got everything we need? The pay-offs ready for transfer?"

"Brief cases are ready, like he needs anything extra." House answered, sarcastically.

"I was just thinking about that. Close the door." House closed the door and sat down opposite his boss. Bigg thought for a second and then leaned in.

He asked in a low tone, "This thing with Mackey taking the route, what do you think that is?"

House thought about it.

"You can't be too sure. But looking at how things are on the Avenue, and knowing what a son of a bitch he is, it seems like he might be changing the rules or worse, writing us out."

"I was thinking the same thing. But we' got a lot of mutual investments, I mean deep investments. You think he would jeopardize exposing hisself?"

"He may not see it that way. Remember he's not exactly the 'leave witnesses behind' type. Now if this is what we think it is, then he may be in the process of tying up loose ends, which mean *us*. But we don't know that for sure, and with this new deal with the Micks coming down the pike, we can't afford to jump the gun. We gotta be cautious."

House sat back in his chair.

Bigg nodded his head in agreement, "Yeah. But that still don't erase what he did. We got a deal out there for transport protection or in the very least no-disruption. This is like a slap in the face, blatant disrespect. I got a rep to uphold." Bigg thoughtfully added, "Naw, I got a feeling this is something else. That other thing you said, 'writing us out'. And like you said, if you wanna start anew, you sever all ties. Then again, ..."

"The phrase 'safe than sorry' comes to mind." House suggested, finishing Bigg's sentence.

Bigg agreed, and then coming to a conclusion in his mind he said, "We play it cool. Play it cool but keep an eye out for strange behavior. If something's not right, we act. 'Cause House?..."

"Yeah Bigg."

"I ain't ready to stop being boss."

First fall

The stack-house was used primarily for processing fabric. It was the third stop in the chain before the product hit the avenue. From the port, to Baltimore's garment district, to the distribution stack-houses, and then on to retail. The stack-house was one of many off-avenue businesses silently owned by Big Shot. It was clean and well used Monday through Friday, but the early hours of this Sunday morning found it and the surrounding area quiet and desolate.

This meeting was to be one of routine assurance; necessary to maintain security through side deals and payoffs and also a mention of a possible future business connection. A cool midst and overcast sky set the course of the morning as Commander Mackey's unmarked vehicle turned onto the street and pulled in front of the stack house. About the same time Big Shot and House exited a car that sat at the opposite end of the block. They had gotten there earlier to confer with their lookouts. Everything was clear. The Commander's subordinate, Officer Wagner, rushed from his driver's side to open his passenger's door. The four greeted with nods in front before entering the Stack-house's wide doors. To any passersby, the foursome looked to be random businessmen overseeing the upcoming week's shipments; and in a way that assessment would be correct.

Once inside, Wagner gave the stack-house a brief visual 'once-over'. There was a small circular table with two opposing chairs that sat just within the beams of sunlight peaking through the high windows. It was otherwise lit by a few clear light bulbs giving it the look of a theater during intermission. Big Shot and Mackey took seats at the table while their subordinates stood few feet behind.

Bigg started, "The numbers are up seven percent with the opium and lone-sharking. Sixteen is even better with ten percent 'Up Top'. The gambling houses are steady, even with the recent rash of stick-ups."

"Good, good." Mackey contented.

"Old man Cleveland Black is on target with the 'fence', only I need that secure path from the east-side."

Mackey agreed, "You get me a map of your path, and I'll be sure to get some good men on it."

Bigg noticed Mackey's assistant Wagner studying him. It wasn't overly obvious but enough to be perceived. He decided to respond to the 'elephant in the room'.

"Commander, let's talk about the dead transporter and more importantly, why I got robbed for the Presstman Street card game's take."

Mackey tried to sound official; brushing it off he said, "Don't worry about that. That was a routine stop. It just got a little out of hand."

"A little out of hand? Y'all killed one of my men's runners and you stole four large."

Bigg's tone did not set right with Mackey.

He responded coldly, "Be clear, anything and everything on the avenue is already mine. You're just renting space. I allow you to earn. Don't ever question me or my actions."

Bigg took the proclamation with a restrained rage.

Exasperated, he said, "Well it's obvious now where we stand. Perhaps that's a talk for another time. For now, I'll have your payment brought in." He turned to House, "Go get the briefcase for the commander, I'm going to take a leak."

In a flash Mackey thought about all other times Big Shot had paid him directly, now someone was bringing the payment in from somewhere else, all while he was conveniently 'taking a leak'. Add to that, the bold way this darkie was speaking to him. It was enough, in Mackey's mind, to confirm that colored girl's earlier warning of a set-up.

He simply said, "Petey?"

Big Shot didn't see the shot, he just heard the bang and watched his second in command, House, slump to the floor. He turned back around to see Officer Wagner holding a smoking gun. Wagner had shot House dead and now had his revolver aimed at him. He froze.

Mackey stood, "He's not going anywhere, neither are you. There will be no set-up today Geechie."

Bigg showed his hands, "What are you talking about. You're setting *me* up. We're supposed to be partners."

"Not any more. Times up."

"Wait, we got arrangements. The payoffs, the kickbacks, the tax. You kill me and you ain't gettin' no more of that! And I got the proof at my house. Something happens to me and that proof finds its way to the press." Bigg bargained.

Mackey signaled Wagner to lower his weapon. Bigg exhaled in relief. Mackey feigned a look of agreement, pulled his service revolver and shot Big Shot three times in the chest. He looked back at Wagner who was walking toward him. They both looked at the two dead gangsters in the stack-house.

Mackey said to his subordinate, "He had a good run, but he had to go. Besides, we can just do business with the next nigger."

"Right sir." Wagner agreed.

As the two officers walked cautiously out onto the street, closing the wide front doors behind them, Mackey said to Wagner, "We gotta find out where he stays. 'Get that proof." And then almost to himself, mumbled, "'Damn shame, but at least there weren't any witnesses." And he was right; except for the two horrified bums watching from the rafters of the stack-house.

The bums climbed down from their crawlspace as they heard Commander Mackey's automobile drive off. Both were in a state of disbelief. Removing his oversized hood and matted wig, Lieutenant Wright silently gave Ross the hand signal to secure the area. Ross never removed his disguise; an over-sized, dirty scull-cap and a filthy, stained, tan overcoat. He would slip out later and mix into the neighborhood maintaining his disguise, but for now, Ross gave the all-clear and the two met at the bodies which laid within ten feet of each other.

"What the hell was that?" he asked rhetorically. "I-I can't believe how easy that was for him. 'Shot'em like it was nothing."

"Important thing was, that we saw it. We saw the whole thing." Wright responded.

"And heard it. What *this* scumbag said." Pointing to Bigg's body, "He referenced that shooting incident by Wagner a few weeks ago, only it seems Mackey did it, probably in cold blood." Ross bit his lip in frustration. "He's gotta go down. He just can't do whatever he wants and get away with it. And we were right here."
Seeing Ross' distress and then looking at down at the bodies, Wright just shook his head.

"There was nothing we could do. He would've killed us if he knew we were here, you know."

Ross nodded, "Yeah, I know."

He bit his lip at the thought of Mackey escaping justice; his justice. He wondered how the events of the night would manifest into a conviction. He asked himself would prison be enough? Would anything short of a bullet in the head be enough? He looked down at the corpse of the man who pulled the strings that killed his uncle, but he wanted the man who had actually pulled the trigger. He wondered if his true justice would ever really be served.

'I can only hope.' Ross thought.

Wright pulled his police radio from under his dirty coat.

"Detective, do me the honor of calling this one in."

He handed Ross the radio. Wright was disgusted by the immoral actions of the commander, yet, in a small way content with the fruits of his investigative labor. That labor, which had stretched back for years, pointed to the partnership, or in the least, an association with a high-level crime figure. Wright knew what kind of man Mackey was from his experience working under him all those years ago at the Western Precinct. The favoritism and corruption he witnessed firsthand was the main reason Wright had applied to the Department of Internal Affairs in the first place. Sure, he and Ross were witnesses to the murders, but Mackey was too well embedded in the higher-level corrupt system to ever really be threatened by the I.A. lieutenant and his colored sidekick. Mackey was a decorated commander of the Western District after all. Wright realized that the struggle ahead would be a difficult one, and longed for justice that may never happen.

This moment of doubt was interrupted by a gargled, bloody cough. They looked down. It was the body of House, Big Shot's second-in-charge. Thought dead, he had in fact been unconscious as a result of his injuries. Wright and Ross looked at each other in amazement; a live witness with first-hand evidence of Mackey's connection with Big Shot's organization. House was quickly checked for weapons and relieved of his back-holstered pistol. As they waited for Internal Affairs Investigations back-up and a sweep team, they tried to revive the semi-conscious gangster. House's eyes blinked open.

To the two apparent bums he saw standing over him, House offered, "You- you g-gotta help me. 'F-f-first... first one of you, you bums, oww!.. to get me to the hospital,... gets a case ...of whiskey."

CHAPTER TWENTY THREE

New King

Pennsylvania Avenue was abuzz with the news that the boss 'Down Bottom' was gone. The almost ten year reigning boss of bosses was dead. Most feared a violent battle to fill the vacuum, but those in the know, had no such misconceptions; they knew who the heir apparent was. The heir apparent knew too. It was Sixteen. And now he held court in the aptly named, 'Bucket of Blood Saloon', a notoriously dangerous bar along Avenue's 'Shop'. Within the bar, he sat in a C-shaped booth and table to the back, smoking a cigar. He'd heard the news of his boss' death just hours after it occurred. Two days had passed and now he strategized, readying himself to assume control of the organization. His moneyman, Scratch, stood at the foot of the table waiting for permission to sit.

"I got messages for you." he said.

Sixteen took a sip from his Cognac, "Talk."

"I just left the old man, Cleveland Black. He sends his blessings. 'Says he retiring. 'Getting too old for the Avenue."

"*Now* he's retiring." Sixteen chuckled. "'Should've done that ten years ago. This here's a young man's game."

"I'm sure he knows that now. Anyway he wants to make a deal. He wants his lieutenant Cholly Word to take over when he leaves, 'wants your blessing and assurances of a smooth transition."

"Not gonna happen. But let them think it is, though. We'll *take* everything from them later."

244

"Got it. Next, the east-side boss is willing to work with anybody as long as the terms stay the same. I've already squared away our deal over in Jew-Town and I'm still waiting for a response from Western."

"Don't expect one, not yet." Sixteen advised.

"Then how we gonna know what's up? Nobody can make moves. We kind of in limbo over here." Scratch said.

Sixteen answered in a strategic tone.

"The avenue is hot, and they're a mess over there right now. The cops have to keep up appearances to make sure they're still seen in a good light, so they're gonna be making a show of force; crackin' heads, disrupting flow, you know things like that. So for the time being, all outward business dealings will have to freeze for at least a week, until the Avenue cools down."

"I'll make it happen." Scratch assured.

Sixteen took a breath, "As long as everybody who *needs* to know, knows whose boss, we can *take* a much needed break. With the recent turn of events, I feel the need to celebrate."

Scratch smirked, "As always, I'm on that too."

An unused Avenue property was modestly decorated and was now being used for an event. It was well lit and mostly used as storage but tables, chairs and old party dressings that were stacked in the basement were put out for the occasion. Years ago the property was some kind of clothier owned by one of the old gangsters, but now Scratch used it for his boss' 'get-together'. The 'get-together' was not promoted as a celebration, but as an 'acknowledgement gathering' in honor of the late and present Avenue boss. Sixteen sat at a low-lit table to the side of a parquet dance floor. He was dressed to the nines, with his navy-blue pinned striped suit and white button up. By his side sat Gene, his number two, also exquisitely dress. Well-wishers milled about and folks eager to get and stay in Sixteen's good graces, came to his table to pay their respects. He, of course, accepted all praise and congratulations like a conquering king.

The crowd had formed into a sort of procession to and from table. There were the criminal attorneys, already hired by, or willing to be hired by Sixteen's ilk. There were the low-leveled political reps, sent to represent where their bosses were too smart to go. And then there were the street chiefs, most of which were already under Sixteen's thumb. Over the years he and Big Shot had been slowly consolidating the Avenue territories through subversion, cunning and brute force.

Also mixed in the procession were those who were just fascinated with the street life. Mostly female, they clamored at the chance to shake the hand of a real life gangster. Sixteen was happy to oblige.

"Oh my goodness." one woman said, "Thank you for showing colored men how to make that money. I want my son to grow up and be just like you."
Sixteen took it all in stride.

The man behind her, a white man, looked like a representative from one of the east-side organizations; Little Italy or perhaps that Lombard Street Jewish mob. He didn't recognize the man and the whites rarely did business with the Avenue. Either way Sixteen was particularly content with this visit. It showed respect and may have indicated that he had officially arrived, city-wide. The white man stared blankly like a palace guard and only made eye contact when he stood right in front of the table. He extended his hand. Sixteen's ego didn't let him stand, but it allowed him to shake.

"Congrats from back east." the man said.

In his other hand he carried a fancy bag. It looked like the type of bag that women gave each other presents in. Sixteen was cautiously intrigued. The man presented the bag with two bottles of top shelf brandy in it.

Pulling one bottle out just enough to show the label, the man said, "Class for class."

Sixteen just nodded in appreciation. The man nodded goodbyes, walked away and out the door. Gene, still sitting beside him took the bag to place it on the floor between them when he noticed a small card inside.

"Hey Six', it's a card in here. You want it?" he asked.

"Yeah, give it here."

Sixteen put the card in the inside pocket of his suit jacket to read later. An hour later the line of congratulators had tapered to a stop. Gene was at the bar impressing two ladies as Sixteen sat alone, finally. Just then he remembered the letter. He retrieved it from his jacket pocket and opened it.

It read,

Mr. Rogers, congratulations. Excuse the usage of a messenger, but I am discreet. I will be at the Slatemore Hotel's bar tonight. At one fifteen am, I'll order drinks for 'two'. Hopefully I won't be alone.

Signed 'L'.

At first Sixteen wondered, then it came to him, 'Miss Vallis. 'L' for Lisa, Lisa Vallis. She finally coming around. Finally realizing who she's dealing with.'

He was enamored with her from the first time he saw her at the Sphinx Club. He had been in passive pursuit of her, sending invitations, and reps, but to no avail. His people couldn't find a background, which to him was a good thing. Any 'history' on anyone was usually a sketchy one and in some cases, especially concerning women, no news is good news. She was rarely, and even then, casually seen; usually on the arm of some high leveled power broker. No one really seemed to *know* her, she was just was one in a few 'elegant' white women attracted to the Avenue.

Of her letter to him, he thought, 'And why not? After all, I *am* the Avenue; and that is one fine white woman. And a man of my position deserves a woman like that by his side; one that looked like royalty. Not like that black cow Bigg was married to'. He was elated, though careful not to let it show. This was the best news he had heard all night. It was already half past eleven so he didn't have time get someone to check the place out. There was no need, anyway.

'This was just a woman, a fine one, but a woman none the less.' he thought, 'I'll just go down to see what's happening, what harm could do. Worst case scenario, I set up a hot date on the Ave; best case, is tonight, I get lucky.'

"Gene, I gotta make a run." he said walking quickly toward the door car keys in hand.

"Hey, where you going? You' leaving your own party? Let me get somebody to go with you."
"Naw, no sweat. Everything's copacetic."

248

Just Desserts

The revolving door was still spinning from the older couple that had just walked through it. Sixteen did not like the 'trappability' of revolving doors so he used the adjacent traditional swinging doors to gain entrance. He now stood in the lobby of the ritzy Slatemore Hotel. It had been, for years, one of the prominent hotels of Baltimore's colored elite and the stay of choice for the upper echelon entertainers. Occupancy this night, however, was relatively low due to ongoing renovations to the Avenue-facing rooms. Only back and side facing rooms were to be used with some exceptions. The hotel itself was most times a starting place for a night's festivities, as at this hour, most had already found their way up the Avenue to trip the light fantastic; wondering back just before dawn.

Along the hotels perpendicular corridor, it's bar sat off to the right just across from the registration desk. Sixteen cautiously entered the bar scanning the room. It was dark and mostly empty; only lovers and drunks sat off in dark corners. Jazz ballads could be heard playing softly thought the hotel's intercom system. Instinct guided his glances to the back service and public exits; no one. Years of experience had taken over his actions, but he relaxed a bit when he saw, at the bar, a single female figure with her back to him. She wore a knee-length black dress with a shoal draped across her shoulders. She was his intended date. He noticed that she wore the pearl necklace he had offered her on one of his earlier advances. Beside her was an empty stool. Sixteen straightened his tie and walked toward the bar. He felt his heart skip a beat when she turned around to meet his approach. Her fair skin glowed softly in the dim lighting and she looked even better than he remembered.

"Miss Vallis." he greeted.

She smiled, "Mr. Rogers, Call me Lisa. I'm glad you decided to come. Join me?"

"Call me Melvin." he responded. "And by the way, my pearls look nice on you."

"Your pearls?" she smirked. "I believe they were a gift from you. An appreciated one."

As he unbuttoned his suit jacket, he noticed her thick thighs peeking from a high spilt in her dress. Lisa looked him up and down with a sexy, mischievous smirk, and then turned back to her drink. Sixteen took the stool to the left of hers and picked up the shot glass that sat in front of him. He shot her a look of inquiry.

"Rum and Coca-Cola, just like the song. My favorite." she answered. "But if you wanted something a little stronger…"

"Naw, this is good." he interrupted. "Now," he gulped down half the glass. "Let's get down to business."

"No business Melvin." she said, "I assure you, this is all pleasure."

"Oh, do tell." he said, intrigued. He looked at her from the side, she was stunning. He couldn't get over how good she looked to him. Her form-fitting black one-piece and matching shoes seemed almost a waste in an empty bar.

"Why the change of heart? I've been trying to see you for a while." Sixteen asked staring straight ahead.

Also staring straight, Lisa answered, "Mostly business, I bring a lot of money uptown to the Avenue."

"Hustling bigwigs," Sixteen said. "Not a bad racket."

"That being, I must be careful who I'm seen with. I have a reputation to protect;

"Well that's the thing, you don't. No rep, no nothing, especially on the Avenue circuit. You're like a ghost on the street. No pun intended."

She chuckled, "Then goal achieved. Like I said I am discreet. And you know the saying, 'A lady in the streets…'"

Sixteen swallowed the lump in his throat.

Lisa turned to him and continued, "To answer your question, there was always an attraction; a physical attraction. But I am an ambitious woman, and romantically as well as professionally, nothing less than an ambitious man will do."

"And me?" he uttered nervously.

She moved closer to him, "And you, Mr. Rogers, have exceeded all of my expectations.' She whispered in his ear, 'Power makes me… *willing*."

Sixteen was frozen.

She finished, "I'm staying in this hotel, tenth floor, room eight. I would like to 'personally' congratulate you on your promotion and talk about future dealings."

She went in her purse, pulled out a five-dollar bill and placed it on the counter in between their drinks.

As Sixteen sat stunned, Lisa stood from her stool, whispered, "Ten-oh-eight" and walked out of the bar. He watched her curvaceous figure walk up the hotel corridor and on to the elevator. As if jumping out of his own body and slapping himself into reality, Sixteen gathered himself and left the bar. He felt he could not get down the corridor fast enough and upon reaching the elevator doors, began slapping the 'up' button as if his life depended on it. On the elevator he checked his breath and hair. Both were good. 'Ping'. The elevator doors opened; tenth floor. Down the hall and to the right he went in haste, traversing room renovation equipment until he stood in front of Room 1008. The door was ajar.

Sixteen pushed the door opened and slowly walked in. The room was dimly lit. It was a basic single occupancy with a bathroom, one closet and a queen-sized bed. Lisa was in the bathroom to the left of the entrance. That door was opened and with a glance, Sixteen could see that she had, just that quickly, change into a long sheer black negligee. For a split second he even thought he saw straight through it to her bra and panties.

'Yes!' he thought. 'She means business.'
He walked further into the room. The closet door was half-opened. His cautious nature made him check it. Light from the bathroom gave him just enough to properly inspect the closet space with a peek. The window shades were drawn with two thick, velvet curtains that hung to the floor on each side. The whole wall was in shadow. A small radio softly played big band ballads.

From inside the bathroom Lisa said, "Take your jacket off and lie on the bed, I've got a surprise for you."

"Surprise?" Sixteen asked. "You ain't gonna go nuts on me, are you?"

"No. I just have this fantasy of being a burlesque dancer. I haven't had the opportunity to act it out. But with you, I feel like I wanna let lose. Oh, and if I do go crazy, don't worry, it'll be the kind of crazy you like."

"Well alright, then." Sixteen responded as he anxiously took off his jacket and button-down. He un-holstered his pistol and placed all three on the floor, then

laid topless on the bed. Lisa came out of the bathroom
sexy but uncoordinated, like a non-pro should. Her
silhouette made her look like a goddess to him; every
curve was accentuated by every movement. More and
more, Sixteen felt that this was perhaps the greatest
moment of his life. Lisa danced toward him, doing her
best stripper imitation and he was like putty in her hands.
Tonight, he would do whatever she wanted. She
positioned herself cowboy style on top of his lap.

"You want me to take my pants off, baby?" he
suggested.
She put her index finger to his lips, "Shhh. Just sit back.
Let me do all the work."
She kissed his neck and caressed his chest as she reached
for a blindfold on the nightstand.
"I want this to be a night to remember." she whispered.

Halfway in ecstasy, Sixteen whispered back,
"Anything you want."

As she slowly gyrated on his lap, she blindfolded
him. Then from the nightstand drawer, she pulled out two
sets of handcuffs. He passively resisted, but the tongue in
his ear persuaded him to comply. She slowly and
seductively clamped each hand to the opposing ends of
the bedpost, then he felt her get up, presumably to get
naked. Most of Sixteen's excitement was in waiting for
what came next in this sexual escapade. It took a moment
to realize that nothing else was happening. He was still
cuffed to the bedpost, blindfolded.

"Baby?" he called. "Lisa? 'You there? What
happened baby? Why' you stop?"
When he got no answer, fear and anger set in.

"What the fuck? Bitch, let me up!"

He struggled for a minute to pull himself free, but the bedpost was too strong; he was trapped. It was then that the blindfold was snatched off and his eyes adjusted to the dim light. At the foot of the bed he saw Lisa standing. He could see her in the light that came from the bathroom. Her face was different; cold, emotionless. Immediately in his mind he thought of all the hapless suckers on and off the Avenue, that got tangled in her webs of deception, only to be busted out at one of the upscale gambling joints or flat out robbed. But no, this couldn't happen to *him*, he wasn't one of those squares from downtown. He was Melvin Rogers, Sixteen in the streets. One of the baddest, smartest, most feared gangsters in the city. He had made his bones doing a hit for Big Shot at the age of sixteen. In fact, that was how he got his nickname, Sixteen, 'cause that was the age, that he took out Bigg's feared rival; the old dude... what's his name, *Pop*. And after that, the rep got even worse. Nobody would even think of doing some jive time petty crime to him. Yet... here he was, trapped, shackled, by this white woman.

"You think you gon' get away with this? You set me up." he hollered in disbelief.

"No she didn't, I did." a voice said.

It was a dramatic entrance, like the end of one of those Noir films. From out of the shadow, stepped a young brown skinned woman. She too was dressed in all black with a matching black purse. Confused, Sixteen just looked.

The woman spoke, "Years ago, you killed a man on Pennsylvania Avenue." She pulled a Smith & Wesson .38 revolver from her purse. "His name was Pop."

Sixteen thought, 'Cool Pops. Damn! I was just thinkin' 'bout that nigga. Oh shit!'

He pleaded, "Hold up little lady. Wait a minute. That wasn't personal, that was just part of the game."

"I know." She aimed the gun at him. "So is this."

Still cuffed to the bedpost, he began thrashing himself around in an attempt to break free, "Who the fuck is you?!"

As she held a pillow in front of the gun, she answered, "His niece. You can call me, Ruthie." She emptied six shots into Sixteen's chest.

It seemed to Ruthie like minutes had passed; actually it was only seconds, precious seconds. As she looked down at Sixteen's bullet-ridden, bloody, lifeless body, Lisa, who had been standing off to the side, called to her.

"It's done. Let's go."

They were confident that the muffled shots didn't attract too much attention on the barely occupied floor, but were careful to cover up and move quickly just the same. The two gathered belongings, left the room, closed the door and took the elevator to the lobby.

On the elevator, facing forward, standing side by side, Lisa noticed Ruthie's blank stare.

"You OK?"

Almost to herself, Ruthie stoically answered, "I thought I would feel different, and I do, but in a weird way. Now I know what I'm capable of. I mean I'm glad Sixteen's dead, but in the end, it didn't bring my Uncle Poppy back. Nothing can. Nothing ever will."

Lisa grabbed her hand, "Your uncle, he lives on through you. And Mr. Rogers, at least that's one less scumbag on the street. Let's just hope a worse one doesn't pop up in his place."

Exiting the elevator, Lisa walked a few steps behind Ruthie as to give the perception that they were not together. Once outside, they stood facing opposite directions.

Over her shoulder, Lisa asked, "Well, what now?"

"I got a few more things to handle."

"See you on the Avenue then?"

"Probably not. After this, it's not much here for me, and at the same time, there's too much here for me. I don't think the Avenue is the life for me." Ruthie closed her eyes as a rare breeze kissed her face, bringing memories of her home on the 'Hill'. "Yeah, I'm going back to the country, to sit on my porch."

"Sounds good. Save a space for me."

"I will."

Lisa turned and gave a quick hug. "See ya around Ruthie."

Ruthie hugged back tighter, "Thank you for everything, Ellisa."

She started to walk up Pennsylvania Avenue, but stopped.

She turned to Lisa and said, "One more thing, tell your uncle Nikos I said, thanks."

CHAPTER TWENTY FOUR

Aftermath

Pennsylvania Avenue's underworld and Western Police District had been rocked by executions and revelations of murder and corruption. The Commander Mackey of the Western Precinct and his subordinate Officer Wagner had been indicted on the charges of murder in the first degree, attempted murder, corruption, and racketeering on the testimony of a high level operative in a criminal organization and two upstanding officers. Medals were awarded, promotions were accepted and honors were bestowed; still red-tape, systematic racism and high level corruption quietly won the day.

Through slick lawyers and powerful friends in high places, the Commander's charges were lowered to involuntary manslaughter and malfeasants of the law. He would receive a small mention in the press and suspended indefinitely with pay until the trial, but time would eventually erode the memory of deeds past. Commander Mackey would not go to jail, but his position on the force was unsure. Back at Baltimore City Police Department-Central Office, Downtown, Detective Ross sat the desk of the newly promoted, former Lieutenant Wright. Reading the Baltimore Sun Newspaper, he was disgusted by what he saw.

Newly commissioned *Corporal* Wright walked in and sat behind his large oak desk. "I see you're reading the official news."

257

Ross looked up, "'Mackey walks'? Yeah. Very disheartening."

"Nothing we didn't expect, Detective. At least we exposed that sonofabitch. Spotlight's on him now, he won't be trying anymore funny business; for a while anyway."

"Lets hope not."

Wright tilted his head in thought, "Join me on the roof, will ya?"

A few minutes later, on the roof of Central Headquarters, the unofficial gathering place for the rank and file to talk, relax and blow off steam, Wright and Ross leaned over the roof's four-foot boundary-wall looking down onto the street below. The cityscape seemed majestic yet calming; opposite from the bustling streets ten stories down. It was a quiet, monumental occasion. It was the first time a colored cop or person, had been to the roof to enjoy it. Ross took it all in.

After breathing the fresh air Wright started, "What's your deal kid? Why a cop?"

Still looking over the edge Ross thought, then answered, "I just wanna make the city safe for those who can't..."

Wright interrupted, "No, I mean your *real* reason." He gestured his hands to his chest. "What's your drive, your passion. 'Cause I gotta say, your persistence, it makes me believe that you got other motivations."
Ross shrugged.

Wright offered, "No pressure kid, I'm just wondering."

"No, I'll talk." Ross said, then staring off, "Why a cop, eh? You know it's funny; your motivation can be like something you can't remember, until you think about it, then you can't forget it. I guess it was the classic, 'I lost someone, I wanna make it right' thing. My uncle, he was in the life on the Avenue. I think he loved the streets, but he didn't what that for his family. That's the side I saw of him, the caring side. My pop was a Great War vet, went crazy and shot himself in '29, so my uncle kinda watched over us. He always talked about moving us somewhere better but his plans didn't happen soon enough. He got killed, and me and my mother were left to struggle, eventually ending up on the streets before moving with relatives on the east side. I experienced both sides, from having to not. I know, the street life has its codes, but he was my uncle. After a while, I figured it was my time to be selfish. I'd been a giving, selfless person all my life, even as a kid. Always making sure everybody else was alright, that they were safe and had everything they needed. I guess that could be a reason I joined the force. But even after, one time, just once I wanted to give in to my one selfish impulse; one that over the years grew into a quiet obsession. The obsession to make those responsible for my uncle's death, pay. So to make an earlier correction, it was more obsession than motivation that drives me. Speaking of which, sir, I was kind of thinking the same about you. I've done a little homework, you seem out of the blue, but you obviously have an interest."

"Very perceptive." Wright answered, "As a matter of fact, I do. Since we're sharing... thinking back, ah, I think it was in '33 maybe '34, I ran across this kid in a stake-out raid; 'had him red-handed. Took him to Western to have him booked and wouldn't you know, the little bastard's being set free by guess who?, non other than out esteemed Commander friend. When I was dumb enough to question him about it, him gave me such a scare. From that day, until I left, he watched me like a hawk. I got the worst assignments, was shunned by fellow officers and he made my life there miserable. My saving grace was your old Captain Warren who, I guess sympathized with me and signed off on my transfer to Central. Warren made it look like I was moved for my incompetence, but in fact, I was placed there to sharpen my police skills and develop a relationship with Internal Affairs Investigations. He would be my contact within Western as we waited for a way in. And that way finally came in the form of the newly promoted colored officer from Eastern District." he said referring to Ross.

Ross modestly shrugged it off. "No sir. I just do my job. It's nothing."

"Nothing?!" Wright continued. "The way you've handled yourself in your investigations, at the station and in the field. The way you saved my ass in that warehouse. Your bravery in stepping up as a witness, even your grace in the face of set-backs. That's damn good police work, from a damn good human being."

"Huh, that 'stepping up as a witness' thing probably isn't the smartest career move. I had it bad before. Can you imagine?"

"Not necessarily." Wright consoled. "In Mackey's hopefully extended absence, interim commander Warren has been tapped. He'll look out for you. Not to mention, your success has prompted the higher-ups to hire two more colored officers by the beginning of the summer."

Ross was pleasantly surprised and had no words. He struggled between embarrassment and pride.

Wright noticed and extended his hand.

"Your a class act and a good cop, Ross. A credit to us all."

Ross accepted. They shook.

"Thank you, sir. I appreciate it."

"And every good cop deserves to have someone in the foxhole watching his back. I know it's been tough for you, but I want you to know kid, you're not alone out there or in here; not anymore. I'll always have your six."

"And I, you sir."

The Hill

A few miles outside the city limits in Cockeysville, Maryland, Ruthie and Doris sat out on the back porch of a small farmhouse. The house was a modest, brown-shingled, two-storied cottage with a half-acre back yard. In the yard by a barn was an older woman who knelt in a patch of dirt tending to her kale and carrots.

"You alright out there, ma?" Ruthie yelled, "You're movin' kinda slow."

"Please" her mother hollered back, "I'm in better shape than both of y'all youngins' put together."

Doris hollered jokingly, "Hold up Miss Lil, this is between y'all. I ain't got nothing to do with it."

Lillian waved her hand and went back to her gardening. It was early spring and unseasonably mild, light winds blew across the yard and porch. It had been a little more than a month since, in the city, Pennsylvania Avenue had been rocked by scandal and murder. The radio news said one of the newer younger gangsters had even been found murdered in a prominent Avenue hotel. Police had no suspects or motive, but didn't seem too motivated to investigate either way. It was chalked up as part of some underworld power struggle. Ruthie and Doris sat relaxing in two lawn chairs. Between them was a small table on which sat a pitcher of lukewarm lemonade.

"Ooh that wind feels good. Just think, city folks don't never get to feel this." Ruthie said.

"Yeah. I guess this is the life, unless you want excitement." answered Doris.

"Too much excitement in one life-time is not good for you, trust me."
They sat in silence for a moment.

Then Doris suggested, "You aren't coming back, are you?"

Staring off to the distant edge of their land, Ruthie answered, "I don't know, I don't think so. It's like being torn between two parts of yourself. But, for at least the foreseeable future, I'm not budging."

"I hear that. You're lucky." Doris said with some sadness.

"Well it's not like *you* don't have a choice. You got enough money saved up, and your rent is paid through the end of the year. Ain't no rush to get back, you can stay here as long you want to. In fact, I would rather you do stay; you're family. I can't do all this relaxing by myself. Besides, you need time away from the Avenue just about as much as I do." After a thought, "Speaking of reasons why, how' you feeling."

Doris breathed deep as she looked up, "I miss him. I still can't believe he's gone. And to think those crummy cops killed my Joe," her eyes began to well, "My Joe Baldy. He's gone."

The two embraced hands as tears rolled down Doris' cheek.

She continued, "At least we know what happened to Joe. We *still* don't know where Mil is. Do you think they got him?"

With a thought and a knowing look, Ruthie reach in her dress pocket and pulled a letter. She hesitated then passed it to Doris.

"I haven't shown this to anybody." Secrecy was implied in her statement.

Doris accepted, unfolded and read the letter.

It read,

My Ruthie, I miss you so much. By now I'm sure you heard what happened to Joey. Tell Dorie I'm sorry and that she should know that he loved her very much. He used to talk about her all the time. Those police killed my best friend and now I'm on the lamb. I am so sorry I couldn't say goodbye before leaving. I can't tell you where I'm going, just know that I'm safe and I'll be alright. You are the best thing that ever happened to me, but for now, this is goodbye. I hope you experience all the good things in life. I love you. Milton.

Doris stared down at the letter for a moment after finishing it. Her thoughts hung heavy with the last connection to her beloved, Joe.

"I guess we both loss out, huh?" she said in a tearful chuckle.

Ruthie looked down at the photograph she had pulled from the letter. It was the one she and Mil had taken on the Avenue during the holidays. It was a happiness from a lifetime ago. She smiled. Then she looked out into the yard; her mother still working in her kale patch, the newly grown grass waving in the breeze, flying insects buzzing about and a small toolshed at the far end of the lawn.

She answered, "I guess some would say yeah, but when you look around, at the bigger picture, where we ended up, in a small way, I'd say we won." She looked to the sky, "Ain't that right Unc?"

Also looking up to the sky, Doris said with a smile, "Yeah Mister Uncle Poppy." She thought and then added, "You still got a funny name."

The ladies enjoyed the warm spring early evening, and many more like it, and life from then on was good.

Life Goes On

Baltimore City as a whole was gearing up and continually mobilizing for the war effort. Thousands poured in from the city and surrounding regions to work at the Sparrow's and Locust Point steel plants, which sent its newly built battleships, bomber planes, armaments, not to mention their sons, off to war.

Pennsylvania Avenue was Pennsylvania Avenue. By day a bustling colored metropolis, shoppers going to and fro, people patronizing restaurants and traffic jams. By night, neon lights, billboards, celebrities, jazz, glitz and glamour; and of course, more traffic. The expected street war from the power vacuum never happened; ...well kind of. The Shop (the mid-avenue territory), was inherited by Cleveland Black's well-respected 'next-in-line', Cholly Word. He was by default, now boss of bosses on Pennsylvania Avenue. Factions of the Avenue's 'Up Top' and 'Down Bottom' organizations broke up into smaller gangs and did business with an uneasy but cordial working relationship. However, there were reports of some of the smaller gangs being consolidated behind a brash, young, relatively unknown newcomer. The combined gangs themselves were a new breed of ruthless gangsters; but the strangest of the reports were that their leader was a woman. A young one, known simply by her street-name, Jacks.

To the people from the neighborhoods off the Avenue, the recent events of murder and scandal became, over time, little more than rumor to be speculated upon and gossip to be disputed. All and all, people loved, laughed, fought, cried and lived. And life went on like life always does, on Pennsylvania Avenue.

Epilogue

"...And pick me up a couple of cans of that corned-beef hash, will ya'?"

"Sure hon'."

From his front door, suspended Commander Sherman Mackey made a request for the grocery store list to his wife Sheila. He stood enjoying the breeze that flowed from his opened back door, through the house and out the front. His wife was on her way to the local market to pick up a few things. Usually she did her shopping on Saturday afternoons with her neighbor friend Betty, wife of the Fire Chief, that lived just across the street.

Theirs was a modest two-storied, three bedroom porch-front row home complete with front and back neatly trimmed lawns. Their street, the twenty-four hundred block of Calverton Heights Avenue had become sort of an oasis in an already nice part of town. Its residents, mostly the professional, authoritative types, migrated to the neighborhood, which began to take on a air of prestige. Some of its residents assured that it was among the safest areas in the city.

Sheila would be doing her shopping alone today. They had run out of eggs so she was off to the store to get some along with pork chops, flour and of course, some corned-beef hash for her husband. They had been running low on food because Mackey was home all day now and was snacking more and more in his idle time. He would be spending more time at home until that messy situation at Western Precinct was done and resolved. But Mackey rather enjoyed his time off and regarded it as sort of a

266

vacation. He thought about his former underling, Officer Wagner. Wagner wasn't as lucky as Mackey, his connections not as strong. He was facing time, and would have to take the fall, but he would keep his mouth shut. He was a good kid and he would be taken care of. Mackey felt bad for him.

'Comes with the territory.' he thought.

Friends and neighbors had heard and read the news of Mackey's alleged corruption and connection to colored gangsters, but most had dismissed it as the liberal media framing their honest, hardworking, red-blooded friend. If anything, to them he was a leader, a keeper of the peace, a protector from the more uncivilized elements of the city. That *colored* element, which was rarely seen around the neighborhood, except in capacities of servitude; maids, landscapers and laborers. So it wasn't uncommon to see a colored face, every now and then, just as long as it wasn't too common.

"I might be a while." Sheila said from the side walk, "Alice is probably at the store and you know how she likes to talk." she warned.

"Take your time, hon. I'm gonna listen to the Senator's baseball game on the radio."

He nodded, she walked. As he turned and closed the front door, he heard a noise coming from the kitchen. He walked back to investigate. The back screen door had banged up against the metal porch rail.

"Goddamn wind." he grumbled and pulled the door closed.

Walking back to the living room Mackey half-noticed the vegetable basket with some celery sticks, a small potato and a carrot lying on the counter in front of it.

267

'I guess she *would* leave a mess, trying to see what we need from the market', he thought. "Women."

In the living room, he grabbed his newspaper and sat down in his favorite chair. Flipping through the pages he saw news of the Japanese advance in the pacific, he saw Mayor Jackson's support of the war bond drive.

"Goddamn Japs."

He saw news of a street-car accident on the city's east side, then scanned to an article about colored activist protesting unequal wages at Armco Steel Plant.

"Goddamn nig..."

Mackey would never know what made him look up. There was not an out of place sound to be heard. But when he did, his face turned chalk white. Off to the side of him, standing in the dining room's archway was a colored man wearing a pork pie hat and a dark tan trench coat.

Somewhere between fear and anger he found to power to ask, "What the hell are you doing inside my house?"

The man had sneaked through the back door when Mackey was at the front. He was horrified to see the colored man raise and aim a revolver, with a potato shoved on the nozzle, right at him.

The man's face was blank and exhausted as he said plainly, "This is for Big Joe Baldy."

He pulled the trigger.

The blast from the revolver put a hole in Mackey's forehead and splashed his brains all over the wall and furniture behind him. The shooter was Mil, and the ten seconds that followed felt like hours. He didn't know if Mackey remembered who he was; he didn't have time to wonder. He forced himself to move. What was done, was done, and it was now time to go. He dropped his gun hand down to his side. He did not know if the muffled shot had aroused a neighbor or passerby, so he pulled his pork-pie tight and low, raised his trench collar and walked briskly out the back door. Mil moved quickly down the back alley and up two blocks to the main street. He had made a quick change as he walked, taking off his trench and hat revealing his Naval Pea coat. He dumped his old wearings into a public trashcan and then walked normal paced to mix into the everyday crowds. He put on his government issued scully cap and hailed a taxi.

In seconds, a cab pulled up. The gruff driver half examined the rearview mirror.

"Where ya goin' Mack?"

Mil responded, "Navy depot, down at the harbor."

The cabby turned to look back from the front seat, "You a sailor, eh?"

Thinking about the old life he was leaving behind and the new life that lay ahead, Mil exhaled and answered, "I am now."

The End.

ABOUT THE AUTHOR

Author J.A. Rich is a native of Baltimore, Maryland. Shy and reclusive as a child, J.A. loved to escape into books and television. He was fascinated by the Science Fiction/ Fantasy genres and a fanatic comic book aficionado. He authored many short stories, honing his skills as a writer. J.A. also emceed and performed at many spoken word and poetry venues around Baltimore city.

The son of historians, J.A. has a deep interest and is well versed in Baltimore City history and culture. He first came up with the idea of writing Pennsylvania Avenue, hearing the stories of his father's sisters who grew up along the Avenue in the forties and the fifties. Fascinated, he threw himself into recreating stories from that long gone world of yesteryear.

J.A. has expressed interest in writings from five to six different novel genres with possible stories branching of from each. Those genres range from Horror to Science Fiction to Drama, and of course History; of which, with genealogy has him in the planning stages for an epic story like none ever written before.

His one wish is to bring the reader into the worlds that he conceives, so that they can see as he sees and experience for themselves. So relax, grab one of J.A. Rich's novels and join the journeys of the mind, in books.

Pennsylvania Avenue- a Novel

Made in the USA
Middletown, DE
15 August 2016